D1391388

PUFFIN BOOKS

THE SERPENTS OF ARAKESH

V. M. Jones lives in Christchurch, New Zealand, with her husband and two sons. Her previous novels are *Buddy*, which won the Junior Fiction and Best First Book Awards in the 2003 New Zealand Post Children's Book Awards, and *Juggling with Mandarins*, winner of the 2004 Junior Fiction Award. *The Serpents of Arakesh* is the first book in *The Karazan Quartet*.

www.karazan.co.uk

THE SERPENTS OF ARAKESH

THE KARAZAN QUARTET

V.M. JONES

PUFFIN

For my son Bryn, with love

PUFFIN BOOKS

Published by the Penguin Group
Penguin Books Ltd, 80 Strand, London WC2R 0RL, England
Penguin Group (USA) Inc., 375 Hudson Street, New York, New York 10014, USA
Penguin Group (Canada), 10 Alcorn Avenue, Toronto, Ontario, Canada M4V 3B2
(a division of Pearson Penguin Canada Inc.)
Penguin Ireland, 25 St Stephen's Green, Dublin 2, Ireland (a division of Penguin Books Ltd)
Penguin Group (Australia), 250 Camberwell Road,
Camberwell, Victoria 3124, Australia (a division of Pearson Australia Group Pty Ltd)
Penguin Books India Pvt Ltd, 11 Community Centre,
Panchsheel Park, New Delhi – 110 017, India
Penguin Group (NZ), cnr Airborne and Rosedale Roads, Albany,
Auckland 1310, New Zealand (a division of Pearson New Zealand Ltd)
Penguin Books (South Africa) (Pty) Ltd, 24 Sturdee Avenue,
Rosebank 2196, South Africa

Penguin Books Ltd, Registered Offices: 80 Strand, London WC2R 0RL, England

www.penguin.com

First published in New Zealand by HarperCollins Publishers (New Zealand) Ltd 2003
First published in Great Britain in Puffin Books 2005
1

Copyright © V. M. Jones, 2003

The moral right of the author has been asserted

Set in 11.5/15 pt Monotype Plantin
Typeset by Rowland Phototypesetting Ltd, Bury St Edmunds, Suffolk
Made and printed in England by Mackays of Chatham plc, Chatham, Kent

British Library Cataloguing in Publication Data
A CIP catalogue record for this book is available from the British Library

ISBN 0–141–38200–7

CONTENTS

PROLOGUE

Appearances – like many things – can be deceptive.

They looked like a tramp, a bodybuilder, a bank manager and a businesswoman, sitting at a long polished table. There was a whiteboard at one end, and crystal tumblers of iced water and a small bowl of peppermints at each place. Laptop computers chattered over the quieter hum of air conditioning.

Of the four, Veronica Usherwood looked most at home. An ostrich-skin briefcase was stowed tidily beside her chair. Her hair was immaculately cut, as smooth and glossy as starling feathers. Her flawless skin was enhanced by the merest suggestion of dusky blusher on high cheekbones, and dark lashes framed her cool, pale eyes. She wore an elegantly tailored suit and gave the impression of being composed, elegant and completely in control . . . if perhaps a little aloof.

Quentin Quested looked like a tramp who'd wandered into the room by mistake. His baggy corduroy trousers had what looked suspiciously like a gravy stain on one knee, though it was difficult to be sure – they were dark brown and covered in cat hair. His shirt was wrongly buttoned under his shabby waistcoat and his pale, knobbly face wore its usual expression of vague surprise and childlike curiosity. It was hard to imagine he could see very much at all through his smeared spectacles; harder still to believe that inside his bony, freckled head was the most brilliant mind on the planet.

If you were asked to pick which of the four in the room was one of the wealthiest people in the world, he'd probably be your last choice.

A safer bet would have been Withers, who, being an accountant, had an air of columns and figures correctly calculated, and healthy bank balances.

Shaw looked exactly like what he was – a body-guard, bald as a badger and built like a bull. The smooth dome of his head topped a broad, heavy face, his curiously immobile features at odds with alert, deep-set eyes that flicked constantly round the room, missing nothing.

A laptop computer rested in front of each person. The computers were networked so that whoever was talking – Withers, as it happened – could share the information on their screen with their colleagues.

'To summarise,' Withers was saying in his dry, papery voice, 'we can clearly see the profits from *Quest for the Golden Goblet* have already outstripped *Dungeon Quest*.'

He took a small sip of water from the glass at his elbow, and dabbed his lips with a clean white hand-kerchief before continuing.

'Moving on, I am sure you will find this graph of

the comparative sales of the entire Quest series inter-esting.' On every screen but one, a three-dimensional graph appeared, with five lines of different colours zigzagging their way skyward.

On Quentin Quested's screen a cloaked figure was climbing a vertical cliff using what appeared to be suckers attached to its hands and feet.

'This is all very well, Withers,' Veronica Usherwood commented crisply. 'But it isn't what we're here to discuss. I called this meeting to establish whether our new promotional strategy for *Quest for the Golden Goblet* has been successful.'

A manicured fingernail rapped a key. There was a brief tussle between conflicting commands and Withers' graph was replaced by the opening screen of the Quest website.

Dawn, in a landscape of strange and rugged beauty. Above the distant silhouette of a mountain range twin moons, one silver and one gold, were suspended in a purple sky. Beside them shone a single star. A light mist hung in the air and for a moment it was almost as if a breath of the damp freshness of that morning found its way into the stuffy room, bringing with it the promise of a new day waiting to unfold and a distant universe waiting to be explored.

There was silence.

Veronica Usherwood clicked on the twinkling point of light. Instantly it zoomed to the foreground: a full-colour photograph of a computer superimposed on a twinkling starburst. Raising one delicate brow, she ran her eye over the words.

Buy your copy of Quest for the Golden Goblet *NOW and be in to win!*

Your very own state-of-the-art Nautilus computer system . . .
The full Collector's Set of Quest adventure software . . .

A once-in-a-lifetime chance to attend a two-day gaming workshop with Quentin Quested – and test-drive his latest top-secret breakthrough in computer-game technology!

'During the month the promotion has been running sales have increased by two hundred and thirty-three point three, three recurring percent,' Withers was saying.

Shaw grunted and stretched. He reached for a peppermint from the bowl beside him, popped it into his mouth, and chewed it with a crunching sound that made Veronica Usherwood wince. 'If *percent* means out of an 'undred, then 'ow can yer 'ave *two* 'undred an' wotsit percent?'

Withers leaned across the table, putting the tips of his fingers together to form a bony tent. 'I shall enlighten you, Mr Shaw . . .'

'Oh no you don't, Withers,' snapped Ms Usherwood. 'This meeting was scheduled to end at three thirty, and it's already twenty-five past. We've established that the competition has been successful in terms of sales. But what we haven't discussed is the other, *primary* agenda.'

'Yer mean . . . gettin' the right kids fer the job?'

'Thank you, Shaw. That is *precisely* what I mean.'

A witch-like cackle suddenly issued forth from Quentin Quested's computer, making everybody

4

jump. Hastily, he pressed a key, giving the others an apologetic smile.

Ms Usherwood sighed. 'We're discussing the competition entries, Q,' she said patiently.

'Ah, yes,' said Q, rubbing his nose. 'Most interesting, Usherwood.'

Withers called up a spreadsheet and scrolled rapidly to the bottom. 'As of two thirty this afternoon,' he announced, 'we've had a total of twenty-nine thousand, six hundred and fifty-four entries. Should you wish, I am able to provide a detailed breakdown by age, geographical location and gender . . .'

'That won't be necessary, thank you, Withers. I think we've established that Q will have plenty of children to choose from. And remember, we still have almost a month to run. Q, have you made any further progress with the computer programme to select the finalists?'

Q was keyboarding frantically, his fingers a blur of speed, and appeared not to hear.

Veronica rolled her eyes and sighed, rose gracefully and reached down for her briefcase. Regretfully, Withers turned off his computer. Shaw pushed back his chair and lumbered to his feet. 'Still sounds ter me like somethin' outta cloud cuckoo land,' he muttered. 'With due respect an' all, it just don't seem possible.'

To everyone's surprise, Q looked up from his keyboard, hands momentarily suspended in mid-air. His eyes were focused and startlingly bright behind the cloudy lenses, and for a moment Veronica wondered whether he might have been listening all along.

'Oh, no, Shaw,' Q said softly, with a gentle smile, 'there's no cloud cuckoo land about it. It'll work, you'll see.

'*It has to.*'

AN AUTOBIOGRAPHY

'You may begin. And I'd like to remind you all – especially *you*, Adam Equinox – that I expect silence during this exercise, and a well-thought-out and *legible* piece of work.'

I tipped my chair forward so all four legs were on the ground again. It made a dull thump, and Miss McCracken shot me an irritated look. I ignored it.

All round me kids were rummaging in their pencil boxes and finding their places in exercise books. At the desk beside mine, Nicole was scribbling busily – it looked as if she'd done half a page already.

Outside, across the playground, I could see the street. A bus had just drawn up at the bus stop. Eventually a little old lady appeared at the door, holding a walking stick and a whole bunch of shopping bags. As she teetered at the top of the steps I could practically hear her thinking: 'What now? How do I *do* this?'

Painstakingly she moved her cane into her other hand – the hand carrying all the shopping bags. Slowly, like a chameleon reaching out to grab a branch, she stretched her free hand towards the handrail.

'*Adam!*'

Miss McCracken was standing in front of my desk, glaring at me. Her arms were folded across her chest and her mouth had that pinched look it gets just before she sends you to the Principal's office.

I sighed, opened the desk and dug through looking for my English book. It should be easy to find – I'd done an Amazing Maze on the cover. Yup – there it was. I banged my desk shut. Nicole glanced across with a small frown, flipped over her page and carried on writing.

From somewhere close by, I heard the stuttering roar of a motorbike starting up and accelerating away. I couldn't see it, though. Imagine wind in your face; all that speed and power . . . the freedom to drive away – head off wherever you wanted . . .

I checked on Miss McCracken. She was back at her desk, but she was watching me out of the corner of her eye – and I could practically see steam coming out her ears. Reluctantly, I picked up my pen. It had one of those globs of dried ink on the end, so I wiped it on the top corner of the page before I started.

Right, Adam: let's do it! First off, I looked up at the whiteboard to remind myself what we were supposed to be writing about.

My Autobiography, Miss McCracken had written, and underneath: *Name, Physical description, Family history, Birthplace, Date of Birth, Parents, Siblings, Early memories, Likes, Dislikes, Hobbies, School friends, Future ambitions*.

At the top of the page I wrote: *My Autobiografy*.

I didn't underline it the way Miss McCracken had on the board. I went one better and wrote it in this real cool bubble writing. When I'd finished, I tipped back my chair again to admire it. Pretty darn good. I stared down at the blank page, then up at the ceiling, chewing my pen. Risked a quick look over at the road. The bus had long gone. I half expected to see the little old lady creeping along the footpath, but she was gone, too.

I dragged my thoughts back to the empty page.

Describing yourself – that's *hard*. How about starting with my hair and working my way down? I sighed. My hair – a shaggy, dark thatch I gave up on years ago, when I realised it would never shine like other kids', no matter how much I brushed it. Eyebrows to match – level and dark, as though they've been drawn on with two bold strokes of a wide black pen. Skin that turns goldish in winter, and brown as a nut the moment I go into the sun for more than two minutes. My weird eyes, so pale and clear they look like they don't belong to me. I thought about my long legs, my strong arms, my broad shoulders and the height that makes most people think I'm a couple of years older than I really am. I pushed my hair off my forehead with the back of my hand, and gave my head a thoughtful scratch.

Then, painstakingly, I started to write.

My nam is Adam Equinox. I am twelv yers old. I am cwit big and prity strong. I hav dark brown hare, my skin is kwit brown to. My eyes are gray grey lite blu.

I read over what I'd written. So far, so good. With

a glance up at the board to see what came next, I ploughed on.

I was born in – I hesitated for a second, looking up at the ceiling again for inspiration – *Yoogowsarlvia. My dad is the oner of a wold famus sircus cald Equinoxes. He is also the loin tamer. My mum doz a act on the hy trapeez. Wen I was littel we traveld all over Yorup. I lernd to look after the elefants wen I was ony 4. At nite I yoosd to sleep with the loins in ther caj. I dident haf to hav a bath becas the loins yoost to lik me cleen with ther tungs.*

I laid down my pen, rested my head on my hand, and gazed down at what I'd written. I wasn't reading it, though. I was imagining the lions' rough tongues as they licked me clean, feeling the blast of their hot breath in my face. I was seeing the elephants turning heavily towards me when I came to tend them in the grey dawn, their huge feet moving almost soundlessly through the deep, fragrant straw.

With another part of my mind I was picturing my mother, a slim figure in spangled silver, swooping like a bird on the trapeze high overhead, unreachable as a star.

Walking up the hill with a bunch of guys after school, I didn't say much, as usual. Home time – what a laugh.

One by one the guys peeled off, unlatching gates into small, tidy gardens; barging through front doors left on the latch for them as three o'clock came around.

By the time I reached the end of the road, I was the only one left. Ours was the last house. A narrow, overgrown path was just visible winding away through the tangled trees. For a moment the thought of the forbidden ravine with its hidden caves drew me like a magnet. But I was late as it was – I didn't dare risk it.

Reluctantly, I swung open the white wooden gate, banging it shut behind me. I scuffed my feet through the gravel on the way up the drive, little bits of stone working their way through the splits in the toes of my shoes. Dragging my bag behind me, I trailed up the red concrete steps and into the hallway, kicked off my shoes and hung my bag on its hook. Took out my lunchbox, went through the dining hall to the kitchen, and dumped it with the others on the pile on the servery. As usual, I was one of the last back.

I glanced at the clock in the hallway. Three thirty – half an hour till afternoon tea and homework. The big house had the empty, echoing feeling that meant everyone was outside, round the back. *Weekdays, three to four – supervised playtime, weather permitting.*

Five minutes later, I was kicking a soccer ball against the tool-shed wall when I heard the familiar singsong chant:

'*Adam Equinox*
Stupid, dumb, ugly ox
Can't read, can't spell
Can't do anything very well.'

I didn't look up. Didn't have to. I knew exactly who it was, and I didn't want to see his angelic little face with its chubby pink cheeks and its frame of golden curls.

Geoffrey Dempsey.

A stone hit me on the back of my neck. Today Geoffrey didn't intend to be ignored. Blat! Blat! Blat! I kicked the ball harder, hoping to drown the stupid rhyme as it came again . . . and again.

Another stone – and this time, it stung.

I felt my hands clench into fists. I gave the ball one last hard kick and wheeled round, scowling. Geoffrey hopped nimbly back out of harm's way, his face beaming with malicious delight.

He giggled, hopping from foot to foot, ready to run. 'Hey, Adam, I thought you might be bored with the old one, so I've been working on an improvement.

'*Adam Equinox,*
Born in a shoebox,
Can't read, can't write,
Sucks his thumb every night!'

I'm not sure what happened next. All I remember is a kind of red haze and a roaring sound. And next thing I knew, my head was full of this harsh panting sound, like someone sawing wood, and some kids were pulling me off Geoffrey, who was flat on his back.

His smug little face was covered in blood, and the smirk had been wiped right off. His curly locks were tangled in the dirt and his eyes were puffed and swollen. He had his arm up in front of his face, and he was whimpering and staring at me like I was some kind of a monster. I was kneeling over him, gasping and shaking, holding his neck with one hand. My knuckles hurt.

As the red haze faded away and everything came slowly into focus, I saw two black lace-up shoes on the ground beside Geoffrey. Slowly, my gaze travelled up. Past two stick-like ankles in thick brown stockings. Past a tartan skirt and a starched white blouse. Past a scraggy neck like a chicken's . . . and up to Matron's face. The look on it came as no surprise, but even so, my heart sank.

Half an hour later, instead of doing my homework, I was standing on the footstool in Matron's office. My head was beginning to ache.

In the comfortable armchair in the corner opposite the filing cabinet sat Geoffrey. He'd been cleaned up and changed into fresh clothes, but there was a plug of dried blood in one nostril, and his eyes were red and puffy. He was halfway through his second lolly, which he was eating very slowly with wet, sucking sounds.

Matron stood in front of me. Matron is hard and stiff and cold. She has short frizzy hair like steel wool, and a face like a trap. Everything about her is bony and seems to push you away. Even when I was little and she used to pick me up, her fingers kind of poked and pinched and hurt. Now I'm bigger, she does the poking and pinching and hurting with her mind.

'For once in your life, Adam Equinox, tell the truth! Admit that you attacked Geoffrey without provocation, apologise to him, and you can get down and go and do your homework.'

'I won't,' I said, for what seemed like the hundredth time.

Her face tightened. 'You will,' she said. 'Geoffrey, dear, I know this is upsetting, but I'd like you to explain just once more what *really* happened.'

There was a pop as Geoffrey took the lolly out of his mouth. 'I was walking round the back to the tool shed,' he said, in the babyish voice he always put on for Matron's benefit. 'I saw Adam playing with the soccer ball, and I asked him if I could play too.' He gave a little hiccuping sob, and screwed his face up like he was about to cry. 'He told me to . . . he swore at me, Matron, but I don't want to tell you what he said.' Matron's face darkened. 'I told him it was wrong to use language like that. And then he . . . he . . . chased me . . . and . . .'

'There, there, that's enough, dear. Adam, you know I will not tolerate bad language, violence, dishonesty or defiance. This is your last chance. If you want dinner tonight, you will own up and apologise to Geoffrey, *now*.'

It should have been easy. It would have made my life easier, that's for sure. But somehow I just couldn't manage to convince myself to take the easy way out.

Closing my eyes, I tried to imagine the fatty smell of Tuesday's cottage pie sharpening into the clean, metallic tang of engine oil. In the darkness behind my eyelids an engine throbbed and bubbled into life, and an endless highway unfurled towards the horizon.

A Wish and a Prayer

So for me, Tuesday night turned out not to be cottage-pie night after all. Instead, I went hungry, and caught up with my homework in the empty dining hall while the other kids watched TV.

Eight thirty was bedtime. Two minutes to shower and change into pyjamas, then teeth, toilet and bed. Matron stood at the door of our dormitory with her hand on the light switch. 'Straight to sleep and no talking,' she said. 'And as for you, Adam, you'd better remember your prayers – and in your shoes, I'd pray to God to make me a better boy, or who knows where you'll end up.' With that she snapped the light off and banged the door behind her.

There was a soft snicker from Geoffrey, and then silence. No talking after lights out was an unbreakable rule.

I turned over on my side to face the wall, and lay very still. Gradually, the brittle silence relaxed into the sounds of sleep – the creaking of bedsprings as someone burrowed deeper under the covers; a few soft snuffles; a gentle snore from Frankie in the next bed.

When I was as certain as I could be that no one else was still awake, I reached out and felt for the knob of my bedside drawer. Millimetre by millimetre I eased it open just enough for me to slip my hand inside. I reached in and felt right to the back. Up against the back corner of the drawer my fingers found my pencil torch.

The torch was one of my most precious possessions. I'd got it two terms before, when there'd been a reward system of auction points through the school term. I'd ended up with less points than anyone: only sixty-two, while some kids had way over two hundred. There had been heaps of really cool stuff to bid for on the last day of term. Packets of sweets, school-lunch vouchers, Get Out of Sin Bin Free cards – I could have done with one or two of those – and even a couple of small, cheap-looking computer games. I'd looked at the stuff laid out on the teacher's desk and desperately wanted it all. But the one thing I wanted more than all the rest put together was the torch.

Luckily, it was almost the last thing to be auctioned, when the other kids had spent most of their points. They kept asking me, 'Come on, Adam, when are you going to bid? What are you going to go for?' I just tilted back my chair and smiled. The torch had my name on it, though I was the only one who could see. I snapped it up for fifty points, and was left with just enough to buy a sherbet fizz to eat on the way back to Highgate.

The torch was the size and shape of a fat ballpoint pen, and came with two AA-size batteries. Now they were starting to wear out, so these days I only used it when I really, really needed to. Like tonight.

Before I turned it on, I groped in the drawer for the other things I wanted. When I'd found them all, I slipped deep under the bedcovers. Leaning up on one elbow, I made a low kind of tent under the bed-clothes. My finger felt for the little button on top of the torch, and I pushed it forwards. The softest glow illuminated my tent, and I felt private and cosy and safe.

First, I buried my face in the shawl for a moment. It was soft and light as thistledown. I closed my eyes and breathed its special smell in deep – a faint, powdery, almost spicy perfume. I tucked it snugly in beside me.

Next, I laid my little brown *Bible* flat on the sheet. All of us had one, but mine was different. It opened up automatically to the usual place. The newspaper cutting was yellowish, brittle, and completely flat. The edges were thin and kind of frayed-looking, and in some places the words were so blurred you could hardly read them. That was from when I was little, and liked to rub my fingers over it before I went to sleep. Nowadays, I was more careful . . . but I did allow myself to reach out and touch it very gently with the tip of one finger. Then I read it, though I knew the words off by heart.

Baby found in shoebox

A newborn baby boy was found abandoned on the steps of the Highgate Children's Home on Friday.

'The baby appears to be several weeks premature,' said

Inspector Neville Pope, who is leading the investigation into the baby's identity. 'He's strong and in good health, though somewhat small due to his early delivery.'

It is thought the baby was left on the steps of the home early on Friday morning, probably only hours after being born. He was warmly wrapped, and appeared to have been fed before being abandoned. The discovery was made by the cook, Mrs Mary Maddock.

'We found him at about six in the morning, when I was putting out the milk bottles,' Mrs Maddock told reporters. 'I heard a sound I thought must be a kitten, and found the box tucked away in one corner of the porch. I brought it inside, and there he was, warm as toast despite the cold morning. We're calling him Adam Equinox, just until he's claimed. Adam because it's a good Biblical name, and Equinox because he was born on the day of the Equinox – 22nd September, the day when the sun is in the sky for exactly 12 hours, and night and day are equal.'

'We're hoping to resolve this matter soon, as we have more than enough on our plates,' commented the Matron, Miss Agnes Pilcher.

'The baby is of dusky complexion, with dark hair and unusually pale eyes,' said Inspector Pope. 'The only clues to his identity are the cream-coloured lambswool shawl in which he was wrapped, and a silver penny whistle and unusual ring found in the box with him. Other than that, all we have to go on is the box itself, which is similar in size and shape to a large wooden shoebox.'

Anyone with information regarding the baby or his mother, who may be in need of medical assistance, should contact their local police station. Until further information comes to *light, the baby remains in the care of the Highgate Children's Home.*

My fingers felt for the ring, and I slipped it on. It gleamed in the faint torchlight with a mysterious, silvery lustre. I ran my thumb over its strange surface – smooth on the back, thick and deeply ridged at the front – almost as if it was incomplete, or had been made to fit into something. It was still way too big for me, but I loved the comforting weight of it on my finger. For the thousandth time, I wondered if it would ever fit me . . . and whose hand had worn it.

Dreamily, I reached out and stroked the silver penny whistle lying on the threadbare sheet, and smiled. There had been one other gift, one that neither Cook, nor Matron, nor even Inspector Pope had known about. It was the gift of hearing music in my mind; of giving the penny whistle a voice and making it sing.

Was it my imagination, or had the dim beam of the torch become even fainter in the few minutes it had been on? Quickly, I switched it off and put it back in the drawer, sliding it right to the very back with the penny whistle and the ring, and replacing the *Bible* at the front.

I lay down on my right side so I was facing the wall with my back to the room and snuggled the shawl into its place under my cheek. My fingers felt for the lacy edge, and started rubbing it in small circles just under my lip. I could feel my body relaxing, turning heavy and loose, and my mind starting to drift. Without meaning to, my thumb crept into my mouth.

I closed my eyes and began to pray.

Dear God, please bless my mother and father, wherever they are.

Please help me learn to spell and read real well like other kids.

Please let there be something I'm good at, and somewhere I belong.

Please help me to be strong.

And then, as I wavered on the fringes of sleep, an extra thought, half wish, half prayer, formed in my mind.

Please let something wonderful happen to me. Please don't let my life always be like this.

CAMERON'S BOOKMARK

'Duncan, will you please hand the exercise books out. Now, children, on the whole I was very pleased with your autobiographies.'

Miss McCracken was in a good mood. Maybe I'd have a decent mark for a change. I thought back to my story, and how vivid and realistic it had been. No doubt about it, that story was something pretty special! Instead of the sinking feeling I usually had when we got work back, I felt a tentative little squiggle of excitement deep down.

I didn't let it show, though. My book landed in front of me upside down, and I made sure not to seem in any hurry to turn it over. After a moment or two I casually flipped it right way up. In the corner, right by the exit of the maze, Miss McCracken had written in red pen: *Do NOT deface your exercise books!*

Well, never mind that. With a rising feeling of excitement, I opened the book and leafed through. There it was: My Autobiography. Next to the bubble writing, Miss McCracken had written: *Simple underlining is sufficient, thank you, Adam.*

I hadn't realised there'd been the beginning of a smile on my face until I read the comment at the end of the story, and felt my face drop as the smile dissolved away into nothing.

This assignment required a factual account, not a flight of fancy. Yet another shoddy piece of work. Fail. See me.

I felt like I'd been punched in the stomach. A hot wave of humiliation swept over me. My face burned and my ears had that ringing feeling they get after they've been boxed.

Miss McCracken was standing up at the front of the class, smiling and talking, nice as pie. 'Top mark went to Nicole, for a sensitive and well-constructed five-page essay. It isn't often I award ninety-five percent, so well done, Nicole. I'll be asking you to read your autobiography to the class shortly.

'First, though, I would like you all to review the comments I've made, and reread your work in the light of my remarks.'

The smile disappeared and her face tightened.

'Adam Equinox, I will see you now. And bring your book with you.'

I slouched up to her desk, the exercise book dangling from my hand. I couldn't believe that for a second I'd felt proud of my story. Didn't I know better by now?

Miss McCracken looked at me and sighed. 'Adam, surely even *you* must see that this simply isn't good enough?' She licked one finger and snapped the pages over till she came to my story. 'Just look at it. A complete dog's breakfast. Look at the spelling –

when you can read it, that is. For goodness' sake, you have a dictionary! And all of seven lines long. You simply don't try. You have no self-respect, no drive to succeed. You . . .'

'Still,' I muttered, 'you've got no right to call my work shitty.'

'*What?*'

'You've got no right to call my work shitty! It's OK for kids to say that kind of thing, but teachers are supposed to be different!' I was talking loudly now – almost shouting. I felt really, really mad. It was just so unfair!

Miss McCracken had gone pale and moved behind her desk. 'Adam, I didn't call your work . . .'

'Yes, you did!' I yelled. 'Look!' I stabbed the word with my finger. 'Here it is, right here. *Yet another shitty piece of work!* And you say I don't try! How do you *know* whether I try or not? You don't *care* about me *or* my shitty work – all you care about is giving high marks and gold stars to the people who write five pages!'

I was really yelling now. I felt great! I picked up my book and shoved it under her nose. She recoiled as if it might bite her. 'You know how much I care about you and your red pen?' I grabbed the book in both hands. 'This much!' With a twist of my wrists, I ripped the book in half. It felt wonderful. I dropped the two halves on her desk.

There was a long, awful silence.

I could feel every pair of eyes in the room on me, but I didn't look round. Miss McCracken and I both stared down at the pieces of exercise book lying on her desk. And all of a sudden I didn't feel so great. Slowly, I looked up at Miss McCracken. Her face was deadly white, with bright pink blotches high up on both cheeks, as if she'd been slapped. To my horror I could see tears in her eyes. Worst of all, she looked . . . almost afraid.

I stood there with my head sunk between my shoulders like the stupid, dumb, ugly ox Geoffrey said I was. And I plodded after Miss McCracken to the Principal's office without another word.

I spent lunch time taping my book together and rewriting my story, checking every single word in the dictionary. It took the whole hour. The problem with dictionaries is that you need to know how the word is spelt before you can look it up.

For once, I didn't mind. More than anything I just wanted to be by myself. I felt tired and sad and sick to my stomach. I didn't eat the peanut butter sandwich or the apple Cook had packed for my lunch, even though I felt hollow from having no dinner the night before.

After lunch was silent reading. I really like reading, though I'm slower than the other kids. There are always some words I can't figure out, but I just skip them, and let my mind make pictures instead – like watching a movie in my head. Often, I imagine how I'd end the story if I was writing it. Some nights I even dream I'm reading and the words flow easily like water in a stream. I make up the whole rest of the book in my sleep and read every word without one single mistake.

Today, I was halfway through an adventure book about a plane that crashes in the middle of a jungle. I found my place, tipped back my chair, and began to read.

Next to me, on the other side from Nicole, Cameron Harrow was also finding his place. I squinted across to see what he was reading, but all I could see was that his book looked a lot thicker than mine, and the words were smaller and closer together. Next to his book on the desk lay his bookmark, a coloured card with pictures and writing. I craned over to see. 'Psst – Cameron,' I hissed. 'What's that?'

'*Adam . . .*' said Miss McCracken wearily.

Cameron gave me a quick glance and shook his head. We both stared at our books again.

I quite liked Cameron, even though he was a bit of a nerd. He was real rich – at least his parents were. He came to school in a silver sports car, and went to Laser Strike for his birthday parties – not that I was ever invited. But he didn't show off about it and though I sensed he was wary of me and kind of kept his distance, he was never mean like some of the other guys.

Just as I was finally getting into my book something slid onto my desk. I blinked. It was Cameron's bookmark. I snuck a glance over at him. He smiled, and winked. I winked back. I put the card inside my book and pretended to carry on reading while I looked at it.

It was some kind of a computer-game registration

card. One of those things you fill in when you buy stuff – like a guarantee. *FILL THIS IN AND STAND TO WIN!* it said in large letters across the top.

It was more than just a registration card. It was a competition. I frowned, trying to figure it out. If you bought the game – called *Quest for the Golden Goblet* – you were eligible to enter the competition. You had to fill in the card and send it off. And it was reply-paid, so you didn't need a stamp. The prize was a once-in-a-lifetime chance to be one of five kids who got to go to a special 'Gaming Workshop' – whatever that was – with the guy who'd invented the computer game. That, and a state-of-the-art home computer system!

COMPETITION VALID FOR PURCHASES DURING THE MONTHS OF MAY AND JUNE ONLY, it said in big letters. *CUTOFF DATE FOR ENTRIES JUNE 30.*

It was the twenty-seventh today.

I wondered if Cameron was going to enter. I would if it was me – it would be cool to go to a gaming work-shop, *whatever* it was, just to get away from Highgate, Matron and Geoffrey. But people like Cameron didn't have problems like mine. And I guessed Cameron probably already had a state-of-the-art computer.

When we were packing up our bags to go home I handed the card back to him. 'Looks pretty cool,' I said. 'What's it all about, anyway?'

'Well, obviously you've heard of the Quest computer games.'

'Not really,' I admitted.

'You *haven't*?' He thought about that for a minute, and you could see the exact moment it all made sense – yeah, obviously Adam Equinox wouldn't have stuff like computer games in the children's home. Cameron blushed. 'Yeah, well, anyhow,' he carried on quickly, 'it's this real wicked series of games – role-playing interactive adventure-type stuff, in this virtual world called Karazan.' He gave me a quick look through his thick specs to check I was still with him. I nodded – I'd heard guys talking about it. All the kids in the class seemed to have computers and be really into that kind of stuff. And who could blame them? It must be like having a whole different world in your back yard. What wouldn't I give for that?

'Anyhow,' Cameron was explaining, 'the guy who developed the Quest series is the most awesome computer-game wizard in the history of the universe. He's called Quentin Quested – a total genius, but a major recluse. He lives in some huge, isolated mansion, hidden away at the back of beyond, and he has the biggest library of computer games in the world.'

He tucked the card back into his book, and slipped it into his bag.

'The competition winners get to go there for two days and test-drive his latest game – and take home a free computer. It tells you all about it on the website. It sounds pretty cool,' he hooked his bag over his shoulder, 'but I reckon the chances of winning wouldn't be great – practically the whole world will enter. And even if I did win, I couldn't go these holidays, because I'm going away with my family.'

He shrugged, and gave me a grin. 'But the entry form makes a great bookmark.'

'You're not going to enter?'

'Nah,' he said casually, pushing his chair in under his desk.

Suddenly a thought hit him.

'Hey, do you want it?' Quickly, he took the book out again, pulled out the card and handed it to me. 'Good luck,' he grinned, 'but don't hold your breath.'

'Page two hundred and eight, page two hundred and eight,' I could hear him muttering as he headed for the door.

A House of Leaves

After school I went straight back to High-gate, dumped my bag and my lunchbox, and headed for my secret hide-out. The worst thing about living somewhere like Highgate is that there are people watching every single thing you do. Most of the time it doesn't matter, and you get used to it, especially when you've lived with it all your life.

But sometimes it can be pretty annoying. Like when you get a really, really bad mark for your homework, and next thing you know someone's peering over your shoulder and sniggering. Or when you just need some space to think things through and be alone. Or when you've got something private to do. Like today.

No one knew about my hide-out. It had been my special place for years, and my biggest fear was that someone would find it and take it over, or tell Matron.

It was right in the middle of the shrubbery at the side of the house. To get to it, you had to burrow through the middle of a huge old flax bush, the secret entrance to a kind of tunnel I'd made by pushing through over the years. It twisted and turned through dense leaves and between thick, woody trunks till all of a sudden you were through – right up against the brick wall of the house, completely hidden by the shrubs in front and on both sides and overhead. The clearing had grown bigger over the years, same as the tunnel . . . same as me, I guess. It was big enough so I could sit leaning against the wall with my legs stretched out in any direction. I could even lie down if I curled my legs up a bit.

It was awesome. Being in there was like being in a totally private, completely secret little room – a house of leaves. It had a damp, earthy smell and the light was greenish and dim, like in a jungle. It was always cool, even in the middle of summer, and in winter it was freezing.

I'd often thought about moving the special things from my bedside cabinet to my hide-out for safe-keeping. But I was afraid they'd get wrecked when it rained, and anyhow, I needed them close at night.

As I crawled through the tunnel, I realised I still had an apple from my lunch in my pocket. Suddenly I was ravenous. Even though the apple was softish in places, with little black dents in the skin, it smelt wonderful. Everything tasted better in my hide-out. I ate every scrap, even the core, and spat the pips away into the undergrowth.

Time for business. I took the white card and the ballpoint pen out of my pocket. This was one time I was determined my handwriting would be its very tidiest, with no spelling mistakes. That shouldn't be too hard; most of it was totally straightforward stuff like name, address, and telephone number.

Carefully, I brushed some rotting leaves and twigs away to make a clean place on the ground, laid the card down and began to fill it in.

It all seemed pretty simple until the last line. *Please explain, in twenty words or less, why you believe you should be selected for this unique experience.*

I gnawed on the pen, my mind a complete blank. What was I supposed to say? Was there some magically right answer that would give you a better chance of being picked? Well, why *did* I believe I should be selected? I knew I wouldn't be – like Cameron said, the chances were practically non-existent. But after all . . . I scribbled: *Sumwun has to – it mite as well be me.*

Above my head I heard the window of the staff room slide open, and Matron's voice: 'A cup of tea would be *most* welcome, thank you, Cook.'

Having the staff-room window just above my hide-out was a problem in some ways – when the window was open, I had to be extra careful not to make any noise. But there were advantages. I got to know about things before anyone else and sometimes I heard things I was pretty sure Matron would have classified Top Secret. If I was ever found out, I'd be dead meat – we'd had it drummed into us over and over again how wrong it was to eavesdrop. But I reckoned it wasn't eavesdropping so much as military intelligence – because at Highgate, the more you knew, the safer you were.

I slipped back through my tunnel, crept away from the entrance, stood up and dusted myself off. I could hear voices and laughter from the lawn on the other side of the house. There were probably ten minutes or so before afternoon tea – long enough to slip out and post my card if I ran all the way to the postbox, although there'd be trouble if I was caught.

I was out of breath by the time I reached the postbox. I took the card out of my pocket and looked at it one final time. I wondered who would look at it when it reached its destination. I imagined it lying in a clean, manicured hand . . . a red pen like Miss McCracken's poised over it, ready to mark it with an angry red cross.

Suddenly the card seemed grubby, and I noticed one corner was crumpled from being in my pocket. And now that I looked at it again, I had a sinking feeling that *well* should only have one 'l'.

But it was too late to worry about that now – it would look worse with heaps of stuff crossed out than with one tiny mistake nobody would even notice. Quickly, I dropped the card through the slot of the postbox and raced back to Highgate.

A LETTER

It was dumb luck that I was in my hide-out when Matron went through the mail just over a week later. And it was even luckier that Cook was in the staff room, having a cup of tea before she started making dinner. Because if Matron hadn't told Cook about the letter, I wouldn't have heard about it either. At least, not until it was too late.

It was Thursday – sausages and mash day – and one of those warm, muggy afternoons, so the staff-room window was open.

At first, I didn't pay any attention to the voices drifting over my head – it was like having the TV on in the background when you're busy doing something else. Which I was – carving a little wooden horse out of a hunk of wood, using a craft knife I'd borrowed from the art room at school.

I don't know whether it was the sound of my name, or the sudden change in the tone of Matron's voice, that made me sit up like an ant had bitten me on the bum.

'What on earth . . . A letter for *Adam Equinox*!'

'Really, Matron? Now who'd be writing to him, I wonder?'

Cookie's cool. She's pretty much on my side, but she needs her job, so she doesn't often show it. At least when *She* – as she calls Matron – is anywhere near. It was Cookie who kept the newspaper cutting for me when I was just a baby, and it's Cookie who sometimes slips me crackers and apples when Matron's not around.

Matron sounded grim. 'We'll soon find out.'

There was a short silence. I imagined Matron slicing open the envelope of *my* letter with her little brass letter-opener. There was absolutely no doubt at all in my mind who the letter must be from, and what it was about. It was from Quentin Quested – it *must* be!

I felt a wild surge of excitement. Could I possibly have been chosen? Why else would he write to me? I willed Matron to read the letter out loud, so I could hear what it said.

'*Well.*'

'What does it say, Matron? Who's writing to our Adam, then?'

Matron's voice was as sharp as a knife. 'Seems the sly little so-and-so has entered a competition – and not only that, he's been picked as one of the finalists. It says he's to go up north for the final selection process.'

'Well, isn't that nice! Lovely for the wee boy to have a bit of a change, I'd say,' said Cook comfortably.

'You don't for a moment think I'm about to let him

go, do you? Where do you imagine that boy would have got hold of an entry form for a competition like this? I'll tell you where: he *stole* it. And I'm not prepared to reward that kind of behaviour. There is no question of Adam going anywhere, except into my office to be disciplined for this.'

My head swam. I felt dizzy, and as if I was about to be sick. Chosen as a finalist – and not allowed to go!

'On the other hand . . .'

I listened, desperately hoping Matron was about to change her mind. It had never happened before, but as Cook always says, there's a first time for everything.

'It does seem a shame to give this chance up altogether. After all, there's a computer to be had, if we play our cards right. I wonder . . . perhaps it might be more appropriate to let Geoffrey go. He'd certainly have a better chance of getting through any selection process than Adam.'

'But Matron . . .'

'But Matron nothing,' she snapped. 'Don't you have work to do in the kitchen, Cook? And it's high time I called the children in for homework. Yes,' – and I've never hated Matron as much as I did at that moment – 'I think this opportunity will do very nicely for Geoffrey.'

I don't know how long I crouched under the window, as if I'd been turned to stone. It can't have been long, though – dazed and numb as I was, I knew that if Matron had gone to bring the children in, it would only be minutes before I'd be missed. The last thing

I needed was for anyone to come looking for me.

Gradually the numbness was replaced by a weird feeling of disbelief. This was my one chance, the special, magical thing I'd been praying for, and Matron was going to give it to *Geoffrey*.

Suddenly, like someone flicking on a switch, an idea formed in my head – a plan so perfect and complete I blinked. I backtracked and played it through my mind again. Would it work?

One thing was for sure: I had nothing to lose.

I turned round to face the wall and slowly raised my head up through the leafy ceiling to the level of the windowsill. I peeped through the open window and into the room. It was empty, and the door was closed. On the round wooden table in the centre of the room were two cups and saucers, beside a pile of letters.

In a second I'd boosted myself up onto the window ledge and hopped through. I was over to the table like lightning, rifling through the letters with hands that shook, looking for the one addressed to me.

It jumped out at me – Master Adam Equinox – on a fancy envelope with the same Quest logo as the reply card.

I put the other letters back. Vaulted back over the windowsill, and in less time than it takes to blink I was crouching in my hide-out again, the precious letter in my hand. I burned to open it but there was no time. I laid it carefully on the ground at the edge of the clearing and covered it over with dry leaves. I prayed it wouldn't rain.

I slithered back through the tunnel and raced across

the lawn towards the house, my heart hammering as if I'd run a million miles.

Of course, there was a price to pay. It didn't take long for Matron to discover the letter was missing, and you can guess who was the number one suspect.

There was a search of all the dormitories. All the beds were stripped, and the mattresses turned upside down. Our school bags were tipped out, and the rec room and the homework room turned inside out.

I had a two-hour grilling in Matron's office, ending with being sentenced to my toughest punishment ever: no dessert or TV for a month, with a strapping thrown in for good measure. But I didn't care. All I was worried about was whether Matron would connect the open window with the letter's disappearance, put two and two together, and discover my hide-out. I waited with a feeling of doom – but it didn't happen.

What did happen was that Matron found Quest Incorporated's phone number from Directory Enquiries. She told them I had chickenpox and couldn't come, and asked if she could send Geoffrey instead. She told me herself, while I stood on the footstool in her office and she tried to get me to admit I'd stolen the letter.

How can you steal something that belongs to you?

It was Cookie who told me they'd said no, the place in the finals wasn't transferable. Especially once Matron had admitted the letter had gone missing under what Cook called *mysterious circumstances*.

It was two days before the dust settled enough for

me to visit my hide-out again. Two whole days before I was able to retrieve my letter, and at long last read what it said.

Dear Adam
Congratulations – you're a winner!

Yes, it's true! You have been chosen from over 40,000 entries as one of the finalists in the Quest Golden Opportunity Competition.

Only five of the ten finalists will win the ultimate prize – two unforgettable days working with software genius Quentin Quested, and a Nautilus computer system of your very own. But even those who miss out on being one of the final five will win a full Collector's Set of Quest adventure software, with every title in the award-winning series.

Here's what you have to do to take up this amazing opportunity!

Simply arrive with your parent/s or guardian/s at Quentin Quested's country retreat (full directions and map on reverse of this letter) between 4 p.m. and 6 p.m. on the afternoon of Saturday 13 July.

A welcome cocktail party and orientation will be followed by a night in luxurious Quested Court.

The final selection process will take place during the course of the following day, with the names of the successful five being announced at a celebratory banquet that evening.

The five unsuccessful finalists will be presented with their consolation prizes, and will be free to return home.

The chosen five will bid farewell to their guardians, and will remain at Quested Court for the following two days, taking part in a top-secret programme of computer-related activities that will take them to the cutting edge of the adventure-game world, and beyond.

The two-day workshop will conclude at 6 p.m. the following Tuesday evening.

Once again, congratulations on being a winner! We look forward to meeting you. Please do not hesitate to contact us directly if you have any queries, or wish to discuss any aspect of the above.

Your companions in fantasy and adventure,

Quentin Quested and the Quest Team

I must have read the letter about twenty times. It was just too much to take in. I had no idea what it all meant – what would the final selection process involve? I hoped there wouldn't be any tests, like at school. What if I won my way through to the final five? What would it be like, being somewhere that wasn't Highgate or school? The whole thing was huge and terrifying and more exciting than anything that had never happened to me.

Because there was one thing I was absolutely certain of: I was going to be at Quested Court on Saturday 13 July. No matter what it took – if I had to hitch a lift, stow away on a train, or walk the whole way – I was going to be there.

And no one – not even Matron – was going to stop me.

My Secret Mission

In the end, I told Cameron.

I had to – no matter which way I looked at it, I was going to need help. He was the only person I felt I could trust, apart from Cookie – and I didn't want to get her into any kind of trouble.

I told him at athletics practice. We'd both been knocked out of the high jump – I'm no good at it, and Cameron is one of those guys who trips over his own feet. I sidled up to him. 'Hey, Cameron,' I said in his ear. He jumped about a metre, and looked at me kind of warily from behind his specs. Cameron likes to stay on the right side of the teachers, and you could see he wasn't too sure I belonged on the same side. I gave him a reassuring grin, and stood close so I could mutter in his ear.

'Hey – you know that bookmark you gave me?'

'Yeah?' he said cautiously.

'I filled it in and sent it off, and guess what?' Suddenly I felt shy about telling anyone my amazing news – almost as if telling might make it vanish in a puff of smoke, or something crazy like that.

'What?' He was interested now – he'd stopped leaning away and was really listening.

'Well,' I hissed, looking round to check no one else was within earshot, 'I got a letter saying I'm in the final ten!'

That got his attention all right. His head whipped round fast enough to dislocate his neck. '*Wicked!*' he goes, real loud.

'*Shhhh!*'

'Sorry,' he whispered. 'Adam, that is just *so* cool – you're not kidding me?'

I guess he could see I wasn't. He grinned. '*Wicked!*' he said again.

I hadn't expected my news to be greeted with this much excitement – in fact, to tell the truth, I'd had a niggling worry he might try to claim the prize. But he seemed really happy for me. It made me like him even more.

'It *is* wicked, huh? Only thing is, though –'

Quickly, without going into too much detail, I filled him in on the problems with Matron, and how I'd had to take the letter. I wasn't sure he'd approve, being such a goody-goody, but all he said was, 'You nicked it? *Wicked!*'

'Yeah,' I told him, one eye on the sports teacher. 'I'm going, I've made up my mind about that. Only problem is, I have to figure out how, without Matron smelling a rat. I've looked at the map on the back of the letter, and it's about four hundred kilometres. I could hitch, I guess –'

He interrupted me: 'We can't talk about it now – Mr Thomas is giving us funny looks. How about you come home with me after school tomorrow? Bring the letter and we'll make a plan. The whole thing is just way, way cool – you *have* to do it! And hey –' he was really getting into this now, 'we could play *Quest for the Golden Goblet*, too – that way, you'd get an idea of what the whole thing's about before you go. Would you be allowed?'

Matron didn't like it, but there wasn't much she could do about a telephone invitation from Cameron's dad – other than get a look on her face as though she was chewing a lemon when she told me I could go.

There's only one word to describe that afternoon at Cameron's.

Wicked!

For starters, somewhere along the line Cameron stopped looking at me as if he expected me to bite his arm off. For the first time I could remember, I felt like maybe – just maybe – I was making a friend.

His dad picked us up in the silver sports car. It had a CD player, loaded up with music kids our age like, not old-fashioned, fuddy-duddy stuff. We turned it up loud and opened the electric windows; Cameron's dad made a face, and some comment about it being lucky we didn't have far to drive. He was real cool, not how you'd imagine a rich person at all.

Their house was like something you'd see on TV. I started to take my shoes off at the door – there were these real pale, soft-looking carpets – but Cameron laughed, threw down his bag in the hall and walked through to the kitchen.

We raided the pantry, and found some dough-nuts and these huge nectarines with stickers saying they came from California, and chocolate biscuits with crunchy stuff inside. I couldn't believe we were allowed. 'Won't your dad be mad?'

Cameron just laughed. 'That's what it's here for!' I could see he was enjoying himself.

He dug out a bag of popcorn, and we popped it in the microwave. It was magic. We sprinkled on some salt, and piled it on the plates with the rest of the stuff. Then Cameron grabbed two cans of cola from the fridge – a whole can each – and we headed off to his bedroom.

Cameron flopped down on one of the chairs at his desk, and gestured to the one in front of the com-puter. 'You take the driver's seat.' I sat down. 'Right,' he said, 'business first.'

It took us an hour to put together a plan we both felt sure would work. As Cameron said, this kind of chance didn't come more than once in a lifetime – you wouldn't want to mess it up. It was amazing how easy everything was with the Internet. I'd been worrying myself sick about how to find out about buses and train schedules, but all we needed to do was type in the information we wanted to know, press a key, and there it was.

We put together every detail of what Cameron called my 'secret mission', making sure the bits con-nected and it all made sense. The way we worked it,

I'd get to Winterton station at about five on the Saturday evening.

Once we were happy with it, I said, 'Well, I guess I'd better copy it. Have you got a bit of paper and a pencil?' The prospect of writing it down didn't appeal to me at all. I was sure the moment Cameron saw my terrible writing and spelling, he'd remember I was the class dumbhead. He'd stop being friendly and realise it was time I was getting back to Highgate.

'Nah, we'll do it the lazy way,' said Cameron, flicking on the printer, and printing it all out easy as pie.

As I folded it up carefully and put it away in my pocket, I had a sudden, sickening thought. It felt just like one minute I'd been strolling along with my hands in my pockets and next second I'd dropped off the edge of the planet. Reality, I guess.

Cameron was nattering away, but he must have sensed something, because he stopped and gave me this look. 'What's up?'

I looked away. I felt ashamed and miserable and utterly hopeless. 'Nothing,' I mumbled.

'Yeah, there is. Come on, Adam – why have you gone quiet?'

'It's just . . . it's just that . . .'

'Just that what? Whatever it is, let's sort it out quick – we've still got *Golden Goblet* to do before you leave, and it's half past four already!'

There was this big lump blocking my mind – pride, I guess. With a huge effort, I moved it over to the side, out of the way. 'It won't work.'

'What do you mean, it won't work?' he said impatiently. 'Of course it'll work – we've just spent the last hour making sure it'll work perfectly!'

'You don't understand,' I said hopelessly. After all, how could he? This house – the computer – the car – the food – every single thing about Cameron was so different from me that we might as well have been in separate worlds. He could never understand the kind of problems that existed for me. How *could* he? How could we even *begin* to be friends?

Cameron looked at me from behind his thick glasses and said: 'What don't I understand?'

So I blurted it out. 'We forgot about money. It would all cost money, all the buses and trains and stuff.'

Cameron carried on staring at me, waiting for more. 'So?'

'I don't *have* any.' I was mad at myself for not thinking of it before . . . and ashamed to have to admit it in front of Cameron.

He looked at me as though I'd slapped him in the face. A blush crept over his cheeks, and his glasses kind of misted over. He looked down. He's ashamed, too, I thought. Ashamed he ever invited me here.

'I'm sorry,' he said, so softly I had to struggle to hear him. 'I never even thought. Of course you don't have any money.' He gave me this little glinting shy glance. 'I don't suppose . . . I don't want to offend you, or anything.' He took a deep breath. 'But I have heaps. I can give you, or lend you, or whatever, enough to pay for the train fares and stuff, and a bit

45

extra, without even noticing. Would you let me? As my contribution to your secret mission?'

I thought about it – for about a millisecond. I'm pretty good at recognising when I have a choice, and when I don't. 'Well, thanks, I guess,' I said, 'but it's a loan, right? I'll pay you back the second I have money of my own. Only thing is . . .' I found I was grinning at him, 'don't hold your breath, OK?'

'OK,' he said, and held out his hand. I held out mine too, and we shook.

'Deal,' he said.

'Deal.' But in my mind, I wasn't really shaking on that. In my mind, I was hearing *friend*.

It sounded like the best word I'd ever heard.

MATRON STRIKES BACK

What with end-of-term tests and athletic trials, the next few days passed in a blur. Before I knew it, it was Friday. The last day of school – and the day before I was due to set off. I still couldn't believe it was really going to happen – and that was another reason I was glad I'd told Cameron. Without him counting down the hours with me, I reckon I'd have written the whole thing off as a crazy dream.

Miss McCracken handed out our reports, along with the usual lecture about them being addressed to our parents – *and guardians*, with a meaningful look at me – not us, so we must on no account open them.

We took all the artwork and projects off the walls and everyone was given theirs to take home. Cameron rolled his up carefully and asked Miss McCracken for a rubber band to keep them all together.

I screwed mine up and tossed them in the bin.

'*Adam!*' said Cameron. 'Why did you do that?'

Anyone who looked at my stuff for more than a millisecond wouldn't need to ask. It was rubbish – even Miss McCracken didn't pretend any different, always sticking it up way off in one corner, or behind a pot plant. 'I don't keep that kind of junk,' I told him. 'Don't have the space.'

At last the bell went. On the way to the door, Cameron gave me a dig in the ribs. 'Hey, Adam – good luck!' He pushed a piece of paper into my hand. 'This is my e-mail address. If you get the chance, let me know you made it. You can tell me all about it next term – don't forget a single detail!' Cameron was going overseas for the holidays with his family, and wouldn't get back until a couple of days before the new term.

Once the other guys had peeled off home and I was trudging up the last stretch of the hill on my own, I dug my report out of my bag and opened it. Not that I really cared what was in it – but experience had taught me it was better to know what it said in advance.

Language, said the first heading. I slowed down and screwed up my eyes, trying to read Miss McCracken's writing. It wasn't so great – especially for someone who moaned so much about other people's. *Adam has a wide-ranging vocabulary, though an unfortunate tendency to use it inappropriately.* Huh? *His verbal skills do not extend to his written work, which remains poor. Spelling and presentation have shown no improvement over the past term.*

I sighed. This wasn't looking good. *Reading. Adam remains a reluctant reader, lacking the fluency we would expect at this age. He is easily distracted, and frequently disrupts silent reading periods as a result.*

48

Roughly, I shoved the report back into its envelope and stuffed it into my pocket. *School's over*, I thought. *Don't think about all that – think about tomorrow, instead. This time tomorrow you'll be almost four hundred kilometres away from school. And Miss McCracken. And Matron and her precious Geoffrey.*

All through dinner that thought was going round and round in my head, as comforting as a heartbeat: *This time tomorrow, I won't be here.* I usually looked forward to Friday's steak, egg and chips, but today my stomach was churning, and the food seemed to stick in my throat. I ate it all, though – I reckoned I needed to keep my strength up for the morning.

I planned to leave right after breakfast, as I needed to be at the bus stop by nine thirty. The bus would take me to the station, where I'd catch the ten-thirty train. One change at Cranmer, a short wait, and I'd be at Winterton by late afternoon. From there it looked like an easy walk to Quested Court.

Matron's voice cut into my thoughts. 'Children, your attention, please. Those of you being collected for the holidays need to finish your packing and wait in the recreation room for your guardians. Those on washing-up duty go through to the kitchen and begin. As for the rest of you, trays away as usual.' Then her eyes fixed on me like a laser. 'Adam Equinox, I will see you in my office.'

My heart sank. What now? It couldn't be the report – it hadn't been any worse than expected, and Matron didn't usually make a fuss about that kind of thing.

Desperately sifting through everything I'd done – and not done – over the past few days, I slouched down the passage to Matron's door and waited outside. Her heels came clacking after me. She opened the door, marched in and sat behind the desk. I followed her. There were chairs on my side of the desk, too, but I knew better than to sit. They were for visitors; I was expected to stand.

Matron slid open her top drawer and took something out. For a heart-lurching second I thought it was my Quentin Quested letter . . . but when she slapped it down on the desk I saw it was my school report.

'I have had the pleasure of reading your term report,' said Matron. 'Its contents will come as a surprise, as naturally you haven't read it.' I flushed – even I could see the rip in the envelope where I'd torn it open. 'I am most disappointed. Listen to your teacher's closing comment: *Adam is a boy who makes no effort whatsoever to apply himself, and takes no pride in any aspect of his school work. He has poor social skills and is a negative influence on his peers. He is disruptive in class, undisciplined and lacking in consideration and a fundamental sense of responsibility. Adam needs to learn to apply himself, and to develop a sense of self-respect.*'

I felt my face burn. It wasn't true! I wasn't like that! However much I pretended not to care, it hurt to hear that Miss McCracken thought I was so hopeless.

But there was worse to come.

'This is unacceptable, Adam,' said Matron, her voice like ice. 'Your behaviour and poor performance reflect directly on Highgate, and thus on me. I have no alternative other than to punish you for this shameful report. I have thought long and hard about what action would be most appropriate.'

I waited.

Matron looked me dead in the eyes, and smiled.

'I've decided you will be confined to the boys' dormitory until lunch time tomorrow: a period of quiet contemplation to assist you in improving your attitude and behaviour.'

Her eyes were like flints. Suddenly I saw this was about much more than the report. This was about the letter from Quentin Quested.

Like a fool, I'd believed Matron had forgotten. But now I knew she hadn't: she couldn't be sure I'd taken the letter, but *just in case* she was going to lock me up like a prisoner until she knew it would be too late for me to do anything about it.

That night I cried myself to sleep. I hadn't done that since I was a little kid and I thought I'd developed a hard enough shell for it never to happen again. I was wrong. I stuffed my shawl into my mouth and bit down on it so no one would hear. Most of all, I didn't want Geoffrey to know.

When I woke up, it was raining. My head felt swollen and stupid, and my eyes were puffed up like a boxer's. I turned to face the wall, so no one would see. After a while Matron came clacking over to my bed, and stood there for a minute in silence. I lay with my back to her, ignoring her.

'Sulking, are we?' she said. 'Very well: you can stay

there with no breakfast, if that's what you'd prefer. And since you will doubtless feel the same at lunch time, perhaps you'd better miss that, too.'

Her heels clicked away to the door. I heard it snap shut behind her, and the sound of the key in the lock. It would have been a luxury to cry in private, but I had no tears left.

I spent the morning wondering what the time was, and imagining the ten-thirty train to Cranmer pulling away from the platform without me. And playing my penny whistle. And thinking.

When Matron unlocked the door again after lunch, I did my best to look as hang-dog and miserable as possible. I must have done a pretty good job, because she gave a satisfied nod and said, 'Get dressed and come through to the recreation room. Outside play is cancelled because of the rain. You will sit with your back to the television, and read a book.

'And Adam . . .' Her lips twitched into a small smile. 'Don't *ever* try to get the better of me again.'

One thing about Matron – she loves a good exit line. She turned on her heel and clacked off in the direction of her office.

The second she was gone, I leapt out of bed and grabbed my bag. I was already packed, dressed and ready to go, my plastic waterproof over my sweat-shirt. I crept through the dormitory door and down the passageway past Matron's office. The door was closed. I reached the rec room and slipped past with my heart in my mouth. To the front door – edged it open, praying it wouldn't creak. Slid through.

I'd imagined myself slinking through the garden like a spy, making the most of the cover of trees and bushes on my way to the gate. But the moment the door closed behind me, I was off down the drive like an Olympic sprinter, gravel spurting out from under my feet and rain in my face, heading for the tall white gate and freedom.

HOUDINI

I ran all the way to the bus stop, my heart thumping and my bag banging against my back.

Luckily it was downhill almost all the way, and there weren't too many people about. I kept looking back over my shoulder as I ran – I had this crazy vision of Matron pelting after me, blowing a whistle like a policeman.

Just as I reached the bus stop I heard a swooshing sound and there was the bus, along with a wave of water that soaked my shoes and the bottom half of my jeans. With one last glance back along the road, I swung on board and dug in my pocket for the money Cameron had lent me.

'Who're you running away from?' My heart lurched. I looked at the bus driver wildly, but he was grinning. 'Just made it, eh? Good weather for ducks! Where to, son?'

'To the station,' I mumbled, 'please.'

I squelched to the back of the bus and flopped onto a seat next to the window. Closed my eyes and sat back, trying to catch my breath and waiting for my heart to stop hammering and the sick feeling to go away. It was partly hunger – I'd had nothing to eat since last night.

Gradually, I started to feel a bit more normal. The bus was way cool. It was all lit up inside, and the windows were fogged up – I had to rub a little peep-hole to see out. It was great watching other people scurrying through the rain, while I went roaring past in the warm, dry bus.

I wished I could stay on it forever. I had absolutely no clue what I was going to do next. I'd missed the only train that made the connection to Winterton. I'd burnt my boats at Highgate – there was no going back. Could I hitch a ride to Winterton? Sleep over in a doorway in the station, and catch the same train tomorrow?

I dug in my bag and took out Cameron's print-out, guaranteed to get me where I needed to be exactly when I needed to be there. All blown to bits by Matron.

Well, there wasn't much I could do about it now. I folded it up and put it back in the bag – there wasn't any point keeping it, but I didn't want to throw it away.

I put my feet up on the seat in front, rubbed a bigger clear patch on my window and sat back watching the world go by.

I was sorry when we arrived at the station. It was the last stop – the few people left on the bus shuffled off, and the driver turned off the engine and reached for his newspaper.

There were a couple of other buses parked up and a big car park, about half full. I could see the station building over to one side, with a sign saying *Ticket Office*. Beyond it, the railway lines gleamed in the rain, reflecting the red lights of the signals. Over on the other side of the car park was a road – a pretty major-looking road by the looks of it, with a fly-over leading round and up to a motorway, where I could hear the steady roar of traffic.

I also noticed something else. Something that grabbed my attention as surely as if it had sprouted legs and arms and started waving and yelling '*Over here!*'

It was a roadside café, all lit up with a big neon sign that said *Open*. Through the rain I saw a sign below saying *All day breakfasts*. And I didn't have to read at all to figure out the smell wafting across the wet tarmac.

Bacon.

My feet headed off towards the café, and the rest of me moseyed along. Didn't have much choice, really.

Five minutes later I was sitting in a booth, my wet clothes gently steaming in the warmth and a Truck-driver's Special in front of me. Two fat sausages, just about bursting out of their skins. French toast with maple syrup. Two halves of grilled tomato. Two fried eggs, with little crispy bubbles at the edges, and runny golden yolks. And a humungous pile of bacon, with crunchy-looking fat all curled and crinkled at the edges. The waitress took one look at my face when she put the bacon on, gave me a grin and a wink, and dumped on another couple of rashers. 'For luck,' she said.

I needed all the luck I could get, but I didn't care about that now. I took a long, luxurious slurp of my hot chocolate, and dug in.

For the next little while I don't think I'd have noticed if a truck had driven through the middle of the café, or even if Matron had suddenly appeared jangling a pair of handcuffs in my face.

It was the best breakfast I'd ever had – I hadn't known breakfasts like that even existed! I thought about asking the waitress if I could come and live there – clean the floors or something, and have Truck-driver's Specials for breakfast, lunch and dinner, every day.

But as I slowly started to warm up and think straight again, I realised what I really wanted. What I really, really wanted was to get to Quested Court.

I mopped up the last bit of egg yolk with the last morsel of French toast, and popped it into my mouth.

Up at the counter, the waitress was serving a man and a tall skinny girl with plaits, who looked about my age. They picked up their trays and came towards me through the tables, looking for an empty one. As they passed, I snuck a glance at their plates. The girl was having a mammoth muffin and a cola, and the man just had a cup of coffee. I felt sorry for them – they didn't know what they were missing.

It was only when I heard them start talking that I realised they'd taken the booth behind me. It sounded as if they were continuing a discussion they'd been having in their car – the kind that isn't much fun for anyone.

'I *still* don't see why they had to cancel,' the girl said. She had a posh accent, and one of those whiny voices.

The man sounded tired. 'Well, they *have* cancelled,' he said. 'This rain doesn't look like letting up – and even if it does, there's no way the ground would dry out overnight. Not enough to make it safe for showjumping.'

'But Houdini is at his absolute *peak*, Daddy,' she whined. 'I just *know* he would have won. And now we'll have to wait *weeks* for the next show.'

'I know, darling,' said the poor dad. 'It's just one of those tough breaks.'

'We've come all this way for nothing,' she moaned. 'And now we've got the whole long drive back. It's so *boring*.'

'Well, we have the book tape,' said her dad hopefully. I grinned. The poor guy was trying his best! If I was him, I'd tell her to belt up . . . or put her in the back with the horse.

'How long will it take to get home?'

'It's just under three hours to Cranmer, and then another hour and a half or so to Winterton . . . so I'd say four and a half hours – maybe five, given the weather.'

It was as if the names appeared in the air above me in fluorescent neon, flashing on and off like the café sign.

Cranmer. *Winterton.*

Without even thinking, I slid out of the booth and headed for the door. I'd noticed a public toilet on the way in – I paid a quick visit, but I didn't waste any time. How long could it take to drink a cup of coffee and eat a muffin?

I pushed through the glass doors and stood in the shelter of the awning, scanning the car park. There were trucks, parked mostly over to one side, and heaps of cars near the station entrance. Suddenly I saw it, almost hidden by a caravan: a big, grey four-wheel drive, with a horsebox hitched behind.

I ran up to it, glanced quickly over my shoulder to check no one was watching, and tried the little door in the side. I expected it to be locked but it opened easily, and I slipped inside.

A surprised whooffle and a sweet smell of hay, horse and leather greeted me. It was pretty gloomy and it took a moment for my eyes to adjust. But the horse was easy to see – he was white, and shone out of the dark like a ghost. And anyhow, he wasn't about to be ignored. He pushed at me with his nose, looking for attention.

I put one hand flat on either side of his face, and whispered urgently to him. 'Hey, buddy – hey, Houdini. Don't give me away, huh?' He blew down his nostrils at me. The end of his whiskery nose was pale pink and soft as velvet as he nibbled at my sleeve.

I stroked his neck. It felt how I'd imagine silk would feel, only warm and alive. He was so beautiful. If *I* had a horse like that, I'd never moan about anything ever again.

I could see more easily now. On the other side of the horse was a whole bunch of stuff – a couple of buckets, what looked like a saddle and a saddle blanket, and a spare rug. I ducked under the horse's neck and burrowed in under the rug, leaving a tunnel to breathe through. It smelt dusty and I hoped it wouldn't make me sneeze.

Suddenly I heard voices outside.

'Don't you think you should check on Houdini, darling? He may need more hay.'

'Oh, *Daddy* – he'll be fine. Let me in – I'm getting *soaked*!'

I heard two car doors slam in quick succession, and the sound of an engine starting up. The horsebox gave a lurch, and started to move.

We were off!

I popped my head out, spread the blanket over me, and snuggled down deeper into the hay.

Houdini reached down his head and gave me a gentle nudge. I gave him a wink, and in the dim light I could almost have sworn he winked right back.

QUESTED COURT

It was warm and dark in the horsebox, and I was snug on my bed of hay under the rug. I felt full and safe, and most important of all, I was back on track. So with the gentle rocking of the horsebox, and the soft humming of the wheels on the road, I drifted off to sleep.

Next thing I knew, I was jolted awake by a rattling crash as the horsebox ramp hit the ground. It gave Houdini a fright, too – he threw up his head and put his ears back and did a little kind of dance with his front feet.

Quick as a flash, I pulled the rug over my head, leaving a tiny peephole. What now? I'd been planning to slip out the side door as soon as we arrived.

It was almost completely dark. The girl stomped up the ramp and gave Houdini a rough shove. 'Move *over*, stupid!' Obligingly, he shifted over to make room. 'Why can't you stay where you are till morning?' she asked him crossly.

I wished he could have, too – it would have made my life easier.

'Oh, *gross*, you've done a poo, you yucky thing!

Daddy will try to make me clean that up, if he sees it. Come *on* – get out!' She untied him, grabbed his halter and gave his chest a shove. He started backing away down the ramp with little, stiff steps. You could tell he didn't much like it – his ears were still cocked back, and his eyes were rolling backwards trying to see where he was going. He was being very slow and careful. 'Hurry *up*!' snapped the girl.

I figured she'd probably take him to his stable, shut him in and maybe fetch him some hay and water before she came back to the horsebox. I'd have a good chance of slipping away while all that was happening. I tensed under my rug, ready to run.

At last he was down. They turned away and clopped off, Houdini's pale behind disappearing round the side of the horsebox. Cautiously I wriggled out from under the rug. I grabbed my bag and tiptoed softly towards the open ramp.

Suddenly the girl appeared round the side of the horsebox. She was looking back over her shoulder as she walked, talking to someone, presumably her dad. I froze.

'Oh, just put him in the stable and close the door. Rogan can see to the rest in the morning.' She was halfway into the horsebox – about a metre away – when she looked up and saw me, standing like a statue in the gloom. Her eyes bulged and her mouth fell open. She lifted her hands up to her face, and let out this ear-splitting shriek.

I'd been going to run the second she saw me, but when I saw her there, white as Houdini's backside and

62

rooted to the spot with horror, I couldn't resist it. I twisted my face into this real mean snarl, and lifted my hands up like claws. 'Graaaagh!' I growled, taking a couple of steps towards her. That got her moving. She spun around and ran for it – right into the pile of horse poo. Both her feet skidded out from under her, and she fell smack on her back in the middle of it with a juicy squelching sound.

I was out of there. As I hurtled away down the drive I heard one startled shout of '*Hoy!*' before I was flipping a right and pelting away down the road into the darkness, grinning and whooping like a maniac.

My first mad dash soon settled down to a steady jog. I laughed out loud. I felt like a million bucks. It was raining pretty hard and I had no clue where I was headed, but just at that moment, I couldn't have cared less.

I must have gone along the road for twenty minutes or so before I came to a sign. I crossed over and stood in front of it, rummaging in my bag for my torch and the letter. First up, I shone the torch on the sign to see what it said. *Winterton, 5*. There was an arrow pointing off to the left. *Hamley, 45*. I turned the letter over, and shone the torch on the map. It took me a minute to figure out exactly where I was. Quested Court was on the outskirts of Winterton, six kilometres along the Hamley road. All I had to do was follow the side road for a bit, and I'd be there! I couldn't believe my luck.

I flicked off the torch, tucked my precious letter

away in my bag again before it totally disintegrated, and headed on down the Hamley road with the rain in my face.

I walked for what seemed like hours. The map had said six kilometres, but trudging along on foot in the pouring rain, I had no idea how far I'd gone.

When I figured I must be getting close, I started paying more attention to the houses I was passing. I couldn't see most of them – there were just gates, mostly closed, or gateposts, some with surnames or the names of farms. Every now and again I'd see lights shining through trees, or a car would swoosh past. Apart from that, I could have been the only person on the planet.

Then came a long stretch of road with nothing – no farms, no houses, just a tall, dark hedgerow rambling along beside me, and what looked like woodland on the other side of the road. I began to worry that I'd missed it. And then at last I saw twin stone gate-posts up ahead, each topped with a massive stone sphere. I squelched up to them, hoping this was finally it. Sure enough, the words *Quested Court* were carved into a flat stone plaque set into the left-hand post. The gateposts flanked wrought-iron gates that looked as though they meant serious business. Through them, I could see a long, overgrown driveway winding between the trees.

The gates were fastened with a thick steel chain and a hefty padlock on the other side. Without much hope, I reached through and tested it. Locked.

Fastened onto one of the gates was a notice. I squinted at it through the rain. *No trespassing*, it said. *Guard dogs loose.*

I realised I was shivering. I felt cold, tired and wet. My feet were sore, and the Truckdriver's Special seemed a long, long time ago. An icy little trickle of water cruised down the back of my neck. *Come on, Adam*, it seemed to say. *If you stand here feeling sorry for yourself, you're only going to get colder.*

I tossed my bag up over the gate, gripped a metal upright in each hand, and started to climb.

When it finally came into view, the house was way more awesome than I could ever have imagined. I rounded the final bend of the driveway, and there it was – more like a castle than a house, with a dozen or so expensive-looking cars pulled up at the front.

The big windows on the ground floor were brightly lit, and friendly squares of light glowed on the other floors.

I stepped forward . . . there was a smashing sound in the undergrowth behind me, and something hit me squarely in the back and knocked me onto my face in the mud. Instinctively, I covered my head with my arms; I could hear a low, guttural growling, and feel hot breath on the back of my neck.

I was too scared to move; too scared to cry; too scared to do anything except lie with my face squished into the mud and wait for the dog to shred me to pieces.

His muzzle was nearer now; I could feel his cold

nose sniffing, and his stiff whiskers tickling the back of my neck. I held my breath.

I felt a hot tongue lick my ear, and heard a worried, almost apologetic whimper. And then I did start to cry – great, hiccuping sobs that seemed to go on and on. I sat there and bawled like a baby, while the dog whined and licked my face and clambered all over my lap with his huge, muddy paws.

He was the size of a tank, black and fearsome, with a studded leather collar and teeth like a tiger. But his eyes were as soppy as a spaniel's, and his ferocious-looking face was creased with embarrassment and concern. When eventually I got up, he wagged his little stump of a tail and walked the rest of the way to the house pressed against me, glancing up into my face every few seconds. He was so big I could walk with my hand on his back without even having to bend down.

We scrunched past the cars, and up to the huge, arched door. I took a deep breath. The dog watched me with his warm, brown eyes, tongue lolling, grinning encouragement. I lifted the heavy knocker, and let it fall once, twice, three times.

Then I put my hand on my new friend's neck again, and waited.

AN UNEXPECTED VISITOR

The door opened, and I blinked in the sudden spill of light. An enormous man was silhouetted against the brightness. I felt so dazzled that for a second I had the crazy impression he was a giant.

'Well, my giddy aunt,' goes the giant. 'What 'ave we 'ere? Where in carnation 'ave you come from, young feller? But never mind that, come in outta the cold. And as fer *you* –' he bent and scratched the dog behind one ear – 'Call yerself a guard dog, yer old shandy-pants?'

A huge hand was on my back, gently propelling me into a flagged hallway the size of a soccer field. I shuffled in, digging in my sodden bag for my letter.

'Please, sir,' I said, my voice sounding thin and quavery. 'Please, sir, Mr Quested, I'm Adam Equinox, and –' my fingers found the letter at last, and I held it towards him. It looked very damp and dog-eared – 'and this is my letter.'

The huge man stared at me, making no attempt to take the letter. He scratched his head.

'You're *Adam*, are yer?' he said at last. 'The wee

boy with the chickenpox? And bless yer barnacles, sonny, I'm not Q – I'm Shaw.'

My head was spinning. What was Q? And why was the big man telling me that he was sure he wasn't it?

'You'll not be wantin' to go to the party in that state.' He opened one of the heavy wooden doors off the hallway, and ushered me through into a room I realised must be a library. It was lined with books, stretching from floor to ceiling. In one corner was a massive wooden desk with a computer. A fire was blazing in an enormous stone fireplace, with battered-looking leather armchairs on either side. On one of the chairs, a small cream-coloured cat was curled up asleep.

I took a couple of steps into the room, and gasped. Shuffling towards me through an ornate golden door-way opposite was a creature that could have come straight out of the fantasy world of Karazan. It looked half animal, half human. A bowed, shaggy head covered in matted hair, with spikes of straw sticking out at odd angles. A face so streaked and smeared with mud that it gave the impression of being some kind of weird war paint. Its clothes were a dirty brown, like old sacks, and the creature was so filthy it was impossible to make out where they ended and its skin began. Weirdest of all was a visible aura around it of wavering steam, like something out of a horror movie. I gaped, and rubbed my eyes. Surely I must be dreaming? Maybe the whole thing was one long, incredible dream!

And the creature in the mirror gaped right back at me and rubbed its eyes, too.

The man – his *name* was Shaw, it turned out – went and fetched a lady with a face like a hawk, and they hustled me up a staircase, along a couple of corridors and into a bedroom the size of the entire boys' dormitory at Highgate.

'This is the room you'll be sharing with Richard Osborne, one of the other finalists,' the lady told me. She pointed to a door over on one side of the room. 'In the bathroom you will find soap, shampoo and towels. I suggest you have an extremely thorough bath. While you do that, I'll see what I can arrange in the way of clean clothes. Leave yours in the laundry basket, and we'll deal with them later. Once you're presentable, we'll introduce you to Q. No doubt he'll have his own ideas about how to cope with your unexpected arrival.'

I guess I must have looked confused. The woman reminded me uncomfortably of Miss McCracken, though I could tell she was trying to be kind.

Shaw gave me a grin and a wink. 'Usherwood's the real boss,' he whispered. 'We all jump when she says jump, even Q.'

'*Ms* Usherwood, if you please, Shaw.' She gave him a small frown and me a cool, rather distracted-looking nod, and away they went.

I peeled my clothes off and left them in a soggy clump on the bathroom floor. There was something I guessed must be the laundry basket, but it was made of white wickerwork and I didn't have the nerve to put my clothes anywhere near it.

I must have stayed in the bath for half an hour, wallowing in the hot water and shampooing my hair into a lather that flew around the room like snow. At last, reluctantly, I got out, wrapped one of the thick, fluffy towels round my waist, and headed through to the bedroom.

There, laid out on one of the beds, were clean clothes: a pair of jeans, a dark blue T-shirt, and a hooded grey sweatshirt. Way cool – all the kids at school wore hoodies on mufti day, but at Highgate my chances of getting one were about the same as flying to the moon. I guessed the clothes must be borrowed from one of the other finalists. I picked up the sweatshirt and held it up to check the size. Underneath it was a pair of boxers – real satin ones. They were black, with a picture of Bart Simpson doing a brown-eye, and the words *Kick my butt*. I grinned, wondering what Ms Usherwood made of *that*.

Just when everything was starting to feel more normal, the door opened a crack, all by itself. I froze, and clutched my towel tighter round my waist. What now?

Round the edge of the door, at about waist height, came what looked like a chopstick. It wavered about for a second or two. I watched, mesmerised. Then the door swung open a bit further, and in popped a little girl.

I guessed she must have been about five. She had on bright lime-green leggings and no shoes. Her toenails were painted purple. She was wearing a white top – none too clean – with little pink and purple flowers. Her face was thin and serious-looking, framed with honey-coloured hair cut in a blunt bob, topped off with a plastic headband with two pipe cleaners sticking up from it, a bit like a moth's antennae.

The little girl waved the chopstick, did two skipping steps sideways, and dropped me a curtsey. Her head-gear fell off, and she reached down and grabbed it and quickly jammed it back on, shooting me a glance to see if I'd noticed.

I pretended I hadn't.

'I am Fairy Princess Fenella Foo-Foo,' she announced. 'And who, pray, are you?'

I wasn't about to be outdone by a five-year-old.

'I'm Crown Prince Adam Equinox,' I told her grandly, and bowed. 'And I am charmed to make your acquaintance.'

'Good,' she goes, and nods, as if I've passed some kind of a test. Then she trots across and hops onto my bed. 'I'm Hannah Quested, *really*,' she admitted. 'Who are you, really?'

'Oh, I'm just Adam,' I told her.

She nodded again.

'I know that. I came to look at you.'

'Oh, yeah? What's so interesting about me?'

'Usherwood said you were a *real little savage*,' she told me, and her face lit up with sudden mischief. 'I wasn't supposed to hear. I've never seen a savage, so I wanted to come and have a look.'

'And what do you think?'

'I think Shaw's right. *He* says you must be a magician, because Sabre didn't gobble you up. Anyhow, I *like* savages,' she said, wiggling her toes. 'Have you unpacked?'

'Nah,' I said.

'All the others have. Shall I help you?'

'I don't really need much help, thanks all the same.' I lifted my bag onto the end of the bed, and opened it. 'This is all I brought.'

Unfortunately, the first thing to emerge out of the bag was my spare pair of Y-fronts, grey and sad-looking. Her eyes brightened. 'Q has ones like that,' she told me.

'Who's Q?' I asked, though by now I was pretty sure I knew.

'Q is Q,' she said. 'He's Quentin Quested. He's my daddy.'

'And who's your mummy?' I asked. 'Is it Usherwood?'

She giggled, and rolled her eyes. 'No, of course not, silly,' she said scornfully, 'though sometimes I think she'd like to be. But *I* wouldn't, and neither would Tiger Lily, so it won't happen. No. My mummy was a gold-digger, but now she's gone. And Q doesn't care because he has me, and I don't care because I have Q and Nanny and Withers and Tiger Lily . . .' a slightly doubtful look crossed her small face, 'and Usherwood and Shaw, too, I suppose.'

I was battling to keep up with all this. 'Who's Withers?'

'Oh, he does the sums and counts all the money.

And sometimes he reads me stories. He's nice.'

I fished out my spare T-shirt. It was wetter than the Y-fronts, so I took it through to the bathroom and hung it on the warm towel rail.

Hannah was still there when I got back, admiring her toenails.

I took out my shawl. It felt a bit damp, but it seemed OK. I gave it a sniff. It smelled the same as always.

'Is that your blanky?' asked Hannah.

'Yeah, I guess it is, in a way.'

She nodded approvingly.

'Tell me about the other kids,' I said. I figured I might as well make the most of my uninvited visitor.

'Well, there are cool ones and not cool ones,' she told me. 'There's one called Genevieve. That's her real name, *really*. I wish *my* real name was Genevieve,' she said wistfully.

'Yeah, and who else?'

'Well, there's a fat piggy one who has a whole suitcase full of sweets and doesn't share.' No need to ask what she thought of *him*. 'And there's a mean foxy boy, and a big boy like you with hair like an ants' nest, and there's Richard, whose clothes those are, and heaps more. But five of them will go home tomorrow, after you've done the test.'

My stomach gave an uncomfortable lurch. 'Oh, yeah?' I said casually. 'What test is that?'

'The Quest Test, of course. Q made it up. He's good at making things up. Is your daddy good at making things up?'

'Hard to say,' I muttered. I took the *Bible* out of the bottom of my bag, and put it in the drawer beside the bed.

'Is that all you have?'

'No, I have a couple more things.' I took out my penny whistle. Normally I would rather die than show it to anyone, but somehow Hannah didn't seem to count. Her eyes grew very round, and her face even more solemn. 'Can you play it?' she whispered.

'Not much use having it if I didn't play it.' I put it up to my lips and played a few bars of one of my songs.

'More,' she said, when I stopped.

So I finished the song.

'You're not a savage,' she whispered. 'And I don't think you're a magician. I think you *are* a prince, *really*. I'm going to tell Q.'

She hopped off the bed and ran out of the room, slamming the door behind her.

Q

O nce I was dressed, there was a brisk rap on the door. Feeling a bit shy, I called, 'Come in.'

The door opened and in came Ms Usherwood. It struck me for the first time how smartly dressed she was – not what I'd call party clothes, but a tight dark skirt and jacket, almost like a uniform. She stopped dead in the doorway, staring at me as if she'd never seen me before. There was something in her eyes . . . a look of surprise, of confusion, almost . . . as if whoever she'd expected to see, it wasn't old Crown Prince Adam Equinox in his borrowed finery. 'Well, you certainly scrub up well,' she remarked dryly. 'I'd hardly have recognised you. Give you a year or two, and you'll be fighting the girls off. Now, are you ready to meet Q? I dare say you're hungry – we'll see what we can do about that. Follow me.'

Obediently, I trailed after her. She marched back down the same corridors we'd come along before, down the stairs to the door leading into the library. This time I was in a better state to take in my surroundings: the deep carpets, the rich wallpaper and the paintings – mostly men and women in old-fashioned clothes – that hung on all the walls, and peculiar moulded ceilings so high I had to tilt my head to see them.

Outside the library she paused, nodding over to one of the doors opposite. 'The reception's in there. All getting on like a house on fire, but I dare say it'll be a different story tomorrow, once the selection's been made. Well, in you go.'

I gave my jeans a hitch up, and pushed my hair out of my eyes. Suddenly I felt a flutter of nerves. Ms Usherwood gave a little laugh, almost like a snort. 'Oh, don't worry, Adam, Q wouldn't notice if you walked in stark naked. He doesn't see that kind of detail.'

She swung the library door open and gave me a shove. 'Adam Equinox, Q,' she announced, and closed the door behind me.

This time a very different boy was reflected in the gilt mirror. Curious though I was to see the famous Q, I could hardly drag my eyes away from my reflection. I looked way cool. If you hadn't known, you'd never in a million years have guessed I lived in an orphanage and usually wore hand-me-downs. I looked like the kind of dude whose dad owned a mansion with a swimming pool and a tennis court, with a couple of limousines parked out the back. No wonder Usherwood had stared. I squared my shoulders, lifted my head, took a deep breath . . . and suddenly I wasn't the least bit nervous about meeting Quentin Quested.

My eyes swivelled round the room. The first person

I saw was Hannah, sitting in one of the chairs by the fire, the cream-coloured cat asleep on her lap. She gave me a solemn, measuring look.

A man in the chair opposite was levering himself to his feet. 'So you are Adam Equinox,' he said, holding out his hand. I shook it firmly, looking him in the eye like Matron told us to when we were introduced to someone. He didn't seem interested in shaking back, though – he held my hand in his gently, as though it might break, and smiled at me with a curious, questioning expression.

He was nothing like I'd imagined. He was tall and thin, and his clothes hung on him like a scarecrow. He had on these old corduroy trousers – none too clean – and a checked shirt with a frayed collar and the top button hanging by a thread.

The weird thing was, though, that his scruffy clothes didn't matter. My eyes were drawn to his face – such an odd, knobbly, ugly, interesting face that I knew at once I would never forget it. He reminded me of a very kind, clever tortoise. His skin was pale, and faintly freckled – the sort of skin that belongs to red-haired people, though it was impossible to tell what colour his had been from the few faded, cottony tendrils that floated round his bald head. A pair of smeary rimless glasses sat askew on his crooked nose, and from behind the glasses peered eyes of a startling blue. His expression was honest, friendly and had a peculiar innocence that reminded me of Hannah.

He was drawing me closer to the fire. 'Hannah, my sweetheart, hop up and let Adam sit there.'

'But I have Tiger Lily on my lap!'

'Well, perhaps Adam would like to have her on *his* lap – if he likes cats, that is. And *you* can sit on *my* lap.'

'She may not stay with Adam,' warned Hannah. 'You know how fussy she is.'

I sat in the huge old chair, which folded itself round me in a wonderful, luxurious embrace. Hannah put Tiger Lily on my knee, and there was a tense pause while she decided whether to give up her place by the fire on principle, or settle down and continue her snooze. I gave her a stroke to help her make up her mind.

Q sat in the other chair, and Hannah snuggled down on his lap. Tiger Lily started to purr.

'She likes you,' announced Hannah, and craned her neck to look up into her dad's face. 'What did I tell you?'

Q smiled. 'I've been hearing all about you,' he told me. 'But first, I must tell you how glad I am that you could come.'

'How glad *we* are,' corrected Hannah.

Q stroked her cheek. 'Now, you will be interested to know I've had a phone call from a Miss – Miss – oh, lord, what was her name again?'

'Miss Pilcher,' Hannah supplied.

'Yes, that's it, Miss Pilcher, of . . .'

'Highgate,' said Hannah.

'Yes, Highgate.'

My heart sank.

'She seemed upset,' said Q. That would be putting

it mildly – she'd more likely be ballistic, and I was pretty sure she'd have let Q know in no uncertain terms. In fact, I wouldn't have been surprised if he'd been sitting there with singed eyebrows, and Quested Court a smouldering ruin around him.

But Q seemed unperturbed. 'It appears there was a misunderstanding about my invitation,' he went on.

'*And* about the chickenpox,' goes Hannah, rolling her eyes.

'Yes, that too. In view of the inconvenience, I have made a . . . ah . . . strategic donation to Highbury . . .'

'High*gate*.'

'Thank you, Hannah, to Highgate, which seems to have smoothed things over. I think you will find all will be well, even when you return.'

And something about the way he said it made me believe that maybe it would all be OK, after all.

'Now, are you hungry?'

'Yes, I am, a bit.' I suddenly realised I was starving, but even as I admitted it, I found myself hoping desperately I wouldn't have to go through to the reception and meet all those strange people. I really didn't feel ready for that.

'Chatterbot, could you run through to the kitchen and ask Nanny to organise something for Adam – something simple he can have in here, by the fire? Tell her he needs something *substantial*.'

'Something *substantial*,' she repeated. 'How about a fairy sandwich? That's white bread with hundreds and thousands. Would you like that, Adam? It's my *best*!'

She slid down and trotted over to the door.

Disappeared for a second, then popped her head back round. 'Q, *what* was that word again?'

'Substantial.'

'Sub*stantial*, sub*stantial*,' she chanted, disappearing again.

We both sat there smiling at the closed door. 'Cool kid,' I said.

'She is the light of my life,' said Q simply. I wondered what it must be like to be the light of someone's life; to be loved like that.

'Now,' said Q, 'tell me. Are you comfortable? Do you have everything you need?'

'Yes, I'm fine. I've borrowed these clothes from someone called Richard, till my own are dry.'

'Good, good,' said Q vaguely. 'More importantly, is there anything you need to know? Any questions?'

Well, of course there were heaps of questions. Like, what would happen tomorrow? What about the test? Would it be hard? Would there be a spelling one? What were the other finalists like? When would I meet them? Were they all super-cool and rich and clever? Did it matter that I didn't know a single thing about computers? How would I get back to Highgate, if I wasn't chosen? And what would happen if I was?

I made a kind of gulping sound, and opened my mouth without the least idea which question was most likely to come out.

'Was it just luck that my card was picked?' I heard myself ask.

'How interesting you should ask that, Adam,' said Q. 'Of all the finalists, you are the only one to whom it seems to have occurred. Very few things in life are just luck, and this certainly was not. The entire selection process has been carefully orchestrated, in a way that will become more apparent as your visit progresses. Because of the numbers involved and the distance factor, the criteria employed in the initial selection were less specific than they will be in the later stages. But they were critical, nonetheless. Yes, critical.'

'Huh?'

He beamed at me, took off the specs, and polished them on his jersey. 'In answer to your question, Adam: no, you're not here by chance. You have qualified to be here, just as the other nine have, and your chances of progressing further are predetermined, just as theirs are. It is a question of correctly identifying the final five, rather than randomly selecting them. There are patterns to these things; it's just that, being caught in the weave, we find the pattern hard to see.'

The door opened and in came Hannah, backside first. She bent down, and picked up a tray from the floor outside the door.

'*I* said fairy sandwiches, and *Nanny* thought a pie,' she said. 'So, you've got them both. And look! There are two sandwiches!'

'Yup, I see there are.' I smiled at her. 'I think you'd better have one of them, don't you?'

TEN FINALISTS

In the end, I didn't ask any more questions. Eating my supper and listening to Hannah chattering happily away about the special magnet on Tiger Lily's collar that opened her cat door, I found my eyelids growing heavier and huge yawns almost dislocating my jaw. When at last I'd licked my fingers and polished off the last few flakes of pastry, I was more than ready to let Hannah show me the way back upstairs to my room.

There was still no sign of my room-mate, so I gave my teeth a token scrub, and stripped down to the boxers.

Then I fell into bed, and plummeted straight into a dreamless sleep.

I was woken by the sound of a curtain being pulled back and a bright bar of sunlight falling across my face. I pushed myself up on one elbow, squinting and shielding my eyes.

'Oops – sorry,' said a voice, and the sunlight disappeared. A stocky blond boy about my own age was standing by the window in boxers and a T-shirt, grinning at me. 'Great that it's a nice day, though,' he said. 'You're Adam, aren't you? You missed a whole lot of fun last night – we played flashlight in the garden once the rain stopped. It was awesome. This boy called Jamie fell in the lake.' He sat down on the end of his bed and looked at me curiously. 'Is it true you hitched here? That's what the others are saying. And that you . . .' he looked embarrassed. 'Well . . . that you haven't come with your parents.'

I sat up and stretched. 'Yeah, that part's true. I came on my own. But I didn't hitch a ride.' His face fell. 'I stowed away in a horsebox,' I told him with a grin, 'but only as far as Winterton. Then I walked the rest of the way.'

'Honest? That's just *so* cool. I came with my dad – Mum's at home with my kid brother. What do you think we should wear today? I mean, will we be doing, like, tests and stuff inside, or will we be outside? What do you think? Shorts or jeans?'

'Dunno. I only have the stuff you lent me – my other clothes are still wet.' I padded over to the bathroom, planning to give the sodden pile an exploratory poke with my toe – who knew, they might be dry enough to put on. And there they were, clean and ironed and folded in a tidy pile on top of the laundry basket. Like magic.

Once we were dressed, we headed downstairs to the dining room, where Richard said everyone was meeting for breakfast. I felt a twinge of nerves – from Richard's description of last night, the other kids had got to know one another pretty well. I was glad

I didn't have to walk in on my own. Richard must have guessed how I felt – he gave me an encouraging grin as we walked down the staircase, and whispered, 'Wait till the others hear how you *really* got here!'

The dining room was warm and sunny and full of people. A few were standing at a sideboard by the wall, helping themselves from huge silver bowls, but most were sitting at the long table, eating and talking. The moment we walked in, the talking stopped and there was this awful silence. Everyone stared at me – a sea of unfamiliar faces.

Ms Usherwood popped up from the far end, where most of the adults were sitting. 'I'd like to introduce Adam Equinox, everybody,' she goes. 'Adam joined us last night. I see you've already met Richard, Adam. Come and help yourself to some breakfast.'

There was enough food to feed an army. At one end there were platters of fresh fruit – orange, melon, strawberries, grapefruit, and something Richard reckoned was mango. There were cereals, too, and big pitchers of cold milk. Over in the middle were great silver bowls of bacon, kidneys, baked beans and scrambled egg. And at the other end were racks of hot, fresh toast, funny rolls the shape of crescent moons, and piles of sticky pastries with icing.

At first I felt too shy to take whatever I wanted, like Richard said we were supposed to do. But he seemed pretty relaxed. 'Just take it in stages,' he advised. 'You can always come back for more.'

Once we'd helped ourselves, we sat down in two empty seats next to a short, very fat boy with straight blond hair. He had a big plate piled high with about half a dozen pastries, but that didn't stop his little eyes darting straight to our plates to see if we'd found anything nicer. On the other side of him was a woman who could only be his mum – big and billowy in a pale pink floaty dress. She was nibbling on a tiny piece of toast. 'Say hello to Adam, dear,' she told the boy. 'We must remember our manners.'

'Hello, Adam,' said the fat kid, through a mouthful of pastry.

'Introduce yourself properly, son,' growls a fat guy in a suit who had to be his dad. 'Let people know your name – walk tall and stand proud, that's my man.'

The kid swallowed, and held out a sticky hand. 'I am Jamie Fitzpatrick,' he announced obediently. 'How do you do?'

I shook his hand, which felt as sticky as it looked – and sweaty. I wanted to wipe it on my shirt, but I didn't think it would be polite.

At that moment Ms Usherwood stood up at the head of the table. 'Could I have your attention please, while I outline the day's activities.

'The adults will meet outside the main entrance at nine thirty – that's in fifteen minutes. This morning, Shaw will take you on a conducted tour of the gardens. As you are aware, these are normally closed to the public. Highlights of the garden tour include the wild-flower meadow, modelled on the alpine pastures of Switzerland, and the Oriental, South African and traditional English country gardens. You will also be visiting the walled garden, the organic kitchen garden, the water garden, and, of course, Fantasy Glade, which is inspired by landscapes derived from Quentin Quested's Karazan series. The morning will conclude with a gourmet picnic lunch under the oaks on the east lawn.'

There was a subdued murmur of approval from the parents.

'There is a more exacting schedule for the children. The initiatives course planned for this morning has been postponed to the afternoon, to give the course a chance to dry out.'

What was an initiatives course? I looked over at Richard, and he looked back at me blankly.

Ms Usherwood continued: 'Instead, we will be conducting the more formal part of the selection process this morning. I'd like you all to meet in the hall, also at nine thirty, and we will proceed from there.'

Jamie's pudgy hand went up. 'Yes, James?'

'Please, Miss Usherwood, will we need anything? Like a pencil case, or a calculator, or anything like that?'

'No, James, everything you need will be supplied. And now, if there are no further questions, perhaps you will excuse me.'

A babble of excited – and nervous – chatter followed her departure.

A tall, broad-shouldered boy with dreadlocks – Hannah's ants'-nest hair, I'd bet – was talking about the initiatives course. 'I'm not worried about it,' he said, in a loud, confident voice. 'If it's outside, that means it's physical; if it's physical, I'll crack it, no worries. I'm the sprint and long distance champ at my school and I can jump four metres seventy in long jump.'

A pretty dark-haired girl piped up from the other side of the table. 'It's all very well for you, Zach. *I* hope it's nothing to do with ball games. I'm so hopeless, I can't even hit a tennis ball.'

'If there are proper tests, like at school, I hope they're – what do you call it? – mulpital choice,' goes Richard. 'That way, you can always guess the answers.'

'I really enjoy creative writing and essays,' said a plain-looking girl with mousy-coloured hair and ears that stuck out. 'I'm OK with comprehension tests and stuff. Just so long as it's nothing to do with *worms* . . .'

'Do you think it might be arm wrestling?' asked Richard hopefully. But everyone ignored him.

'Are you scared of worms, Genevieve?' said a thin-faced, red-haired boy in the corner. 'Wish I'd known that last night!'

'Well, I'm praying it's nothing to do with maths,' muttered Richard. I was liking him more every minute.

'But maths is so *easy*, Richard,' said Jamie loftily. 'It's all logic, plain and simple. Personally, I'm an all-rounder, so I'm hoping the tests will cover as wide a range as possible. I'd describe myself as more of an academic than a sportsman, though.'

'Focus on the positive, James,' chips in his dad. 'With a positive attitude, the sky's the limit.'

This reminder that the grown-ups were listening

put a sudden dampener on the conversation. I pushed my chair back. 'What about you, Adam?' asked Genevieve. 'What are you best at?'

There was a ghastly silence while I thought frantically. Everyone was looking at me, but my mind was a complete, total blank. What was I best at? What was I even *slightly* good at? I felt my face burn. The silence stretched longer, like a rubber band about to snap.

Suddenly a shrill voice piped up from the door. 'Adam is good at *everything*! At mountain climbing and wrestling and leapfrog and stories and sailing and . . . and *jousting*!' shouted Hannah triumphantly, with a little jump for emphasis.

There was a startled pause. Then everyone laughed, and there was a general pushing back of chairs as people headed off to get ready for the day.

I wished with all my heart it was true.

THE QUEST TEST

'**N**ow,' said Q, peering at us through his cloudy glasses, 'if you'd please turn on your computers . . .'

We were sitting in a big, air-conditioned room on the ground floor. The blinds were drawn over the long windows, and the room was bathed in cool fluorescent light. There was a clean whiteboard up at the front, where Q was standing. Over on one side was something round draped in a black cloth, standing on a pedestal.

Something about the room gave me a familiar, sinking feeling, and it didn't take me long to figure it out. It reminded me of a classroom. The desks were bigger, though, with plenty of space between, and on each one was a computer. Up at the front was a desk the same as ours, also with a computer – for Q, I supposed.

Beside each screen was a glass, a jug of water and a little bowl of wrapped peppermints. I wondered if they were for us – and whether we were allowed to help ourselves. At his desk across the room Jamie unwrapped two in rapid succession, and popped them both into his mouth.

Keeping an eye on what the others were doing, I felt along the side of my computer for the on-off switch. The screen flickered, and then lots of white words flashed past too quickly to read. Another flicker, and the screen turned blue, with about ten little brightly coloured emblems on it. One of them seemed familiar: it was the logo of *Quest for the Golden Goblet*, just like the one on Cameron's computer. My heart leapt – maybe we were going to play computer games!

'I'd like you all to click on the icon at the top left, please,' Q was saying. Quickly, I checked to see what everyone else was doing. They were using the mouse. Tentatively, I reached for mine and gave it a wiggle. A little arrow squiggled round on my screen. I put it on the top left icon, and clicked with my finger, like I'd done at Cameron's.

The blue screen disappeared, replaced by a black one with tiny pinpricks of stars. While I watched, words formed in silver on the blackness:

Welcome, Adam Equinox.

Cool!

'Now,' Q was saying up at the front, 'it's important that you work completely at your own pace. Don't worry about what your neighbour is doing; don't worry if you feel you're lagging behind. This isn't a race. Trust your instincts. And remember, for many of the questions, there is no right answer. Please begin when you're ready.'

Yeah, but how? I looked at the screen. Ah – there

was a little rectangle over on the right, down at the bottom. *Start*, it said. I clicked on it.

What is the next number in this series?

7 3 6 5 12 7 4 9 2

Hopelessly, I stared at the numbers. They didn't make any kind of sense. There was no pattern. Down the bottom, the little rectangle said, *Next*. I reckoned I'd scout ahead a bit, maybe see if there were some easier questions further on. I clicked.

What is the missing letter in this sequence?

r e t u p m o

I sighed. I was beginning to wish I'd never come. *Next*.

Insert the missing letter to form two words.

FRO_ROW

I felt sick and stupid, and my head was starting to ache. The words sat smugly on the screen, and the cursor blinked, mocking me. All round me, the other kids were clicking their mice and tapping away at their keyboards. I risked a glance over at Richard. He was chewing his thumbnail and frowning, but as I watched, his face broke into a relieved grin, and he typed something in and sat back, arms folded. *Next*.

Which is the odd one out?

Tree Mouse Rock Eagle Ant

Quick as a flash, I clicked on *Rock*. *Next*.

A boat will bear the weight of three people without sinking. If Jane weighs twice as much as Simon, and Simon weighs half as much as Rob, and Rob is the tallest, which two can safely travel in the boat at the same time?
I grinned, and tapped in the answer.

Over on the other side of the room, Jamie's hand was flapping in the air. Q went quietly over to him. I heard the murmur of his voice, then Jamie's, loudly: 'I'm first to finish, aren't I? It was *so* easy!' Another murmur from Q, then: 'Well, I *want* to check my answers! My dad made me promise . . .'

More murmurs, then a disgruntled silence. *Next.*

In three days' time, it will be Wednesday. What was the day before yesterday?

I looked up at the ceiling, and counted on my fingers. *Next.*

Please answer YES or NO to the following questions.
I find it easy to talk about how I am feeling.
I often do things on the spur of the moment.
If things don't work out first time, I have another go.
I enjoy solving problems.
I like working in groups.
I can usually tell how other people are feeling.
In a group of people, I am often the quietest one.
I regard truth as flexible, rather than as an absolute.

Frowning, trying to be honest, I worked my way through them all. It took me a while to work the last one out. Then I typed in *No. Next.*

For your birthday, you are allowed to choose between three computer games. Which would you choose?

a) A fantasy adventure game set in an imaginary world.

b) A war game based on strategy.

c) A puzzle game which requires logical reasoning, sequential thinking and pattern finding.

I clicked on *a)*. I was prepared to bet everyone had chosen that answer. *Next.*

In a sticky situation, which of the following would you be most likely to rely on?

a) Your intelligence

b) Your strength

c) Your instincts

d) Your companions.

I chose *c)*. Next.

While playing a computer fantasy adventure game, you find yourself in a position to select only one *of the following objects. Which would you choose?*

a) A rope with grappling hook

b) A cloak

c) An axe

d) A bottle of transparent liquid

e) A book

f) A shield

I thought for a moment, and then clicked on *d)*. Immediately, the cursor flashed and letters appeared like magic on my screen: *W-h-y-?* I blinked. I looked up front, where Q had been standing. He was sitting at his desk, looking at his computer screen. As though he felt my eyes on him, he looked up, and smiled, and nodded encouragingly. I wondered if he had somehow typed the question in. It was crazy, I knew, but nonetheless, the thought warmed me. Painstakingly, I typed:

Rope – eksplor

Cloke – hyde/disguys

Ax – fite

Book – reed

Sheeld – defens

I cood do all thos things anyway.

BUT liqid – heeling, mabe majikal?

So the best.

T-h-a-n-k y-o-u A-d-a-m, typed my computer.

I looked up. Q was smiling at me. *Next.*

In the game, you need to choose a dominant colour for your clothing. What colour would you choose?

I thought. Then, *Brown*, I typed carefully. *Next.*

You are required to choose a character for yourself in the same game. Which of the following would you choose to be?

a) A warrior

b) A magic maker

c) A thief

d) Other (please specify)

I sat for a couple of minutes, thinking about that one. Then I tapped in, *d) Myslef.*

At once the screen flashed and turned blue again, just like at the beginning. It looked as if I wasn't going to have the chance to go back to the questions I'd left out.

I grinned to myself. Maybe that wasn't such a bad thing.

INITIATIVES

'Anyone fer another banger?'

I'd already had two, but I joined Jamie, Richard and Zach for thirds. I didn't get the impression Shaw was counting.

'What will we be doing after lunch, Shaw?' asked Jamie, with his mouth full.

Shaw moved the last few sausages over to the side of the griddle, away from the heat. 'Ah, well, Jamie, that's just goin' ter be a bit o' fun. Get you kids out in the fresh air after bein' cooped up.'

It had turned into one of those perfect days that sometimes follow heavy rain. Everything looked fresh and clean. The grounds of Quested Court – at least, the part where us kids were having our barbecue – were like the very coolest kind of park – lawns like green velvet, a fountain, and huge old trees. Best of all, though, everyone was being so kind. I couldn't remember the last time I'd got all the way through to lunch time without being yelled at.

'Right – all ready? Let's 'ead off, then. Foller me.'

We followed Shaw across the lawn, past tall, clipped hedges and into a forest of pine trees. We were walking in ones and twos, the three girls sticking together. Richard and I were joined by Jamie, whose short legs had to do the occasional skip to keep up. He was puffing slightly, partly because he seemed determined to talk non-stop while he walked.

'I wonder who'll make it into the final five,' he said. 'I'm a logical choice, plus I did really well in the test – a hundred percent, I reckon.' His voice dropped to a breathy whisper. 'Some of those questions were pretty dumb, though. I mean, you just couldn't figure out what you were supposed to say. What did you put for the one about the sticky situation, Adam?'

I sighed. This was exactly the kind of conversation I hated. 'Can't remember,' I fibbed.

Jamie shot me a calculating look. 'Really? I have an *excellent* short-term memory. Hey, wait up, won't you, guys? Do you have to walk so fast?'

Shaw had come to a stop up ahead, where the trees were thinner. Whatever 'initiatives' was, it looked as though we had arrived.

Dotted round the clearing were what looked like half a dozen or so wooden structures. I could see a high wooden wall, a tall pole with a car tyre beside it and a weird-looking net with different size holes in it, strung between two posts. There seemed to be others, too, off between the trees.

Shaw stood facing us, hands in his pockets, looking all set to enjoy himself. 'Right, kids, listen up good. This 'ere's the fun part, so yer don't want ter take it too serious. First off, we'll split yer inter two groups.' He took a piece of paper out of his pocket, and consulted it. 'We've got Kenta –' a slim little olive-skinned girl with straight black hair moved up beside him. He gave her a nod and a wink. 'Zach –' Dread-locks sauntered up beside her. 'Jamie –' Jamie waddled importantly to the front. 'Maria ... and Adam.' Maria was the pretty dark-haired girl who didn't like ball games. 'OK, you lot are one team, the rest of yer are the other.

'There's six obstacles. The aim is ter get yer team over them all as quick as yer can. It 'elps ter work as a group – and that's all I'm tellin' yer.' I gave Richard a grin and he gave me the thumbs-up. I wished we were on the same team, but somehow I didn't think there'd be any point asking to change.

Shaw handed out laminated sheets telling us the order of the obstacles.

Zach pushed to the front and took ours. Jamie's hand went up. 'Yeah, Jamie?'

'Please, Mr Shaw, do we choose a leader? Or will you choose the leader for us?'

'Aha, Jamie – now yer onto it! *I* don't pick the leader ... but mebbe that's part of it ... and mebbe I shouldn't be tellin' yer.' Shaw's broad, good-humoured face creased into a rare smile. But the dark eyes flicking round the group were shrewd and calculating, and I had a sudden feeling Shaw was seeing a lot more than he let on. That there was more to him than he liked to pretend ... and he might be more involved in the selection process than he wanted us to know. 'So, get yer thinkin' caps on. Teamwork an' leadership, that's the ticket – just like the army!'

Zach didn't put his hand up – he was way too cool for that. 'Were you in the army, Shaw? Is that where you learned all this stuff?'

'You bet I was! Officers' trainin' courses, leadership skills, fatigues . . . you name it. Now, on the count of three. One – two – three – and yer off!'

There was a rush for the first obstacle. For our team, it was the pole with the car tyre. Jamie, pink-faced, pushed to the front, determined to shoulder the role of self-appointed leader. 'Right,' he said, 'what do we have to do?'

'There is a notice fastened to the pole,' Kenta pointed out shyly.

Jamie read it out. It said we had to thread the tyre over the pole, and lower it down to the ground. Then we had to get it off again. Simple. Only problem was, the pole was a good three metres high.

Zach took charge. 'I'm real strong, and great at shot-put,' he announced. 'How about I throw it over?'

There was a video camera up in a tree behind the pole, I noticed. A red light on it was glowing and I wondered if we were being filmed. Everyone was clustered round the pole, arguing about what to do. Eventually Zach took the tyre and threw it upwards with all his strength. It knocked against the top of the pole, bounced off, and hit Jamie a glancing blow on the arm on its way down. Jamie crumpled to the ground and started to cry.

Kenta crouched down next to him. 'I plan to become a doctor, Jamie. Let me see where you are hurt,' she said kindly, in her formal little voice.

Zach was standing with his hands shoved deep in his pockets, glowering at Jamie, but I could tell he felt bad about what had happened. Maria had noticed the video camera, and was smiling up at it.

I mooched over to Zach. 'Hey, Zach,' I suggested hesitantly, 'how about if we make, like, a human tower? Say you, then me, then one of the girls, seeing they're lighter. Then maybe Jamie could pass the girl the tyre, and she could put it over.'

His face brightened. 'It's worth a try.' He clapped his hands. 'Hey guys, let's try this.' Quickly, he outlined the plan. I kicked my trainers off and stood on his shoulders and Kenta hopped lightly up onto mine. 'I pursue gymnastics as a hobby,' she said, and you could tell it was true by the light, balanced way she moved.

Jamie picked himself up off the ground, wiped his nose on his sleeve, and passed her the tyre. Over it went, and Jamie and Maria lowered it carefully down. Job done. Same thing in reverse, and it was high fives all round, and on to the next one.

As we worked through the obstacles, a pattern began to emerge. Zach went at everything like a bull at a gate, determined to do everything as much on his own, and by sheer strength, as possible. Maria drifted around on the edges, clapping and exclaiming when things went right, and grimacing prettily up at the video camera when they went wrong, which seemed to happen fairly often. Kenta was shy and quiet, but quick to come forward when there was something practical she could contribute. And Jamie, of course: determined to be the leader, but short on practical ideas that would actually work.

Take the net. The objective was for the whole team to cross from one side to the other by crawling through one of the holes without coming into contact with the strings. It was wired up to this buzzer, which went off when you touched it. Catch was, the same hole couldn't be used twice. Obviously it made sense for one of the big guys to go through a low, easy hole first, and then help the lighter girls through holes higher up. That would leave the low holes free for the heavy guys to crawl through once the rest of the team was on the other side. But it took ten minutes of arguing and people getting stranded on the wrong side of the net with all the holes used up, before this seemed to occur to anyone.

Next, we had to get the whole team across a wide, shallow stream using two car tyres and a wooden plank. There was the usual hubbub of suggestions, everyone shouting each other down. Then suddenly Kenta turned to me and asked, 'What do *you* think, Adam?' To my amazement, everyone quietened down and looked at me. I flushed, heard myself explaining how I reckoned it would work best . . . and in no time flat, we were over.

With the wall, the big thing was to get someone stationed up top who was strong enough to haul all the others up – especially Jamie – with everyone else heaving from underneath. Little Kenta was left till last – with a run and a bounce, she was up and over all on her own. She flashed me a shy smile.

Last of all was a two-strand electric fence – it gave a loud buzz if you touched it, though, instead of an actual shock – which we had to navigate our way over using just a plank of wood. We made a kind of human stile and got across, no worries – and again Kenta was last, running nimbly up the plank while I held the high end, and jumping down to land lightly on the other side.

After all the time we'd wasted, I was amazed when Shaw came up and gave us all high fives and told us we'd finished first. We ambled over to watch the other team struggling with the tyre and the pole, Richard standing solid as a rock as the base of the human tower while Genevieve teetered at the top. At last they did it, and we all gave a great cheer, before heading back for afternoon tea.

The best thing about the initiatives course was that it made us feel as if we'd known each other forever. I'd started the day with a bunch of strangers, but as I took a couple of chocolate-chip cookies from the loaded plate and passed it on, I realised that I felt closer to these kids than I did to anyone at Highgate, or at school. Not counting Cameron, of course. Jamie was reaching for the last biscuit when the dining-room door opened and Q walked in.

'Hello, everyone,' he said. 'I trust you've all had an enjoyable afternoon. Shaw tells me we have some excellent problem solvers, and you have all performed most satisfactorily. Well done.

'Now, there is one final exercise. Will you all please wash your hands thoroughly, and then follow me.'

Mystified, we queued for the cloakroom, and gathered in the corridor. The atmosphere was relaxed compared to the morning – you could see some friendships had been formed, and I couldn't help wondering what would happen that evening, when the selection was announced. The thought made me feel slightly sick.

I glanced at Richard, and he grinned at me. 'Do you need clean hands for arm wrestling?'

Q led us back to the computer room where we'd done the first test. I hoped we weren't in for another dose. But he walked over to the dark, shrouded object in the corner, and told us all to gather round. Then he turned off the light.

The room was immediately plunged into absolute darkness. I heard an indrawn breath, almost like a sob, from someone . . . then there was a slither as the cloth slid away, and a collective gasp from us all.

There, suspended in the darkness, was the most beautiful thing I'd ever seen. It was a transparent glass sphere, perfectly round, about the size of a basketball. I knew it was resting on some kind of stand or table, but in the pitch dark it seemed to be hanging in midair, as if by magic.

Lightning was held captive inside the sphere. Brilliant purple-blue electric streamers danced up from the base in a magical display of light. Ever-changing, utterly silent, totally mystical; so beautiful it took my breath away.

I realised Q was talking softly – had been talking for some time. 'The plasma globe is one of the most beautiful manifestations of plasma. Put simply, plasma is the fourth state of matter – a hot, ionised gas. The pressure in a plasma globe is high – so high that when plasma is generated, it heats up. Since hot air rises, the streamers of light tend to move up the sides of the globe. They keep moving because the charged gas areas keep moving. You can become a return path for a plasma trail by touching the glass surface.'

Q reached out one hand, and laid his palm flat on the side of the globe. Instantly, the blue streamers were drawn to his hand as if to a magnet, glowing and dancing under his palm. He placed his other hand on the other side of the globe, and the streamers divided and flickered between them. I sighed. I could have watched forever.

Even Jamie sounded strangely subdued. 'Do we get to touch it too?' he whispered.

In the bluish light reflecting upwards into his face, I saw Q smile. 'Yes, you do,' he said. 'That's why you're here. Would you like to go first, Jamie? It's quite safe.'

One by one, the kids shuffled forward in the dark and put their hands on the globe. Richard laid his palms flat, just as Q had done, and stood motion-less, gazing soberly at the streamers twisting between them. Genevieve rested the ends of her fingers on the glass, tracing patterns with the lightning as it followed her fingertips. I hung back, imagining the cold blue light playing on my skin through the glass. I wanted to be last.

With some of the kids, the light seemed to be

brighter and more intense. I wondered if it had anything to do with the temperature of your skin, or maybe how sweaty your hands were.

At last, I was the only one left. 'Adam,' said Q, 'it's your turn.' I felt drawn to the globe by an almost gravitational pull. Of their own accord, my hands lifted, spread, and lowered themselves as softly as feathers onto the smooth surface of the globe.

Instantly, the lightning arced upwards in a blinding flash like a thunderbolt. A searing shock jolted through my palms and knifed up into my shoulders, setting them on fire with pain. I was hurled backwards, smashing into whoever was behind me. Fluorescent blue stars spun before my eyes and a weird electric humming buzzed in my ears.

Gradually the room came back into focus. Q was kneeling over me, looking distraught. His mouth was moving. I couldn't hear what he was saying – couldn't hear anything. I dimly realised someone must have turned the light on again. I blinked, and shook my head, trying to clear it. I felt numb. Q seemed very small and far away.

I felt a pair of strong arms lift me, and carry me through the silent group of children like a baby. Shaw carried me all the way up to my room. By the time we reached it, my mouth was still dry and I was trembling, but I felt a lot more normal. 'Well, yer sure are no lightweight,' Shaw grunted, depositing me gently on the bedspread. 'It's good ter see the colour back in yer face, Adam.' He took a blanket from the wardrobe and tucked it round me. 'Old Q and 'is gadgets! Usherwood 'ad a shock off that contraption once. Won't go near it meself, that's fer certain. But we've never seen nothin' like *that* before.'

'That's quite true, we haven't,' said Q, who had followed us in and was hovering anxiously beside the bed. He still looked upset. 'How are you feeling, Adam? I am so sorry – I had no idea the reaction could be so strong. It is extraordinary . . . simply extraordinary.'

I gave him what I hoped was a reassuring smile, but my lips felt numb and stiff. My voice came out kind of croaky. 'I'm fine now . . . but it was weird . . . it felt like an electric shock, and the glass was hot. Burning hot, like fire. How come the other kids didn't get burnt?' I was feeling better by the second. I sat up. 'Was it a power surge or something?'

Shaw paused at the door, listening. 'No, Adam,' Q said, and there was a strange look on his face. 'At least, not in the way you mean.' He put his hand on my shoulder, and gave it a gentle squeeze. 'I'd recommend you lie down for half an hour or so. I'll draw the curtains.'

After they'd left, I lay in the semi-darkness and thought about what had happened. I hoped I hadn't broken the globe. It was so beautiful. Even now, etched on my retina, was a faint after-image of the dancing patterns of light, and of blue stars drifting in the wake of that savage explosion of power.

THE FINAL FIVE

I must have slept, though not for long. When I woke the light in the room was dimmer. My shawl was snuggled into the crook of my neck, and something warm and heavy was resting against my leg. I put my hand down and touched it. A sandpapery tongue gave my hand a couple of businesslike licks. I smiled. Tiger Lily.

But how had she got in? And how had my shawl . . .

I turned my head. Hannah sat cross-legged on Richard's bed, her eyes very round. 'Hi, Adam,' she whispered.

'Hi,' I whispered back.

'Are you OK?'

'Yeah. At least, I think so.'

'I heard Q and Shaw talking about what happened. I brought you Tiger Lily to make you feel better.'

'Thanks. It worked, see?' I swung my legs onto the floor, and stood up. Apart from a kind of stiff feeling in my shoulders, I felt fine.

Hannah gave me a sparkly, secretive look. 'And I brought you something else, too. Look.'

She hopped off the bed. There behind her was a

white, shiny plastic bag. Pinned onto it was a note, in slanty, grown-up writing. I turned on the bedside light so I could read it.

For Adam – a nice surprise to make up for a nasty shock! Please accept these with my apologies. Q.

I opened the packet. Inside were a pair of brand new jeans – the pre-faded kind – and a bright red hoodie. There were two T-shirts with designer logos on the front, one dark green, and the other black. And right at the bottom were two pairs of satin boxers, one a wine-red colour, and the other shiny sky blue.

Hannah was hopping up and down. 'Do you like them? Are you pleased? Usherwood went into Winterton to get them while you were asleep. I wanted to go too, to help choose, but Nanny said I had to rest, and Usherwood said it would take twice as long if I was helping.' She made a face.

I stood gaping at the clothes scattered on Richard's bed. The rich colours glowed like jewels in the soft light. They were the first new clothes I'd ever had, the first present I'd ever been given. For some crazy reason I could feel tears pricking the backs of my eyes. I blinked them away. More to myself than to Hannah, I muttered, 'I shouldn't really accept them.'

'Adam,' Hannah explained patiently, 'don't you know *anything*? When someone gives you a present, you *have* to accept it. If you don't, it'll hurt their feelings. And you have to say thank you, and tell them how much you like it,' she lowered her voice, 'even if you really don't. And sometimes you draw them a picture as a thank-you letter – unless you're big enough to write real words. *That's* what you do when you get presents.'

Well, I know when I'm beat. 'OK, Hannah,' I said, 'thanks for letting me know. And now,' I gave her a grin, 'you can make yourself useful by helping me decide what to wear to the banquet.'

Ms Usherwood stood up at the top of the long table, and daintily pinged her wineglass with her fork. If she'd set off a fire alarm, it couldn't have had a more immediate effect. The entire room was instantly silent, every eye fixed on her. I don't think anyone was breathing – I certainly wasn't.

Following Hannah's instructions, I'd thanked Ms Usherwood politely for choosing the clothes when she came up to my room to fetch me. She hadn't said much in return. There was something unsettling about the way she had looked at me – a thoughtful, measuring stare that made me feel slightly uncom-fortable. I wondered whether it had anything to do with the plasma globe . . . maybe I *had* broken it and everyone was too polite to tell me.

Now, more than an hour later, the table was still groaning with food – hot dogs, pizza, popcorn, nachos, hamburgers and – of course – fairy sandwiches, with crisps and sweets and marshmallows and cake to fill in the gaps, and about ten different flavours of fizzy drink to wash it all down. I'd expected to be far too nervous to eat, but I started off with a chocolate bar, just to be polite, and one thing kind of led to another.

'Ladies and gentlemen, boys and girls,' – Ms

Usherwood's eyes flicked to me, and away again – 'may I have your attention, please. The names of the final five are about to be announced.' The marsh-mallow I was eating suddenly tasted like rubber. It was an effort to swallow; I was afraid I'd choke.

'This is the procedure that will be followed. Five names will be read out. Those five children, together with their parents, will leave the dining room and make their way through to the library. Mr Quested will then address each group separately.

'The unsuccessful candidates will return to their rooms, pack their belongings, and leave immediately. Mr Quested will not enter into any dialogue with the parents of the runners-up. His decision is final, and not open to discussion.

'If you wish to exchange contact information, please do so now, as there may not be the opportunity at a later stage.

'It remains for me to thank you all for coming, and to say what a great pleasure it has been to share your company. Good luck to you all.'

She slipped out through the dining-room door, leaving a sudden babble of voices behind her. Richard was shoving a piece of cardboard into my hand; I saw it was one of his dad's business cards. He'd scrawled his name and phone number on the back. He had a kind of bug-eyed, vacant look, a bit like a stuffed fish. He didn't say anything. Didn't have to – I knew just how he was feeling.

Genevieve and Maria were hugging, Silas and Zach shaking hands. Kenta was standing very still next to her father, neither of them speaking. Jamie was munching a chocolate doughnut in an automatic kind of way. He looked pretty green.

The door opened again, and in came Q, looking miserable. He had a piece of paper in his hand.

'Thank you all for coming,' he said rapidly. 'Especially the children – you have all been wonderful, every single one of you, and if we could accommodate you all on our special course, we would. But unfortunately that's just not possible.

'Now. Please will the following children follow Usherwood through to the library. I will join you there very shortly.' He cleared his throat.

'Genevieve Vaughan-Williams.

'Kenta Nakamura.

'James Fitzpatrick.

'Richard Osborne.

'Adam Equinox.'

There was an odd, uncertain silence. None of us had any idea whether the news was good or bad. Only Zach made a little punching motion with his hand in the air, and whispered, '*Yes!*'

The five whose names had been read out shuffled to the door and into the library. The fire hadn't been lit, and the room looked gloomier and less welcoming than it had the evening before. We stood in a silent little huddle in front of the fireplace, and waited.

Sooner than any of us expected, the door burst open and in came Q. His glasses were sitting at an odd angle, and were more than usually misted over. He slammed the door behind him, and leaned against it.

'Well, that was terrible,' he muttered. 'I should have let Usherwood handle it, instead of insisting on doing my own dirty work. She would have taken it in her stride. So many angry parents! So many disappointed little faces!'

We all looked at one another, light beginning to dawn. There were one or two tentative smiles.

Q took his glasses off, polished them on his jersey, and replaced them on his nose. 'Well,' he said, with a slightly shaky smile, 'this is the easy part. The news for all of you is good. You have been chosen to stay on and work with me for the next two days. Congratulations.'

A tidal wave of relief broke over me, taking my breath away – a rush of joy so powerful I barely felt Richard's spine-crunching back-slap, or Jamie's earnest, sweaty handshake.

Q was moving round the room, fielding a barrage of questions from the parents and shaking the children by the hand. 'No, the test results remain confidential,' he told Jamie's dad. 'I may touch on the mechanics of the selection process with the children later on, but the results themselves wouldn't be of relevance to anyone other than myself.'

He turned back to the rest of us.

'And now, my friends, perhaps it would be appropriate for the parents to return to their rooms and collect their belongings. I'll have a quick word with the children, and then it will be time for farewells and an early night. We have a long day ahead.'

★

Q beamed at us. He seemed to have completely regained his good spirits, and even behind the cloudy lenses I could see his eyes were glowing with pleasure.

'So you are my five finalists,' he said softly. 'Gen, Kenta, Jamie, Richard and Adam. Welcome to what I believe will not only be the most exciting two days of your lives, but quite probably the most significant two days in the history of computer games.

'In fairness, perhaps I should say a word or two about the selection process. It employed a technique developed here at Quested Court; a technique so radical even I was uncertain of its success.

'My greatest concern was that the results would be ambiguous – that the selection technique would not indicate which of you should be chosen. But when your handwriting, birthdate and other personal details, your responses to the computer test, and the video of your performance in the initiatives challenge were put into a programme derived from the Karazan source code, the results were conclusive.'

Q smiled round at our blank faces. 'You could almost say that it was Karazan, not I, that made the final decision.

'*Karazan has chosen you.*'

THE SECRET OF KARAZAN

'Choose a desk, relax and make yourselves comfortable.' Q smiled at us.

Early morning sunshine streamed in through the open windows. The computer room seemed a totally different place – sunny, friendly and familiar. The door was open and a little breeze ruffled the papers on Q's desk.

Tiger Lily appeared in the doorway and paused, haughtily surveying the room with her golden eyes. Then she padded over to my desk and leapt lightly onto my lap. She curled up, tucked her nose into the crook of her paw, and went straight to sleep.

'Are you all ready? Excellent. Then let's begin.

'First of all, I think we need to introduce ourselves properly . . . perhaps say a word or two about who we are, and so on. You will know what is most important to you, and that's what I'd like you to share.

'Perhaps I should lead the way. My name is Quentin Quested, and my friends call me Q. That includes all of you.' Q beamed at us. 'I am fifty-five years old, and have one daughter named Hannah. I live here at Quested Court with a group of special helpers with whom I work so closely they are almost like a family: Shaw, who takes care of my physical safety . . .'

'*Bodyguard!*' Richard mouthed across to me.

'And of course Hannah's nanny, and Withers, whom you may not have met, who takes care of my finances. And Usherwood, who deals with the marketing side of the business.' Q paused. 'On a more personal note, Hannah is my life . . . and Karazan is my world: a world in many ways more real to me than the one we inhabit. Now, who would like to be next?'

Jamie jumped up. 'I will! My name's James Mortimer Fitzpatrick, my friends call me Jamie and I'm eleven. My hobbies are juggling and magic – I did circus arts and a magician course last holidays. I'm an only child. I want to invent computer games and be rich and famous like Q.'

'A commendable ambition, Jamie,' Q smiled. 'Who's next?'

Genevieve stood up, blushing. 'I'm Gen, and I'm thirteen,' she said in a soft voice. 'I've loved fantasy and fairy tales ever since I can remember. I have two little sisters and I make up stories for them. Mum and Dad gave us a computer for Christmas last year, and *Quest to Karazan*. It was the best present ever. And I still can't believe I'm here.' She sat down again quickly.

'Thank you, Gen.'

Richard pushed back his chair. 'Well, you all know I'm Richard,' he said sheepishly. 'I like sport, especially rugby, and computer games. I have two pet mice, and a brother called Thomas. And I hate school.' He grinned round at us, and sat back down.

I looked down at my desk, hoping I wouldn't be next. 'Kenta?'

Kenta rose reluctantly. 'My name is Kenta Nakamura, and I am twelve years old,' she said rapidly. 'I live with my mother and father above our greengrocer shop. My father bought our computer second hand, to assist with the business. My godfather sent me *Quest of the Dark Citadel* for my birthday. It is the only one I have played, but I love it.' She gave Q a shy smile. 'Is that enough?'

'Yes, Kenta, that's perfect. And Adam.'

I stood up, knocking my chair over with a clatter. I picked it up again, blushing like a beetroot and feeling like a complete idiot. 'I'm Adam,' I mumbled. 'I don't know the first thing about computers – or about anything much, really.' There was a stifled snigger from Jamie. 'I can't believe I got through to the final five. I'm worried there's been some kind of a mix-up.' Quickly, I sat back down again.

'You can rest assured, Adam,' said Q gravely, 'no mistake has been made.'

'Now, you must be wondering what we will be doing over the next few days. In order for you to understand it better, I'll need to fill you in on some of the background to the development of the Karazan game world.

'Firstly: who can tell me the names of all the games, in the correct order?'

Four hands went up, Jamie's fingers clicking. I stared down at my desk. I hoped this wasn't going to be like school.

'Kenta?'

'*Quest to Karazan, Quest of the Dark Citadel, Dungeon Quest*, and *Quest for the Golden Goblet.*'

Jamie's hand was flapping again. Without waiting to be asked, he blurted, 'You forgot *Quest to the Desert of the Dead* – it comes after *Dungeon Quest.*'

'Wonderful! Well done, both of you.

'Now, when *Quest to Karazan* was first developed, the technology was much simpler. I doubt any of you realise quite how basic computer games were then – funny, blocky graphics, written captions instead of proper speech, and, above all, *slow.*'

'However . . . two years later came *Quest of the Dark Citadel*. It was vastly superior in almost every way. Increased animation and music capabilities, 256 colour VGA, digitised speech and sound on the CD-Rom version . . . at the risk of becoming too technical, a quantum leap forward in terms of technology. All these advances were taking place pretty much across the board.'

Q took his glasses off and polished them. 'But *Citadel* pioneered a far more important innovation, unique to the Quest series, and one which has remained absolutely secret until this moment.

'Before I continue, I need to remind you all of the confidentiality clause in the agreement you and your parents signed when you arrived. Nothing that is said in the course of the next two days is to go beyond these four walls. If anyone has any difficulty with that, I ask you to leave now.'

He paused again and looked round the room, locking eyes with each of us in turn. No one moved or made a sound. But my mind was buzzing. Was Q really going to tell *us*, a bunch of kids, about a top-secret innovation? Why? And when he did, would we even begin to understand it?

'I called this invention a randomiser,' Q continued softly. 'Effectively, it uses virtual intelligence and a cutting-edge technique called spontaneous evolution to enable the fantasy world of Karazan to evolve on its own, without any further input from me.'

Huh? As I'd expected, Q had completely lost me, and by the blank looks on the other kids' faces, they weren't any better off. But suddenly a familiar little voice piped up from the door.

'Q, you have to use *proper* words. Explain so *I* can understand. Can I come and sit on your lap? And has anyone seen Tiger Lily?'

We broke for pancakes and hot chocolate, and afterwards, Q tried again. This time he had Hannah on his lap, and seemed a lot more relaxed. Tiger Lily had trotted away across the lawn: her beauty sleep over, she was off to catch herself some lunch.

'When I wrote *Quest of the Dark Citadel*,' Q explained, frowning in his effort to keep it simple, 'I built something new into the programme. It was the ability for Karazan to change and develop all on its own, just like societies and civilisations do in real life.'

'This is what I called the "randomiser", and it's what makes my games different each time you play them, with an infinite number of variables and . . .'

'*Q!*'

'Sorry,' said Q. 'This is harder than I thought. Stop me if I get carried away, Chatterbot.'

'You betcha.'

'Well, the most important effect of the randomiser only became apparent when I started work on *Goblet* two years ago. And it was this.' He paused, took a sip of water from the glass on his desk, and continued. 'Karazan had grown into an independent world, parallel to our own. A world with its own physical structure, its own geography, its own politics and population and laws and . . . and universe.'

Q stopped there, and looked round at us.

'Try again, Q,' Hannah suggested.

Q sighed. 'This is going to sound so bizarre, I hesitate to say it. In the simplest possible terms, Karazan has become real. It exists, in exactly the same way as our own world. And I have found a way to travel there.

'That is what you are here to do.'

THE QUEST

We stared at Q. No one said anything for what seemed a very long time.

Gen's hand went up. 'I'm sorry, Q; I don't mean to be rude, or sound as if I doubt what you've just said. I just want to make sure I understand it properly. You said Karazan is *real*? You can actually *go* there – really, not just in your imagination, or on the computer? And that *we* are going to go?'

There was a nervous giggle from Jamie's direction, but I didn't look round. My eyes, like everyone else's, were fixed on Q.

'Yes,' said Q simply.

Suddenly everyone was talking at once. Q held up his hand, and the babble of voices trailed off into a reluctant silence. 'One at a time, please,' said Q. 'Of course you all have questions, and I'll do my best to answer them. Now, Kenta.'

Kenta stood up. 'I have read about something called 'virtual reality'. Is it an extension of that?'

'No, it's far, far more than that. It is . . . one could quite accurately call it . . . *absolute* reality. Jamie?'

Jamie's face was pinker than usual. 'Do you mean

you want to shrink us down and put us into the computer?'

Richard made a muffled snorting sound, but Q answered with extreme seriousness. 'No, Jamie, not at all. The world of Karazan doesn't exist inside the computer. It exists in exactly the same way as our own world does, but as far as I can explain it, in a different dimension.'

Richard's hand went up. 'Have you been? What's it like?'

'No. So far, no one has. For reasons I don't fully understand, adults don't seem able to make the transition between the two worlds – at least, not yet. I've been working on a modification to the programme to overcome this, but so far, I have been unsuccessful. Believe me, if I could travel there myself, I would. Kenta?'

'How did you discover it? And how can you be sure it will work?'

Q rubbed the shiny dome of his head sheepishly. 'I discovered it by accident,' he admitted. 'I was working on a Virtual Reality Enhancer, or VRE – a keyboard toggle to trigger a cybernetic real-time interface between the game and the player. Testing it out, I experienced a bizarre effect, which I knew instantly could have only one interpretation.

'Have any of you ever seen a strobe light? Strobes use the triggered discharge of an energy-storage capacitor through a special flashtube filled with xenon gas at low pressure to produce a very short burst of high intensity white light.'

Hannah gave him a warning frown.

Q continued hastily, 'If you move while the light is flashing, it gives a jerky, almost time-warp effect, close to the one I experienced. In one flash of the light I was in our world, and in the next, I was in Karazan. I alternated between the two dimensions for approximately thirty seconds.'

What Q was saying reminded me of something. Bright, flashing lights . . . The plasma globe. Not wanting to sound like a fool, I stammered out, 'The last test we did. Was that . . .'

Q smiled at me. His eyes were very warm. 'Ah, Adam,' he said, 'I wondered whether you might pick up on that. The plasma globe was the definitive test. The globe was connected to a computer running the Virtual Reality Enhancer, and the purpose of the test was to gauge your individual conductivity potential. You all scored highly and you, Adam, spectacularly so. If there were any doubts remaining in my mind, that test dispelled them. Any one of you could pass from our world to Karazan as easily as walking through an open door.'

His words were followed by another short silence. There was one final question that needed to be asked – and answered. To me, it was so huge, so obvious, it seemed to fill the room. Yet everyone was quiet. So at last, reluctantly, I put up my hand.

'It sounds way, way weird, but if you say it's possible, then I guess we have to believe it. I just wondered . . . how can you be sure that once we're in Karazan, we can come back again? I mean . . . what if it only works in one direction? What if we get stuck there?'

As soon as the words were out of my mouth, Jamie hopped up like a jack-in-the-box. He began talking over Q, who had started to answer my question. His voice was much louder than normal, and slightly squeaky. 'That's *my* question, too. How would we get back again? And what if we couldn't? It sounds dangerous to me.'

He sat back down. There was an awkward pause. No one dared look at Q.

'The points you have raised are very important, Jamie – as is yours, Adam,' he said at last. 'I've battled with the question of whether it's right to send five children into a situation where there are so many unknowns. I still don't know the answer. But one thing is clear: you must decide whether or not you wish to go. And I will accept your decision without reservation.'

'Well, I think the whole thing's cool,' pipes up Richard. 'I bet we could get back OK. I really want to go – it sounds like the most awesome adventure! And it's the whole point of being here, after all.'

Q gave him a grateful smile.

Hesitantly, Kenta spoke. 'I am not sure I understand *why* you wish us to go.'

'Kenta, you have identified the issue at the heart of this entire enterprise. If you are involved – which all of you are, even should you choose not to go – you have a right to know everything.'

Hannah's eyelids had been drooping for a while,

and now she was fast asleep on Q's lap, her head resting snugly in the crook of his arm. He looked down at her tenderly, and gently settled her into a more comfortable position. He smiled at us, and sighed.

'I am asking you to go to Karazan for a purpose. On a quest, if you like. All of you who have played the games know there are five magical potions in Karazan. There is the Potion of Invisibility, the Potion of Beauty and Eternal Youth, the Potion of Power and Invincibility, the Potion of Insight . . . and the Potion of Healing.

'I am asking you to find a phial of the Potion of Healing, and bring it back to me. I'm afraid I have no idea whether it actually exists, or whether it would have the same properties in our world as it does in Karazan. But I'm asking you to try – with all my heart.'

No one spoke. We waited, watching Q, seeing his eyes fill with tears and a look of unbearable sorrow settle over his face like a shroud.

'I am asking you for Hannah,' he said softly. 'Without it, she will die.'

Alt Control Q

'Hannah has a rare and potentially deadly form of cancer. Two out of every three children who suffer from it are eventually cured. But not Hannah.'

I looked at her, curled up like a kitten on Q's lap. With all her zip and sparkle smoothed away by sleep, I saw how thin her face was. For the first time, I noticed her pale, translucent skin and the purple shadows like bruises under her eyes.

'Hannah starts the last of six monthly chemo-therapy courses this afternoon. It is her last chance. All going well, it will continue for five days. She is very brave, but she's also far weaker than she appears; she has been through it before, and she is afraid. I wish I had her courage, her strength.

'But I know what she doesn't: she isn't responding to the treatment. For Hannah, all we can do is pray for a miracle. A miracle, or the kind of magic that exists only in a world other than our own.'

Hannah stirred and murmured in her sleep. There was a scraping sound as a chair was pushed back. Someone started to speak. Crazy though it sounds, it took a moment before I realised it was me.

'I'll go to Karazan, and I'll find the potion if it exists, and bring it back. I'll go on my own, if no one else wants to come. But first we need one person to go to Karazan and come back again straightaway, kind of like a test run. And I'm happy for that person to be me. If I can prove it's safe, then if anyone else wants to go back with me to look for the potion, that's cool.'

Jamie jumped up too, quick as a flash. 'I think Adam's right. He's the logical one to be the guinea pig, especially as he scored so highly in the plasma-globe test.'

Richard chipped in angrily. 'Yeah, right, Jamie – lucky *you* didn't get the highest score in the plasma-globe test, like you keep telling us you did in all the others, huh? Well, Adam, *I'm* not chicken. I'll come with you – on both trips.'

I gave him a grin. 'Thanks for the offer, Rich. But you can't come on the test. That'd defeat the whole purpose! I have to do the first trip alone.' I didn't say so, but unlike the others, there was no one to miss me if I didn't come back . . . and no one to make trouble for Q, either.

'I am with you, also, Adam. As I have mentioned, I wish to become a doctor. If there is something that can be done to save a child's life – I will do it.'

I smiled at Kenta. There was something impressive about her grave little face, so set and determined.

Gen spoke up. She sounded a lot less sure, though, and there was a quaver in her voice. 'If Adam's prepared to go and check it out, and if he comes back OK and it all seems safe . . . then I'll go. If everyone else does.'

No one looked at Jamie.

After lunch the others went outside with Shaw for a game of volleyball, and I followed Q upstairs. We hung a left at the top of the main staircase, and headed to a part of the house I hadn't seen before. We stopped outside a studded wooden door at the end of a long corridor. Q tapped once, opened it, and in we went.

The room was empty except for two long metal racks of drab-looking clothes, and a fat, grand-motherly woman in a flowered apron. She was sitting by the window knitting, but lumbered to her feet as soon as the door opened.

'So this is the boy, Quentin, my dear. Adam, isn't it? Well, now, let's have a look at you.' She put her hands on her ample hips and gave me the once up and down. Then she gave a brisk nod. 'You'll do very nicely, I'm sure. And you were right about the size, Quentin – more a fourteen than a twelve.'

She moved to one of the racks, and started flipping through the hangers.

'This is Nanny, Adam,' Q told me. 'Not just Hannah's nanny, but my nanny too, from when I was a little boy. Nanny's also a qualified nurse, which has made everything easier as far as Hannah's treatment is concerned. Nanny knows why you're here, and what you've agreed to do.'

'And bless you for it, my dear. Though I must

admit, it all seems rather far-fetched to me – I don't really understand computers and other worlds and suchlike. But Quentin, now – he's always had his head in the clouds, haven't you, dearie? More questions and strange notions than any child I've ever known . . . well now, how I do go on! Wee Hannah's all that matters now – and if there's even a chance of something to save that little lamb . . . well, you're a dear boy to try it, Adam.

'Now then, pop this on for size.'

She'd been flipping through the hangers while she talked, and now she held one out to me, with what looked at first glance like a sack on it. I saw it was an old-fashioned tunic and a pair of breeches, made of rough brown cloth. 'And these too, my dear.' Nanny handed me a soft white shirt with long sleeves and no collar, along with a pair of woollen socks, worn leather boots, and a broad leather belt.

I may not be a genius, but by now even I had cottoned on. 'Hey, Q,' I objected, 'you aren't expecting me to *wear* all this stuff?'

Q gave me an apologetic look. 'Although we have a fairly accurate idea of the likely entry point, we can't be sure – and there's no guarantee it'll be deserted. Imagine appearing in the middle of a crowded market-place in Karazan wearing jeans and a sweatshirt! You must admit,' his eyes twinkled, and he gave me his first real smile since the morning, 'you wouldn't exactly blend in.'

He had a point. I took the gear into the bathroom and changed into it. It fitted perfectly, and to my surprise was pretty comfortable. I slung the rucksack Q had handed me over my shoulder.

Looking at the reflection of the tall, rough-haired, olive-skinned stranger in the mirror, I felt the first real stirrings of excitement. I *looked* like someone from another world . . . and for the first time, I began to believe it might be for real.

Q and I were alone in the computer room. I sat down in front of my computer, where the latest version of *Quest to Karazan* was loaded, ready to play. Except this wasn't a game. Suddenly, I felt as if I might throw up. I took a quick sip of water from the glass next to the computer, and swallowed it with a gulping sound.

Q sat down on the chair next to mine. 'Listen to me carefully. The keyboard command to activate the VRE and enter Karazan is *Alt Control Q*. Logically, the entry point should be where *Quest to Karazan* begins: at the foot of the cliffs to the west of the city of Arakesh.' He gestured to the waiting screen. 'The brief flashes I experienced support this.'

He held out something about the size and shape of a cellphone. It had a tiny screen like a cellphone, but where the numbers should have been was a tiny keyboard, like on a computer.

'This is the most important thing of all. It's the smallest microcomputer in the world. Apart from the size and the fact that it's battery powered, its specifications are identical to the PC you've been using. So what do you think you will need to do to return from Karazan?'

I looked at the keyboard. There was the on-off switch, as tiny as a grain of rice. 'Press *Alt Control Q* again?'

'Yes. It works like a toggle. *Alt Control Q* to get into Karazan, *Alt Control Q* to come home.'

All of a sudden I was desperate to go. If I was going to do it, I wanted to get on with it.

Q must have seen my impatience. 'One final thing. I strongly recommend you make your re-entry from the same point you arrive at, as exactly as possible. Mark it if necessary. Logically, the interface between the two worlds will be strongest there.

'Now, give me your hands.' I held out my hands, and he took them. His hands felt very cold, and looked pale in my big, brown paws. His eyes met mine at last. Without his glasses, they were level and direct, the pure, clear blue of a summer sky.

'Adam, be careful. Come straight back. Good luck . . . and thank you.'

There was no more to be said. Q gave my hands a squeeze, and released them. I slipped the tiny computer into my rucksack and fastened it securely.

Slid the straps over my shoulders, and shrugged them into position.

Swivelled round on my chair to face the computer.

Pressed the *Alt* button.

Pressed *Control*.

And with the index finger of my right hand, reached across and touched the *Q* lightly as a feather.

Closed my eyes, and pressed.

IN THE FOREST

Nothing happened.

I'd been expecting – I don't know – a sucking feeling, or a spiral of swirling colours, or maybe even the flashes Q had told us about.

But nothing. Nothing at all.

I sat there like an idiot with my eyes closed, hoping the keyboard command took a while to register, or something dumb like that. I felt sick with disappointment. I was dreading the look on Q's face when he realised his great discovery – and Hannah's last chance – was a load of humbug.

When it was clear that nothing was going to keep *on* happening, I took a deep breath. 'I'm sorry, Q,' I said. 'It hasn't –'

And I opened my eyes.

I was sitting on a low, lichen-covered rock at the foot of a cliff. I was in Karazan.

The hugeness of it overwhelmed me. I buried my face in my hands, hot tears squeezing out from between my eyelids. Shallowly, I breathed in the air of that alien world. It was cool, soft with the dampness of morning mist, and tinged with the faintest hint of wood smoke.

I don't know how long I sat there with my head in my hands. Gradually, I began to notice sounds: the whispering of wind in trees; a sudden bird call, a weird, whistling trill unlike any I'd ever heard before; the far-off thunk of an axe on wood; even further away, the single clear chime of a bell.

I took a deep breath, took my hands away from my eyes and looked around me. It was morning – very early morning, just before dawn. The rock I was sitting on was at the foot of a cliff . . . the cliff I'd been gazing at moments before on the computer screen.

The cliff was slick and smooth like granite. It stretched away above me as far as I could see, and off to each side into the distance like an endless wall. Just like on the computer game, the ground sloped gradually away from the cliff towards a dense forest of strange-looking trees. From my elevation, their tops stretched off into the distance in a nubbly blue-green carpet, with wisps of morning mist tangled among them like cobwebs.

On the far horizon shone a ribbon of brightness – the sea. Above it, ragged bands of cloud were slashed with the first copper streaks of the new day. Beyond the distant edges of the forest, I could just make out the buff-coloured walls of a city.

Closer to hand – less than a stone's throw from the cliff face – a solitary rock reared up out of the grass.

It was smooth and regular in shape, taller than a man, and as narrow as a door.

I registered all this in the instant after I opened my eyes. I could feel my heart hammering in my chest as though I'd run a marathon. My mind was reeling. It had worked! I was there – here – in Karazan! Suddenly, all kinds of unwelcome thoughts were buzzing in my brain. The air – was it safe to breathe? Could the landscape – the world – truly be as real and three-dimensional as it looked? And monsters – what about monsters? I wished I'd thought of asking Q.

Cautiously, I shuffled over to the standing stone. To my relief, the ground felt firm and solid beneath my feet. With my heart in my mouth, I peered round the stone to the other side. Nothing. No monsters, no disembodied arms clutching at me from the stone. Just smooth, grey granite, pitted and scarred with the passage of time.

Tentatively, I reached out one hand and touched it. It felt cold and slightly damp. Real. Putting my face up close, I sniffed. It smelled faintly sour and metallic. I rested my forehead against it, and thought for a moment.

I ought to get out the little computer and go straight back to Q, or he'd be worried sick. But suddenly I had no doubt at all that the keyboard command would work for the return journey. And what Q had called the 'entry point' was so unmistakable, with the lichen-covered rock and the tall standing stone, I didn't need to mark it. I could find my way back, no problem.

If I decided to explore, that is.

I wouldn't go far, just to the edge of the forest. Q would understand; no one could resist going just a little way. I'd only be five minutes.

I could feel the reassuring weight of the backpack on my shoulders. My lifeline, my return ticket. Q had insisted on packing a cloak, in case it was winter in Karazan, and a packet of sandwiches, just in case I was delayed. At the time it had seemed ridiculous, as if we were packing for some kind of virtual picnic.

It didn't seem funny now.

The weirdest thing was how real it all was. I guess I'd thought that Karazan was a fantasy world, so – if it existed – it would be like a cardboard cut-out, or hazy, like a dream. But if anything, I had a sense of height-ened reality as I walked down the slope towards the trees. The ground had a peaty give, and the grass was a shimmery, russet tussock I'd never seen before, its dampness staining the leather of my boots a darker brown. Two pale moons faded into the lightening sky as the reddish-gold sun rose over the distant curve of the horizon.

There was a feeling of spring in the air. Every step seemed to release a new fragrance of damp earth and richness, and a faint, herbal scent that seemed hauntingly familiar, and at the same time utterly new. The air had a purity that sharpened my senses and everything I looked at seemed to have a shining rim of light, as if I'd never seen things properly in focus before.

I paused on the fringe of the forest. Here, the dawn

chorus of birds was louder and I could hear the liquid music of water. Suddenly, a pang of homesickness stabbed through me. Not homesickness for the orphanage and Matron, but a yearning for something or someone I'd never known; a feeling of loss so strong it brought tears to my eyes.

Ahead, the grey light of the new day was swallowed by the shadow of the trees. They towered above me, their trunks stretching up to the canopy like vast pillars, cracked with age. There was no path but they were far enough apart for walking to be easy.

Without consciously deciding to I found myself taking a tentative step into the trees . . . and then another. I couldn't go back yet. I hadn't seen enough. Warily, every sense on the alert, I walked towards the sound of the water.

I'd find something to take back to Q. Something special, to prove beyond a doubt to everyone – and to myself – that Karazan was real.

It didn't take long to reach the water – a shallow stream, clear as glass, flowing rapidly over a stony bed. The chattering, rippling music of the water as it danced over the stones made me instantly thirsty, as if I hadn't drunk for days: my throat felt as parched and dry as sand. I had a water bottle in my pack, but the thought of plastic-tasting juice wasn't as tempting as fresh spring water. I knelt on the bank, feeling the dampness soak into the knees of my breeches. Cupping my hands, I leaned forward over the stream, ready to scoop up a handful and drink.

And then I caught sight of my reflection, shattered

and fragmented in the running water. A black, shrunken face; huge, bulbous eyes and jagged yellow fangs.

I flung myself away from the stream onto the soft, mossy bank, and rolled away into the shelter of the trees. I must have yelled; there was a sudden silence where the birdsong had been moments before. And in the silence I heard words in the sound of the water, a warning that gurgled and chuckled as it tumbled over the stones like broken words stumbling over rotting teeth, whispering over and over again: *Who drinks of me shall be a shrag . . . who drinks of me shall be a shrag . . .*

I ran back the way I'd come, stumbling and tripping and cursing myself for being such a fool. What kind of an idiot was I? Five seconds later and it would have been my true reflection staring back at me. Q would have been waiting in the computer room at Quested Court forever . . . or would he? I had a sudden, vivid flash of a dark, shambling shape clawing its way out of the computer screen, drool hanging in ropes from its rotten gums . . . I squeezed my eyes shut, tripped, and fell headlong onto the forest floor. *Get a grip, Adam. If you're going to freak out like this every time something unexpected happens, you'd be better off sitting by Hannah's bed hoping for a miracle . . . and so would she.*

I took a deep, calming breath, shrugged off my backpack, and dug inside for my water bottle. Bottled fruit juice was fine by me – I wasn't about to eat or drink anything from Karazan until I'd had a crash course in safety from Q.

My hand was shaking so much that a major slosh of juice dribbled down my chin, but after a couple of gulps, I began to feel better. No wonder Q said I should come straight back, I thought wryly. OK, Plan B: back to the entry point, back to Quested Court, and not a word to anyone about what happened. Well, nearly happened.

I clambered to my feet and shouldered my pack. And then, just as I was setting off uphill, I saw it: the most beautiful flower I'd ever seen. It was almost completely hidden in the undergrowth; if I hadn't fallen, I'd have walked straight past. It was about the size of a teacup, and its petals curved outwards like fingers of flame. They were the colour of fire: red and gold and orange and yellow, with a hint of purple at their heart. It was growing on a spindly creeper making its way up the trunk of one of the trees. There was only one flower. I grinned. What could be more special than that? And suddenly a cool thought popped into my head. I'd pick the flower and take it back for Hannah. She'd have started her chemo-whatsit treatment – and I reckoned a flower from Karazan would cheer her up, no matter how lousy she felt. I bet it would smell as great as it looked. I leaned over to have a sniff.

Instantly, the flower clamped onto my face like a burning vice. I gave a strangled yell of horror and pain and fell backwards, tearing at my face. The petals were spreading like molten lava across my skin, sucking on like red-hot leeches. Shrieking, kicking, my eyes squeezed shut, I dug desperately between a petal and my cheek, trying to tear it off. But as my nails clawed and scratched uselessly, I could feel the petal spreading, growing, groping towards my mouth . . .

I yelled again, but with despair this time as the tentacle slipped between my lips, sucking hungrily. I clenched my mouth shut. My face was on fire; I rolled over and scrubbed it desperately into the damp leaves on the forest floor, whimpering and writhing with pain.

And suddenly the burning stopped. I lay face down, scared to move, terrified that anything I did might start it off again. As quietly as I could, I sucked air through the free corner of my mouth . . . sucked air, and waited. Was it resting? Was it dead? Had I somehow managed to kill it?

Something nudged my side – something hard, poking into the softness under my ribs. I whipped over towards it with a jibbering shriek – what was coming at me now? Despite myself – despite my terror of blindness from the groping petals and my horror of what I might see – my eyes flew open.

A rough-clad man was crouched on the ground beside me, a hunting knife unsheathed in his hand, about to prod me a second time with its leather-bound hilt.

Argos and Ronel

'Well, you've been making enough noise to wake the dead,' he grunted, 'and let us hope you have not.' He glanced round warily, tightening his grip on the knife.

My eyes slid to the ground beside him where the vine lay, cleanly severed, limp and oozing sap.

I could feel the flower still stuck to my face: stuck fast, but at least not burning and clutching. I picked at it with the fingers of one hand, pushing myself up into a sitting position with the other.

The man gave an impatient snort. 'Nay, you'll not peel it off, lad, but it will do you no further harm. It is fortunate I happened by and heard your cries.'

He stood, and held out a hand to pull me to my feet. He moved and spoke like a man in his prime, but he was old, though lean and broad shouldered. He had a craggy, swarthy face and tangled grey hair, and the eyes glinting beneath his bushy brows weren't friendly.

'Are you a simpleton, that you wander alone in the forest at dawn – or indeed at any time?' he growled. 'What is your name, and what is your business here?'

With a petal pasted over half my mouth, it wasn't going to be easy to answer, even if I'd known what to say. 'Gmmmff,' I mumbled through the corner that was free, glad of an excuse not to answer his questions.

He scowled. 'Well, whoever you are, be off with you. A lad of your age should know the dangers of the flame vine. Get yourself home, and gather some lanceleaf on your way – that, in the steam from your mother's cauldron, will loose its hold.'

Well, that'd be just fine if I had a mother with a cauldron, or a home to get back to, or the faintest clue what lanceleaf was ... Rubbing at my mouth with the back of my hand, I rolled my eyes pleadingly at him. 'Please, sir – won't you help me?' I asked. It came out as a string of muffled grunts, and he looked at me blankly, shaking his head.

'Perhaps you are simple; you must be, to have been so foolish.' He scowled, and glanced round again. I found myself looking over my shoulder, too – I didn't much like the way he kept scanning the trees, or his comment about the dead.

Suddenly, he came to a decision. 'Well, I cannot leave you here, much as I would like to. Who knows what you have disturbed with your clamour, but the shrags at least sleep deep at daybreak, and they will not venture where a flame burns. The first is our good fortune; we will make doubly sure with the second.' He pulled a rough wooden torch from his pack, and lit it with something I reckoned must be a kind of tinder-box. Though it wasn't nearly dark enough to need the light in the forest, its flickering flame made me feel a lot more comfortable. 'Follow me,' he ordered, 'and keep your nose out of any flowers.'

Ten minutes or so of fast walking brought us to a clearing in the trees. In the centre of the glade nestled a little grey cottage, with a tidy log pile against one wall. A curl of smoke wound up from the stone chimney, its scent mingling with the sweet smell of newly cut timber and the yeasty aroma of fresh-baked bread. An uneven path of flagstones rambled up to the door, where a wooden rocker was set back in the shade.

The man gestured to the rocker. 'Sit there. I do not wish you to enter.' Cautiously, I lowered myself onto the edge of the chair, and waited.

He disappeared inside, and I heard the murmur of voices. Suddenly, his was raised: 'Ronel! Have you no sense? You know it is better that no one sees you, however innocent they may seem!'

'I shall show myself to whomever I please, Argos – and as for you, you have the manners of a glonk to keep a hurt and frightened child outside!' And with that, a figure appeared in the doorway.

After what the old guy had said, and the weird stuff that had happened in the forest, I wouldn't have been surprised if some kind of ghoul had come shambling to the door. But it was a little old lady – and she looked ordinary enough to me. She was dumpy and comfortable-looking, and unlike her husband, most of the lines on her face were clearly from smiles. The deepest were round her eyes, which were as clear and bright as water, with laughter sparkling just below the surface.

She bustled up to me, her face creased with concern. 'You poor lad – you must have been lost in the forest all night,' she said gently. 'Do not be frightened: you are safe here. We have lanceleaf aplenty, and the cauldron is already on the fire.' She touched my face with her fingertips; they felt cool and comforting. The grumpy old man had put me on the defensive. I wasn't prepared for sympathy, and her kindness brought the shock back in a rush. I felt tears spring to my eyes, and when I raised my hand to hide them, it was trembling.

'Poor boy,' she said again, and took the shawl from her shoulders and tucked it round me. It was warm, but soft and light as gossamer. I felt a sudden pang of longing for my own shawl, tucked safely away in a bedside drawer in a different universe . . . a pang of longing so intense I could almost smell its familiar, spicy scent. I shook my head to clear it. If ever I needed my wits about me, it was now.

Her husband appeared in the doorway, 'You are as headstrong as when you were a girl, Ronel! Well, the damage is done. Bring him in, the cauldron has boiled.' Following them into the cottage I had a quick impression of a small room, sparsely furnished and meticulously neat. It didn't seem polite to stare, though, especially as the old guy clearly didn't want me there. Obediently, I trailed over to the hearth, where a three-legged black cauldron was suspended over a bed of glowing coals. A bitter-sweet, herbal smell made my nose tingle and my eyes sting.

'Lean your face into the steam and close your eyes. Do not be afraid. The worst is behind you.'

A warm, damp blanket of steam enveloped my face. I breathed in, and it caught in my throat and made me splutter. Instinctively, I pulled away; a huge hand like a vice clamped onto my neck, holding me still. After a moment I felt a weird, unpeeling sensation on my skin. Something fell into the boiling water with a plop and floated there, like a popped balloon. The flower was off.

I straightened up and gave a huge, shuddering sigh, rubbing my hands thankfully over my bare skin. It felt wonderful – and the pain had completely gone.

'There now, brave lad. Sit and rest a moment by the fire.'

'He can rest outside, if he rests at all. And he can tell us his name and his business, now that his mouth is free.'

But I had other plans. The old man's comment about being a simpleton had given me an idea. I kept my hands over my face, sniffled pathetically and shook my head. The man gave a contemptuous snort. 'What ails you? The flower is gone and you have come to no harm!'

'Aye, you are safe,' said the woman. 'Come, tell us your name, and what brings you here. For none venture here of their own free will – we see no human face from one span's end to the next.'

With a great show of reluctance, I lowered my hands and gestured helplessly at my mouth, shrugging my shoulders and looking as woebegone as I could. Contorting my face with exaggerated effort, I let rip a couple of unintelligible grunts.

The old guy gave a dismissive shrug. 'You see, Ronel, it is as I told you – the boy is an idiot. We will get no sense from him.'

'Even the simplest have feelings capable of hurt, Argos. Perhaps you should learn to guard your tongue, lest it wound where there is no armour.'

'And you are too quick to trust, and have lived long enough to know that all may not be as it seems,' he shot back. 'Stay outside, boy. Come, Ronel: I wish to speak with you in private.'

I perched on the edge of the rocker, wondering if I should make a run for it. I could hear the rumble of Argos's voice from inside the cottage, and the softer murmur of her replies. I thought of Q. He'd be frantic by now – I must have been away for over an hour.

I was about to hop up and make a dash for the trees when I heard Argos's voice again, raised impatiently.

'He must be from Arakesh. Where else could he be from? And that he is five cobblers short of a geld is without doubt.'

A murmur from the woman, too faint to catch.

'You are living in a dream, Ronel. Aye, it is the fourth span, but you know as well as I that it is not until sunbalance that the portal opens, eight moons hence . . .'

I slipped the shawl off my shoulders, keeping a wary eye on the doorway. A portal was a doorway, wasn't it? What doorway was he talking about? Maybe there was some kind of an asylum in Arakesh, and she thought I'd escaped! I grinned. Seemed I'd done a better job than I'd expected!

I'd hung about long enough. I'd have liked to thank Ronel, but I wasn't going to be able to without blowing my cover. And as for old Argos – he didn't deserve too much in the way of politeness, I reckoned.

I slid off the seat, slipped silently to the corner of the house . . . and ran for it. I'd kept my eyes open on the way, and my ears. The sound of the stream had been on my right, and the way through the trees had sloped downhill. I ran steadily uphill, keeping the sound of the water on my left, dodging the tree trunks and making sure I didn't brush against anything. My heart was hammering in my chest, and not just from running; it was with a feeling of overwhelming relief that I saw the trees thin and the cliff face loom ahead.

I came out of the forest almost exactly where I'd left it. The sun was high in the sky, and its warmth felt comforting through the rough cloth of my tunic. But I wasn't about to waste time enjoying it.

Remembering Q's advice, I took the little computer out of the rucksack and sat on the lichen-covered stone. I was out of breath from running; I could feel my heart thudding, and my hands were shaking slightly as I turned it on.

Here goes, I thought.
Alt Control Q.

I was completely unprepared. I'd been expecting an effortless transition, like before. But it wasn't. It was like being battered violently from side to side in a giant kaleidoscope; the pieces of the whirling mosaic were jagged fragments of the Karazan landscape and the computer room at Quested Court. Whirling, flashing images battered my brain like shards of glass, and when I clenched my eyes shut it was worse: a helpless, nauseating juddering, a sick feeling of vertigo and a spinning weightlessness as my mind plummeted through the darkness.

It must have only lasted a few seconds . . . but it felt like forever.

At last, gasping like someone coming up for air after a deep dive, I wrenched my eyes open. I was back in the computer room. The microcomputer was clenched in my hand, slick with sweat. Sunlight flooded in through the windows.

Q was hurrying towards me, his face a picture of mingled worry and relief and a gigantic grin plastered all over his face.

'When you think about it, it's not surprising the time frame is different in Karazan,' Q told me, as we headed upstairs after dinner. 'Common sense suggests the passage of time in different dimensions would be different, too. That fifteen minutes here, for example, would correspond to an hour in Karazan, or vice versa.'

Much to my relief, the time I'd spent away had translated into about twenty minutes back at Quested Court. I'd come clean with Q about my exploratory walk in the forest, but the version I'd given him was carefully edited. And luckily, it didn't seem to occur to him to be angry with me for not returning straight-away – he was way too excited about the fact I'd got through to Karazan, and, more important, come home safely.

The other kids demanded every detail. Without actually fibbing, I tried to concentrate on the positive things . . . to the point of not mentioning the scary bits. After all, they'd all played Q's games on their computers, and wouldn't dream of making the dumb mistakes I had. So I told them about Argos and Ronel, but skated round how the meeting had taken place. I told them how friendly she had been – the less said about him, the better. And I didn't go into any detail about the return transition; they only asked what it had been like crossing over *to* Karazan, assuming, like I had, that coming back would be just as easy.

When eventually their flood of questions died down to a trickle, I could see they all felt reassured, and in the end even Jamie amazed us by announcing his intention to join us on our quest the following day.

Now it was evening, and while Nanny sorted out the other kids with costumes for the morning, Q and I were on our way up to see Hannah. She'd asked for me, Q said: 'But you must be prepared to find her very changed. You mustn't stay long. She's more tired than she admits.'

Hannah was in her bedroom, propped up in a huge four-poster bed that made her look tiny and fragile. A tube trailed like a transparent worm from under her pyjamas to a bag of fluid dangling from a metal stand beside the bed. Her face was very white, and I could see the shape of her bones through her translucent skin. Looking at her, I could easily believe she might die.

Her head was completely bald. Q had tried to prepare me. 'She likes to dress up and pretend. In her imagination she's a little princess, and princesses aren't bald, so she usually wears a wig. But at the moment she doesn't have the energy for pretence. Tonight you will be seeing Hannah as she really is.'

She hadn't heard us come in. She was lying back on her ruffled pillows with her eyes closed, a battered, one-eyed teddy tucked in beside her. Under the covers on the other side snuggled Tiger Lily, purring softly, her chin resting on Hannah's arm.

Q touched Hannah's cheek gently, and without opening her eyes she lifted her free hand, groped for his, and held it.

'You have a visitor, Chatterbot,' he told her quietly.

Hannah's eyes flickered open. She saw me and smiled, a pale shadow of her usual cheeky grin. 'Hi, Adam,' she breathed. There was a chair beside the bed. I perched on the edge of it.

'Hi,' I said.

'Q says you went to Karazan. Is it true?'

'Yeah, it was awesome. You'd love it. Everything is much more real, more . . . bright. It's like you're seeing the world for the very first time. Even the smells, the sounds, are clearer. It's almost impossible to imagine, unless you've actually been there.'

She closed her eyes, and sighed softly. For a

moment I wondered whether she'd slipped off to sleep, but she opened her eyes and smiled at me, and this time the smile was more like the Hannah I knew. 'No,' she whispered, 'I can *exactly* imagine it.'

'Are you . . . OK?' I asked.

'Yup,' she told me, and the bravery of the lie brought tears to my eyes. She rolled her eyes, and pulled a little face. 'Just *look* at me.'

'Real fairy princesses happen on the inside,' I told her. 'The hair isn't the important part.'

She thought about that for a moment. 'Adam?'

'Yeah?'

'When you go back to Karazan . . . be careful. Come back safe. Promise?'

I wondered how much she really knew – about why we were going, and everything that hinged on it. I wanted to promise to come back. I wanted to promise that I'd find the healing potion and save her.

But the courage in her eyes challenged me to be honest. Hannah trusted me, and I knew I should only make a promise I was one hundred percent certain I'd be able to keep.

'I'll be as careful as I can,' I told her. 'I promise.'

I was so exhausted when I fell into bed I was sure I'd sleep the whole night without so much as twitching, never mind dreaming.

But I was wrong.

I dreamed I was sleeping – not in my bed in Quested Court, not in my narrow, creaky bed at Highgate, but in a strange bed in a strange room, somewhere I didn't recognise and had never been before. Although I was sleeping, I could see my sleeping form bundled in blankets, lying motionless in the stillness of the night.

And I could see a shadowy figure, darker than the surrounding darkness, drift silently to my bedside. For an endless moment the figure remained motionless, shapeless, nearly invisible in the blackness.

I almost began to believe it might have melted away.

But then it loomed towards me out of the darkness, hunching over me, sniffing me out – shapeless, eyeless, soulless, blotting out the darkness with a deeper darkness, an endless emptiness . . .

With a sickening lurch, I was awake in an instant, bathed in cold sweat, my heart racing, hardly daring to breathe. My eyes stared blindly into the darkness. The room was utterly silent and I could hear my heart thudding in my ears.

It was just a dream, I told myself. Lighten up. Turn over. Go back to sleep. But the dream hovered too close. I couldn't bring myself to move . . . because I felt a presence in the room.

Without moving a muscle, I swivelled my eyes, searching the room, dreading what I might see. My eyes had adjusted to the darkness, and I could make out the vague shape of the other bed, the chest of drawers, the wardrobe. But apart from those, there was nothing.

Through the wild hammering of my heart, I heard a sound – the faintest rasp of wood on wood, beside my head. For a long moment I lay frozen. Then, summoning every atom of courage I possessed, I murmured sleepily, groaned, and turned over to face . . . nothing.

Nothing . . . that I could see. Turn on the light, I told myself. Just reach out your hand and turn it on. Don't be a baby. Do it. One . . . two . . . three. I reached out my hand, groped for the switch of my bedside lamp, and flicked it on.

Soft light bathed the room. There was nothing there. I heard the faintest, tiniest click: the click of the door being closed, softly as a feather.

My bedside drawer was open the merest crack.

I groped under the pillow for my ring. I'd fallen asleep with it in my hand – for comfort, and to bring me courage for the following day. It was there. My shawl was there too, bundled up under the bed-clothes, where it usually ended up by morning.

I slid the drawer open. My *Bible* was exactly where I'd left it, beside my torch. My penny whistle was there too, hidden away behind them both. With a sigh of relief I pushed the drawer shut – completely shut, as my orphanage training had taught me to do; as I always did, without fail.

I lay down again, and pulled the bedclothes up to my chin. I left the light on. A long time later, Richard turned over onto his back and began to snore.

And a long, long time after that, I finally fell asleep.

Under the Stars

It had never occurred to me that it might be approaching nightfall when we returned to Karazan.

Once again I made the transition effortlessly. When I opened my eyes it was dusk, and I was standing alone on the tussocky rise at the foot of the cliff. Before I had time to wonder where the others were, they materialised one by one. First Gen collapsed on the grass in a heap, then Richard appeared out of nowhere, shaking his head as if to clear it. Kenta followed him, her face screwed up and her head in her hands. Last of all came Jamie, on hands and knees, making retching sounds.

He looked up at me reproachfully. 'You said it was *easy*, Adam,' he moaned. 'I feel like I'm going to throw up.' He rolled over and lay on his back, clutching his stomach.

I was about to answer him when Kenta spoke. 'Look,' she said, pointing, 'the cat has followed us.'

'Oh no! How did that happen?' Sure enough, there at the foot of the standing stone sat Tiger Lily, washing her face with her paw. And then I remembered – she'd been in the computer room when Q had given us our final briefing. She'd been kind of winding herself round my ankles, the way cats do. She must have been touching me when I gave the keyboard command, and been drawn along with me, like a magnet.

Richard laughed.

'I don't see what's so funny,' said Gen. 'OK, here we are in Karazan, but that's about the only thing that's gone according to plan. It'll soon be dark, and I don't fancy spending the night here. And what are we going to do about the cat? We can't take him with us.'

'Her,' I said. 'She's a her.' But no one was listening.

'We must go back again right away.' Jamie's bottom lip was quivering. 'Then we can take the cat back, have a proper dinner, and spend the night safe in our own beds at Quested Court. We can come back again in the morning, after breakfast.'

He seemed to have forgotten we'd just had break-fast, and it already *was* the middle of the morning – in our own world.

But my big worry was Tiger Lily. What if she melted off into the trees and we never saw her again? I flinched – I'd be the one who'd have to explain to Hannah when we got back. I squatted on the ground and held out one hand. 'Kitty-kitty-kitty,' I went enticingly. 'Tiger Lily! Come here.' But every time I crept within reach she'd hop nimbly away, as if it was a game of tag.

Even when the others joined in, we had no better

luck. After a spectacularly unsuccessful rugby tackle, Richard said he was giving up.

'I agree. Anyway, I don't think we should go back – it seems inappropriate to treat travel between dimensions like a shuttle bus, available to take you home every time you meet a minor setback,' said Kenta primly. 'Remember what Q told us? Karazan may well retain some elements of a game world, where everything should be examined and questioned. Much may occur with a hidden purpose that will only become apparent later. Perhaps this is an example. Perhaps the cat is here for a reason.'

'Oh, come *on*,' sneered Jamie scornfully. 'He was smarming up to Adam, and got pulled through by accident. Of course we should take him back. You said I'd never volunteer for anything dangerous, Richard. Well, *I'll* take the cat back home, if we can catch him.'

It was Gen who put her finger on the flaw in his heroic offer. 'You can't. There's only one micro-computer – we all have to travel holding hands, remember?'

'Yes,' agreed Kenta. 'What if you took the cat back, and –' she paused delicately – 'something prevented you from returning?'

There was a short, rather unpleasant silence while everyone thought about what that would mean.

'Let's vote on whether to continue or return,' suggested Kenta.

'Cool,' said Rich. 'I vote to go on.'

'Same here. I say now we're here, we should tough it

153

out.' I didn't say so, but the prospect of spending a night under the Karazan stars was exciting – terrifying, but irresistible. 'After all, we've got our sleeping bags.'

'I vote to continue, but I am uncertain what we should do about the cat. He is a complication.'

'Tiger Lily,' I told Kenta. 'He's a she, and her name is Tiger Lily.'

'That's three out of five for carrying on,' said Richard with satisfaction. 'Seems like the decision's made.'

I would have been happy to make our camp right there, up in the open under the stars. But everyone else said they'd feel more comfortable under the trees, and what if it started to rain? Jamie broke his sulky silence long enough to suggest that we knock on Ronel and Argos's door and ask for a bed for the night, but fortunately no one took him seriously.

We followed the sound of the river down through the forest, past where I'd found the flame vine, and past the place where I reckoned the cottage must be, tucked away among the trees. The further from the entry point we could get before dark the better, the others thought – in the game – the forest held fewer dangers closer to its borders, and was relatively safe near the city of Arakesh.

The ground continued to slope gradually down, and it grew steadily darker. Just as I was about to suggest we call a halt and camp where we were, Richard, who'd scrambled on ahead down a steep bank, let out a triumphant shout: 'Here we go, guys! The perfect camping spot!'

We slithered down the bank after him, the sound of rushing water in our ears. Sure enough, the trees thinned out into a grassy clearing, at one side of which was a wide pool with a waterfall. 'I remember this place from *Quest to Karazan*,' Gen told us, her eyes sparkling. 'There are edible fish in the pool, and the water's safe below the fall.' That meant we'd have fresh water to drink, somewhere to wash in the morning, and the shelter of the trees if we needed it.

Rich was right: it was perfect.

Finding such an ideal spot to spend the night cheered everyone up, even Jamie. Cautiously staying within sight of one another, we scavenged for firewood. Soon we had a merry blaze going, thanks to the lighters Q had issued us with. It was Jamie who suggested we cook something over the campfire, and then try to get some sleep: 'It's what you do to counter jet lag,' he told us. 'Try to adapt to the time frame of your destination as quickly as possible.'

When Gen found a packet of marshmallows in her rucksack, everyone was quick to agree. We toasted marshmallows on sticks over the fire, and for the first time we really talked.

We talked about our quest, and whether the magic potion really existed, and where we should begin our search. We talked about Q's competition, and how we'd felt when we won, and how different the reality was from what we had expected. We told ghost stories, until Gen gave a shiver and asked if we could stop.

And because magic suddenly seemed very real, and

anything seemed possible, we talked about what we would choose if each of us was granted one wish.

'A million more wishes,' goes Jamie, quick as a flash. But he was shouted down. This was serious, insisted Kenta.

'I'd wish to be the greatest rugby player in the world,' said Richard.

'I would wish to be able to attend university,' said Kenta. 'It probably seems a waste of a wish to you, but for me it is an almost impossible dream.'

'What about you, Gen?' I asked curiously. 'What would you wish?'

Gen poked the fire with her stick, and watched as it flared into a flame. Strange shadows danced on her face. 'Promise you won't laugh?' she said shyly, 'I'd wish . . . I'd wish to be beautiful. You know how I love fairy tales? Well, my mother does too. She told me that when I was born, she thought about what gift she would have asked my fairy godmother for, at my christening. "And I'm ashamed to admit, Genevieve, that it didn't take me long to decide on beauty. It can get a girl a long way in life," she said.' Gen sighed. 'Well, it's pretty obvious my fairy godmother didn't turn up. But I've always wondered what it would have been like if she had.'

'Personally, I do not believe that superficial appearance is at all important,' Kenta told her staunchly.

'Yes, I know,' sighed Gen. 'But still . . .'

'OK,' Jamie spoke up unexpectedly. 'Seeing you were honest, Gen, I will be too.' We all looked over at him expectantly. 'I'd wish . . .' I'd have sworn he was blushing, but maybe it was only the firelight reflecting on his face, 'I'd wish to have friends. It's like . . . at school, I get teased a lot. About . . . my size and not being much good at sport. Everyone else seems to have a best friend. But not me. If I could have one wish, it'd be for that.'

We'd caught glimpses of Tiger Lily on and off during our walk, flitting through the trees after us like a pale shadow. While we'd been talking by the fire, she'd appeared on the bank of the pool and found herself a position on a rock, staring intently into the water. Now, the silence following Jamie's words was broken by a gruesome crunching sound. I went over to investigate. She had caught herself some dinner, and was enjoying it as much as we were our marsh-mallows – though I wouldn't have liked to swap.

Soon it looked as though Jamie's jet lag suggestion was paying off: there were more and more yawns, and the talk tailed away to sleepy silence.

'I think Jamie's right,' said Gen at last. 'We should all try to get some rest. It'll make morning come sooner.'

Q had issued us all with identical sleeping bags, moss-green and about the size of Swiss rolls. They were made of goose-down and weighed almost nothing. Q said they'd keep us warm in even the cold-est weather. We agreed we should take turns to be on watch and keep the fire going. Jamie volunteered for first stint, with a meaningful look at Richard, and settled down stoically with his back to a tree trunk.

The rest of us curled up a safe distance away from

the fire. Gradually, silence settled and I became aware of the sounds of the forest – the whispering of the wind in the treetops; an occasional furtive rustling; a sudden chattering alarm call. Once, I heard a long, howling cry, but it was very far away. And once I saw – or thought I saw – pale, glowing eyes staring out of the undergrowth, but the moment I focused on them, they blinked and were gone.

Sleep seemed very far away.

After a long time, I heard muffled sobbing from the dark shape that was Gen. I lay still, wanting to help but not knowing how, trying to decide whether to say anything to her – and *what* to say to a girl who was crying. I saw a small shape slip across to her sleeping bag like a ghost. There was a startled murmur, a rustle, and soon the unmistakable sound of purring.

I smiled to myself, settled deeper into my sleeping bag, and gazed up at the unfamiliar constellations wheeling in the velvet sky above me.

No matter what lurked in the dark beyond our campfire, I had never felt so happy.

FORCE-BACK

'It's humungous!'

'Awesome! A real city, with walls and gates and everything!'

'Why is everyone wearing such dull clothes? And those floppy-eared donkeys with strange mops of hair – they look like lop-eared rabbits!'

'It's like something out of a fairy tale! Do you think that tall building in the centre is a castle?'

We were standing in the dappled shade at the edge of the forest. A strip of open grassland with a few scattered trees lay between us and the sprawling city of Arakesh, with a wide road leading up to the main gates.

From the cliff above the forest Arakesh had looked like a toy town, distant and unreal. Now, it hummed with life. A steady stream of traffic moved along the road, to and from the city gate: mostly people on foot, but the occasional handcart, and one or two covered wagons, drawn by the strange donkeys and the odd mangy-looking llama. Peddlers, perhaps, or farmers, bringing their wares to market.

The gates stood open, but they were flanked by

sentry boxes – and they were manned. The sun glinted off the helmets of two tall guards, and I could make out what looked like a pike leaning against the wall. Though the guards were paying close attention to everyone who entered, they seemed to concentrate on the carts and wagons. Whenever one approached, they'd pull it over to one side and interrogate the owner, rifling through the contents and making notes on a kind of slate. All this seemed to be accompanied by a fair amount of ill feeling on both sides, and angry gestures.

Clustered at the foot of the sentry boxes, and huddled in the shade beneath the city walls, was a ragged band of beggars. They wore hooded grey cloaks and crouched motionless, heads sunk, like resting vultures. Now and then, for no reason I could see, one of the guards would toss a coin towards them; there'd be a brief scuffle, and then one of them would melt away through the gates, presumably to spend his pickings.

Beyond the gates, wisps of smoke were rising from what I imagined must be houses. The faint ringing sound of metal being rhythmically struck travelled clearly through the still air, and I had a sudden, vivid image of a blacksmith at his forge.

It was a real city, full of real people, waking up to another day. Somewhere, a rooster crowed – a simple sound, reminding me of a world that seemed suddenly very far away.

'Adam? Are you OK?'

I turned away so Kenta wouldn't see my sudden

tears. Why would a dumb rooster crowing make anyone feel like crying? 'Yeah, of course, why wouldn't
I be?' I muttered. 'Come on, let's get going.'

The night before, we had agreed Arakesh was the
logical place to start our search. We'd calculated
the city must lie pretty much east of where we had
camped. Jamie had appointed himself official navi-
gator, claiming he'd learned how to use a compass in
Scouts.

So far, it looked as though Q had thought of everything we could possibly need: sleeping bags, food,
lighters and compasses. Even the pocketknives had
come in useful for cutting the green twigs to toast
our marshmallows. We also had torches and a coil
of light, strong nylon rope. 'I have absolutely no
idea what you might need it for,' Q had said, 'but it
certainly can't hurt to have it.' Stowed safely away
in one of the inner compartments of my backpack
were my *Bible*, penny whistle and ring. Crazy though
it seemed in daylight, I couldn't shake the certainty
that there'd been someone – or some unseen presence
– in the room that night. There was no way I was
going to leave my most precious possessions at
Quested Court. Earlier, I'd offloaded some of my gear
into Richard's pack to make room for Tiger Lily, but
I'd kept my shawl scrunched up at the bottom, and
she'd settled down happily in its soft folds for a nap.

We trudged along the rough road towards the
city gate, keeping our heads down and our mouths
shut. That was another thing we'd agreed on: we
would talk as little as possible. We were all aware

that words, once spoken, could never be taken back.

I had a nervous, fluttery feeling in my stomach as we approached the guards. I was certain they would sense something different about us, something that didn't belong.

But we timed it perfectly. Just ahead of us trundled a heavy wagon, laden with produce. With a brusque order, one of the guards motioned it off the road, and both of them closed in on it.

Eyes lowered, hardly daring to breathe, we edged past on their blind side, praying we wouldn't be noticed. But avoiding the guards brought us close to the beggars – too close for comfort. Their hoods obscured their faces, and a rank, putrid smell hung about them. Though they didn't turn their heads, I could feel them watching us, hungry and waiting . . .

The guards didn't so much as spare us a glance. The second we were through the gate we scurried into the shadow of the nearest building. My heart was hammering, and my mouth felt dry. Behind us, I dimly registered the chink of a coin striking cobblestones, and the scrabbling, scuffling sound of the beggars, like ravens squabbling over a crust of bread.

'Right – so far, so good,' Rich whispered hoarsely. Lines of sweat had carved clean paths down his dusty face, although the morning was still cool. He pushed his damp thatch of hair off his forehead with the back of his hand, and made a rueful face. 'The sooner we find that potion and get out of here, the better. Which way now?'

The road branched into three like a trident. The

middle branch was clearly the most well-used – a broad track of cobblestones polished smooth by use, heading straight towards what I imagined would be the town centre. Most of the wagons and carts seemed to be heading that way.

The other two forks wound off to the left and right. Smaller lanes led off them with houses on either side fronting directly onto the street, in earthy shades of ochre, brown, cream and grey. The narrow streets twisted and wound in a haphazard way that made me worry about how easy it would be to get lost.

Even huddled in the shadow of the wall, keeping our voices low and our heads down, we were attracting curious glances from the passers-by. And it was easy to see why – like Argos and Ronel, they all had darker skin and the pale faces of the other four stood out like beacons. 'I hate the way everyone keeps looking at us,' muttered Gen, turning towards the wall. 'Let's get off this main road. At this rate, it's only a matter of time till someone asks us who we are and what we're doing here, and where our parents are. And then what?'

'Yeah, you'd better be our spokesman if anyone challenges us, Adam,' grinned Rich with a wink, and for once I was glad of the dusky skin I'd so often been teased about at school.

'Help – here comes one of those beggar people,' hissed Gen. 'They give me the creeps.'

'In every civilisation there are the downtrodden and unfortunate,' said Kenta earnestly. 'Perhaps these are lepers, or something similar – whoever they are, it is certain they would not choose to spend their lives begging.'

'Well, you can launch a campaign to help them another time, Kenta,' said Rich. 'Right now, we've got more important things to do.'

We took the left fork and followed it deeper into the city, looking about us curiously. Mostly, there were houses on either side, but now and then I saw what looked like an inn, and once caught a glimpse of a grassy courtyard and a splash of bright flowers through a half-open gate. Fat, speckled birds like small chickens pecked between the cobblestones, scuttling away with curious, chuckling cries when we came too close.

We passed two women in aprons standing at their front doors exchanging gossip. They stopped talking and watched us pass, tight-lipped, with narrow, suspicious eyes. Occasionally we'd catch a glimpse of one of the beggars – not squatting at a street corner waiting for a coin, but slipping away round a corner, crouched in an alley, or motionless and almost invisible in the shadows.

It was beginning to seem a long time since breakfast. When we rounded a corner and saw a wide open, grassy square ahead of us with a shady tree in one corner, we headed straight for it and sank down thankfully. To my relief, Tiger Lily showed no inclination to emerge from her snug nest in my bag, but merely opened one golden eye a slit, gave a token purr, and settled back to sleep.

'This must be the village green,' said Jamie, his mouth full of apple. 'Look at all the shops. I'll bet they have a market here, too.'

Gen wasn't listening. 'Oh, look!' she said. 'There's one of those sweet donkey things, and it has a little foal! Can I go and stroke it? If I promise not to talk to anyone?'

Sure enough, tethered to a hitching post on the edge of the green was a donkey, and its tiny foal. The mum was a dusty brown colour, with a mop of black mane in a clump on her head like a feather duster. The baby was creamy white, with a dark brown mane and long, knobbly legs – it did look kind of cute. Their droopy ears gave them both a mournful, gloomy expression.

In the end, Gen, Kenta and I all went over to say hello to them. They seemed friendly enough, and especially liked having their heads scratched. To my surprise, I could feel two little nubs of horn, like a calf's, under the mother's mop of stiff hair.

The girls were ooh-ing and aah-ing over the foal when suddenly the mother stretched her neck out and upwards, pulled her long lips away from her teeth, rolled her eyes, and emitted the longest, loudest burp I'd ever heard. I jumped back; the two girls squealed and shrieked and burst into fits of giggles.

A cheery voice spoke up from behind us.

'You should know better than to tickle a glonk. You be lucky you didn't get a rear-ender!'

I wheeled round, my heart lurching. Facing us stood a boy about our own age, so different from the silent, hostile townspeople that he could have come from another planet.

'What's a rear-ender?' Gen couldn't resist asking.

The dimple in his cheek deepened. He was about Jamie's height, and his face sparkled with mischief and fun. His brown hair was cropped short and stuck up in front in an untidy cow's-lick, giving him a comical, startled air. 'What a question for a lady to ask!' he laughed. 'Well, if you don't know, *I* sure ain't going to demonstrate!'

Right on cue the foal flipped up its fluffy brown bunny tail and let rip an ear-splitting fart. That set the girls off again, of course, and the boy and I grinned at each other.

'My name's Kai,' he told me. 'Who be you?'

'I'm . . . er . . . Adam,' I mumbled.

I didn't know whether to feel relieved or disappointed when Richard rescued me, as we'd agreed to do if necessary: 'Hey, Adam – come over here a minute!'

I gave the boy an apologetic smile, muttered, 'Sorry – gotta go,' and we made our escape.

Kai wasn't alone for long. The village green was like the hub of a wheel, with streets like spokes joining it from every angle. Soon, from all directions, boys came running – almost as if it was break time at school. One of them was carrying what looked like a kind of soft football. With a great deal of jostling and discussion, they quickly separated into two groups.

We watched curiously as the teams ranged themselves into straggling lines, one at each end of the green. Whatever the game was going to be, it seemed slow to start.

Kai strutted out to the front of his team. 'You've got one more,' he called. 'You'll have to choose someone to sit out!'

'Well, we won't, so put *that* in your gob and chew it!' retorted the leader of the other team, a dark-haired, belligerent-looking boy.

'If it wasn't the final, I wouldn't care,' said Kai. 'We're short one, so there ain't nothing *we* can do about it. But you have one extra, so it be your call. Choose your weakest player to be arbiter. But playing an extra man just ain't fair!'

'It's not our problem if one of your players didn't show. It be the way the geld falls – too bad for you!'

'Hob couldn't help it – his pa's sick, and he has to mind the shop!'

'Oh, boo-hoo – hark to the baby cry! Are you playing or aren't you? Because if we don't start soon, we'll all have to go back to trentice, and we'll win by default!'

The two boys stood there, glaring at each other.

Then, taking everyone by surprise, Kai wheeled round and ran over to our tree. 'Can you play force-back?' he demanded.

'Force-back?' We looked at him blankly.

He rolled his eyes impatiently, and glanced up at the sun – his equivalent of looking at his watch, I guessed. 'Aye! *You* know – two lines, kick the fob, try to catch it, *force* the other team *back*. *Force-back!*'

Suddenly, I could hear Q's words in my mind,

as clearly as if he was next to me: *Like a computer game, it'll be about observing, acting and reacting. And sometimes, you'll have to trust your instincts.*

'Go on, Rich,' I said, giving him a shove. 'I bet you can play a simple game of force-back, no problem!'

Richard's face lit up – but his grin was a faint shadow of Kai's, as he held out one hand and pulled Rich to his feet. Talking earnestly, Kai led Richard to his place in the line, and the game began.

Half an hour later a great shout went up from Kai's team, and we watched as Richard was hoisted onto their shoulders and paraded round the village green. I couldn't help grinning, but I was wincing inwardly – this wasn't exactly the low profile we'd agreed to keep. Still, it was hardly surprising: not only had Rich stolen the show with his massive, accurate kicks, but he'd shown the strength and determination of a rhinoceros. Kai's team had scored a crushing victory, and it was almost entirely thanks to Richard.

The other boys straggled away, and Kai and Rich came over to the tree and flopped down, grinning all over their faces and smelling distinctly of sweat.

'You have a permanent place in my team if you want one, Rich,' said Kai, wiping his damp face on his sleeve. 'You are a fearsome adversary. And yet you say you ain't never played force-back before?' He shook his head in disbelief.

Richard reached for his bag, and, before I could stop him, pulled out his water bottle and took a long swig. '*Rich –* ' I said, but it was too late.

Q had given us the most rugged, basic bottles he'd been able to find in any of the outdoor shops in Winterton – military-type canteens, complete with shoulder straps and camouflage netting. I reckoned they were pretty cool, and by the look on Kai's face, he thought so, too.

'By Zephyr,' he breathed, and held out his hand. 'I ain't seen nothing like *that* before. Where did you get it?'

Very reluctantly, with a sheepish glance at the rest of us, Richard handed it over.

Kai was clearly waiting for an answer, screwing and unscrewing the lid and tapping the sides.

'From a merchant in our home town,' I mumbled.

Kai settled himself comfortably. He obviously had no intention of leaving for school, or trentice, or wherever his friends had gone. His gaze was friendly, curious and open. 'Your home town? And where is that?'

There was an awkward silence. Suddenly I had a brainwave. 'Where we are from, it isn't polite to question strangers.'

But Kai wasn't having any of it. He pulled a face and gave me a friendly shove. 'Oh, don't give me that glonk-widdle, Adam,' he said cheerfully. 'Come on – where *are* you from? And where be your parents? And for what purpose have you come to Arakesh?'

He leaned back on one elbow, smiled broadly and waited for us to answer.

Second Sight

Gen made one last valiant attempt to deflect him. 'Shouldn't you be at school?' she asked, sounding rather prim. 'I mean – we wouldn't want you to get into trouble.'

'You women be all the same. From cradle to grave, always yapping at us menfolk to be going about our business,' grumbled Kai good-naturedly. 'In answer to your question, my lady: if I should be anywhere, it's at trentice, and not at *school*, whatever *that* may be. But this week I'm trenticed to my own pa at the inn, and I know the business well enough already, from the wine stains on the floor to the cobwebs in the thatch.'

'Does your father own an inn?' asked Jamie. I could practically see visions of a square meal and a comfortable bed materialising in his head.

'Indeed he does – the Brewer's Butt, in Bend Lane.'

Jamie sniggered. 'Is it really called the Brewer's Butt?'

'Aye, it is – brewer for he who brews the ale, and butt for the wooden cask it's brewed in,' retorted Kai, but there was a mischievous twinkle in his eye, and I wondered whether the name had another meaning in his world, as well as ours. 'And now, it be your turn. Where do you hail from?'

Thanks to Gen I'd had a moment to collect my thoughts. As I started to speak, taking it slowly and choosing my words with care, I hoped I'd made the right call.

'We have journeyed from a town far away, in a distant land.'

Kai nodded. So far, so good, but he was watching me narrowly, and was clearly no fool. And that was partly why I'd decided to stick as closely to the truth as possible – that, and the fact that I liked him, and could tell the others did too.

'Aye, and what be the name of this town?'

'It's called . . . Winterton.'

Kai nodded again. 'Well, I can see *that* be true enough, any road. It be the reason for your pale faces, like grubs that ain't never seen the sun. Well, go on.'

I took a deep breath, and a huge gamble. 'We have travelled here alone, without our parents' knowledge,' I told him. 'You see, we have a sick friend – a friend who is going to die. And we have come to Arakesh to seek a potion that might heal her.' I didn't say the word *magic* – I didn't want to sound like a complete idiot.

Kai's eyes widened, and he glanced round warily. 'Well, my friends, if you seek the Healing Potion, you seek in vain,' he said quietly. 'Unless you bring with you a wagonload of gelden.'

Excitement rippled through our little group like an electric current. Jamie sat bolt upright, his eyes bright. 'You mean it does exist?' he hissed.

'Exist? Of course it exists – as even a hoo-hoo grub from Winterton must surely know,' snorted Kai.

'See the tower up yonder?' He pointed off across the green; sure enough, the tall tower Gen had noticed was just visible above the houses. 'That be the temple – the Sacred Temple of Arakesh. But you'll know this – that's why you're here.'

'No, we *don't* know,' said Richard. 'We didn't even know for sure the potion was real.'

Kai raised his eyebrows, and shook his head. 'Winterton must be distant indeed. Well, then: in the days of yore, more than fifty spans ago –' he dropped his voice again, and glanced back over his shoulder – 'when good King Zane was on his throne, the Potions of Power were at hand to all who needed them.

'There were still the Curators, to hear the applicants and weigh the need, and even in those days, you would only be granted the Potion of Insight if you were a mage, and the Potion of Power if you were a warrior of a certain level. The Healing Potion was for the apothecaries, of course, and those who could afford to paid to use it, according to their means. But it was freely given to us humble folk.' He sighed. 'They say in those distant days common people wore what clothes they pleased, and music and laughter rang through the streets of Arakesh.'

Well, things sure had changed. 'Aren't you allowed to wear whatever you want?' asked Jamie in amazement. 'Do you have to wear, like, uniforms, or something?'

Kai looked at him blankly. '*Uniforms?* Nay, Pinky – unless the uniform colours of the earth be what you mean. For the wearing of colour is a privilege reserved only for Curators and those of noble blood. Within the borders of Karazan, even a lass of three summers playing in a meadow don't dare place a bright flower in her hair, lest it be noted. Yet they say the king wears a cloak of cloth woven like a rainbow and his queens have entire chambers for their gowns alone, with not a single one of the selfsame hue.'

I exchanged a glance with Rich. Thank goodness Q had insisted on keeping our costumes as close as possible to the ones worn by the villagers in *Quest for the Golden Goblet*!

'The gulf between those of high birth and us humble folk is as great as that between the soil and the stars,' Kai was telling us bitterly. 'And what holds the two apart is not free air and the four winds, but fear and pain. Now that King Karazeel rules Karazan, gelden have mouths, and their language is the only one the king or the Curators hear. And it is their weight, more than the weight of need, that sways the balance at the temple.'

Well, I couldn't make sense of much of what he'd said, and by their blank looks I could see the others were also struggling. But even I could tell it wasn't good news. There was a gloomy silence.

'So what it all boils down to is this,' said Kenta slowly. 'The magic potions *do* exist, and you can get

173

them from the temple – that building over there – but only if you have enough money.'

'Aye – ain't that what I just said?'

'How much is enough?' Richard asked bluntly.

Kai gave a short laugh. 'A king's ransom, that be how much – more than I, or you, or even Pa, would ever have, if we worked night and day and spent not a single cobbler more our whole lives long.'

'Do you know anyone who has the potion?' Gen asked hopefully. 'Who might be able to spare us – you know – just a tiny *drop*?'

Kai must have heard the desperation in her voice, because for once he kept a curb on his tongue, and simply smiled at her, shaking his head.

'There must be a way,' I said slowly. 'There *has* to be. At the very least, we should go to the temple and look. Maybe we could – I don't know – sneak in somehow, and . . .'

I didn't say it. I didn't have to. The others were all looking down, picking at the grass. Only Kai seemed unperturbed. 'Aye, there's a thought,' he said, sounding more cheerful. 'To take from the coffers of King Karazeel, the coffers fat with gelden from merchants and farmers . . . and *innkeepers* – aye, that would be no crime in my eyes.' The dimple disappeared. 'But if you were caught . . .' He shook his head. 'King Karazeel makes an example of all who steal from him. It would be the axe and entrails on the walls of Shakesh, children or no. That – or worse.'

None of us asked Kai what he meant – none of us wanted to know.

'Maybe we should just go home.' Jamie's voice wasn't much more than a whisper.

Kai glanced across at him. 'Nay,' he said kindly, 'you should not despair. *Let your boat go with the river's flow; the tide may yet turn.*' He jumped to his feet. 'And now, I'm away to Hob's to tell him of our force-back victory.' His eyes gleamed. 'Will you come with me? He will not forgive me if I deny him the chance to clasp the wrist of such a master of the fob, Rich. And who knows? Hob has a heavy head on his shoulders, and may be able to help you in your quest – and I swear you can trust him as far as an arrow flies.'

Somehow it didn't surprise me that Kai knew the byways of Arakesh like the back of his hand. We followed him through the cobbled streets in the golden sunshine, ducking occasionally down narrow alleyways, and taking a number of shortcuts through what I suspected were private courtyards.

In no time at all he was pushing open the door below a faded wooden sign reading *Second Sight*, and had disappeared inside. I paused outside for a moment to wait for the others, curious to see what kind of place it would be.

The windows fronting onto the narrow lane were of thick, irregular glass, making it virtually impossible to see inside. The fact that they were none too clean didn't help. The others straggled up, and we stood in a cluster round the window, all pretending to admire the invisible merchandise, but really having a whispered conference.

'You shouldn't have told him so much,' hissed Jamie.

'Well, I think Adam did the right thing.'

'It is clear we are unlikely to make any progress without assistance.'

'I like Kai, and I think we should trust him,' chipped in Gen. 'I think we should go on in, meet this Hob, and see where it takes us.'

I looked round at the four faces: Jamie's clouded with worry; Kenta silent and alert; Rich as laid-back as ever; and Gen earnest and intense, her wild hair tangled and a smudge of dirt on her long nose.

I gave them all what I hoped was an encouraging grin, and we headed in.

My first impression was that Second Sight was some kind of a junk shop. Shelves and dusty display cabinets lined the walls, a chaotic assortment of merchandise cluttering every surface. Somehow the light filtering through the window and from one or two lanterns managed to make the whole place seem even darker.

The jingle of the bell above the door was followed almost immediately by a loud crash as Jamie knocked over a suit of armour standing in the shadows.

A skinny, red-haired boy appeared from the back of the shop, Kai in his wake. To my relief, he didn't seem too fussed about the jumble of metal scattered over the floor. 'Happens all the time,' he said casually, giving it a kick. 'Designed to take knocks a lot worse than this. Can't see why Pa don't put it over on the other side with the rest of the weaponry.' He held out his hand to Richard. 'I'm Hob – and I'll wager you're Rich. Thanks for taking my place at force-back.'

He clasped wrists solemnly with each of us in turn, and then led us to the back of the shop after flipping the sign on the door to read 'Closed'. As he did, he winked at Kai, and I wondered what his absent pa would have felt about such flexible opening hours.

'Now,' said Hob, with the confidence of one on his own turf, 'Kai has told me who you are, and why you have come to Arakesh. *I* think the whole thing's really *tempered* –'

'*And* honed!' added Kai, giving him a nudge.

'Aye, tempered *and* honed. And because any friend of Kai's is a friend of mine, and because you won the force-back final for us, I'll help you all I can.' He stuck his hands through the belt of his jerkin, and beamed at us.

We grinned back. Even though it was hard to see how this scrawny urchin would be able to help, it felt good to have another friend.

'Now, you have a heavy head, Hob,' said Kai, in the tones of one acknowledging his friend's long-standing reputation, and Hob nodded in agreement, looking modest. 'And you've read all those books your Pa has –'

'Well, bits of them, and only when he made me.'

'Aye, but more than the rest of us. And you be the one with ideas, when there's a plan to be made.'

Hob scratched his head, and sighed. It seemed like

the responsibility of being the ideas man was a weighty one, but I could see he felt he had a position to live up to, and was clearly not about to admit defeat.

'Well . . .' he said at last, 'we could look through the parchments, and see if there be anything there. We could *even* go through the books –' he slid a reluctant glance over at a bank of shelves crammed with musty-looking leather-bound volumes, 'but that would take a while longer.'

'Aye, let's leave the books,' agreed Kai hurriedly.

Taking a lantern with him, Hob led us over to a tall chest of drawers, almost like a filing cabinet. He produced a key on a string from round his neck, and unlocked it. 'I'll swing for this if Pa finds out,' he told us cheerfully, sliding open a drawer and extracting a dusty folder of thick parchment, which he handed to Kai. He dug out another, and gave it to Gen. 'Here – one for each of you. Find yourself a perch to sit on, and look through the parchments. If you find anything you think might be of help, give me a whistle. I'll put the armour together again and turn the sign round, and then I'll join you. I just hope Pa don't take a turn for the better.'

Even with the light of the lantern, our eyes were burning and our heads aching before half an hour had passed. The thick parchment was dusty and old, and I sneezed now and then as I leafed through my pile, giving each sheet a cursory glance.

Deep down, I was convinced we were wasting our time. We had absolutely no idea what we were looking for, and I had more than a suspicion Hob had made the suggestion of the parchments partly to save face. But at least we were doing *something*, no matter how unpromising it seemed. So, like the others, I worked on, feeling the back of my neck stiffen and my bum gradually go to sleep.

Some of the parchments contained what looked like recipes, and some what I guessed might be spells. There were old maps, some torn and faded, and complicated lists of provisions and equipment. There were whole files of parchments in languages I'd never seen before, and in strange characters it was impossible to read. There were long, complicated legal-looking documents, lists of rules for tournaments, and sheet after sheet of boring-looking historical documents.

Every now and then someone would pipe up: 'How about this?' At first, there'd be a buzz of excitement and a rush to examine the whatever it was they were holding out, but after an hour or so we were all at the stage where we'd say wearily, 'I've just finished a whole file of those.'

I was on my fifth file, and seriously wondering whether to suggest we stopped for a break, when Kenta spoke up.

'What do you think of this?' she asked. 'It seems different from the rest . . .' she paused shyly, 'and it may be my imagination, but it seems my fingers . . . *tingled* when I touched it. But it mentions the balm of healing . . .'

We were on her in a flash. The parchment was

yellow with age, and so brittle it was starting to crumble away in one corner. And, weird though it sounded, what Kenta had said was true: when I touched it, my fingers tingled, as though there was a very faint current of electricity running through it.

'It's in our language, too,' said Gen dubiously, peering at the thick, ornate characters over Kenta's shoulder.

'No, it ain't,' objected Kai. 'I can't read it.'

'Well, that don't mean much,' retorted Hob. 'Let *me* see.'

And gradually, as we squinted at the letters in the dim light of the lantern, we realised we *could* read the writing – and that we had struck gold.

THE PARCHMENT

It was Kenta who read it out, in a voice that sounded thin in the gloom.

'The Balm of Healing rests beneath the towering trees of stone
Guardian of Inner Voices has whispering leaves as home;
Power rings the walls of iron with silk
And Sightless lies in blindness, pale as milk.
Bright Beauty burns with fire eternal as a gem:
An emerald vision age will never end.'

The words settled in the silence as softly as snowflakes.

Then: 'That's all very well,' said Jamie abruptly, 'but listen to this:

'For those who dare defile the steps of five
Lies no escape – they shall not leave alive
Unless bright Serpent Sun to Zenith climb
And fang of light doth pierce the phial of time.'

There was an uncomfortable silence. Then Kai piped up, sounding determinedly cheerful: 'That's only if

they be caught, of course.' But somehow his words had a slightly hollow ring.

'Well,' said Hob soberly, 'there ain't no doubt that this is what you be looking for.'

'Maybe, but I don't understand a word of it,' said Rich. 'Does it mean anything to either of you? Have you heard of the Steps of Five?'

But their blank faces told us the poem meant no more to them than to any of us. And like Rich, none of us could make head or tail of it.

'Why is all the writing so far from the top?' asked Kenta, peering at it.

'And the way the poem is written in circles is strange,' said Gen. 'Let's copy it out so it's easier to read, and then put the parchment back so Hob won't get into trouble.'

But to my surprise, Hob shook his head. 'Nay,' he said reluctantly. 'If it be magical you'd best keep it to hand.'

'What will your Pa say?' Rich objected.

Hob shrugged. 'I'll cross that ford when I find it . . . and mayhap that will be never. Moons go by without Pa opening that cabinet, and I'll wager he don't know all that's inside it.'

'That's the other thing,' said Jamie awkwardly. 'We don't have any money – we can't pay you for it.'

Hob waved his hand airily. 'It ain't mine to sell,' he grinned. 'Take it, and good fortune go with it.'

But Jamie was fumbling in his backpack. 'You've been such a help, Hob. We'd like to give you this, to say thank you.'

He held out his hand. In his palm was the pocket-knife Q had given him.

We each had one – real top-of-the-range red Swiss army knives, with about five different blades, tweezers, a file, a corkscrew, a hoof pick, and even a pair of miniature scissors. I'd never had anything so cool in my life – and Jamie was giving his away.

By the look on Hob's face as he pulled the blades out one by one and tested them on his thumb, he'd never seen anything like it either. 'By Zephyr, this be tempered and honed!' he breathed reverently. 'Be you sure, Jamie?'

'I'm sure,' grinned Jamie.

Kai stood silently in the shadows, watching his friend. There was a tiny smile on his mouth, but something in his eyes . . . Without thinking, I shrugged off my backpack and dug inside. There, under the warm, furry form of Tiger Lily, I found my knife. I pressed it into Kai's hand. 'One for you, too, Kai,' I told him with a grin. 'A token of friendship. From the distant city of Winterton to Arakesh: friends forever.'

'Friends forever,' Kai echoed, his eyes shining.

Hob gave us two thick, creamy sheets of blank parchment to protect the precious poem, and Kenta rolled them gingerly into a scroll, and slid it into her rucksack. We'd agreed the temple seemed the logical place to start our search – the plan was to head straight there, and hope the parchment would start to make more sense along the way.

Hob stood forlornly at the door of Second Sight

184

and watched us head away into the bright sunlight. But as the six of us set off down the cobbled lane, the sound of a bell stopped Kai in his tracks.

It was the same bell I'd heard when I'd been standing under the cliff the first time I'd come to Karazan. Then it had been a distant echo, almost inaudible; now it rang through the streets like a gong, a single chime that sent the speckled birds fluttering up to the roofs of the houses, and had Kai glancing up at the sun.

He pulled a rueful face. 'Well, there ain't no point going to the temple now,' he told us. 'That be the noon bell. It rings once at daybreak, to mark the start of the working day and the opening of the temple, and once at midday, to signal its closing. And as for me, Pa will tan my hide if I'm not back at the inn to help him and Ma with the midday meal.'

The others looked at one another, aghast. 'Does that really mean we must wait another day?' asked Gen. 'Is there no other way?'

Kai shook his head regretfully. I was relieved, though I didn't say so. Digging in my pack had disturbed Tiger Lily, and I could feel her lurching round inside looking for a way out. The last thing we needed was to have her gallivanting round the Sacred Temple of Arakesh, causing havoc and drawing attention to us. Plus, I was keen to have another good look at the parchment, read the poem over again, and see whether together we could figure out what it meant.

Also, I was starving.

So when Kai remarked that the sun would rise

again tomorrow, he was echoing my thoughts. We were walking together through the winding streets in what I hoped was the direction of the gate when suddenly I felt Gen's hand on my arm. 'Adam,' she whispered, 'I just saw another of those beggars disappear round that corner behind us. You don't think . . . it's just . . . I've had a thought I can't seem to shake. You don't suppose it could be the *same* beggar, do you? And that maybe . . . he's following us?' Crazy as her suggestion was, it sent an unpleasant trickle down my spine. Quickly, I glanced behind us, but the street was deserted.

'Nah, Gen, you're just being paranoid,' I told her reassuringly. 'They all look the same, don't they, Kai?'

Kai, who'd been examining the corkscrew on his pocket-knife with a puzzled air, glanced up with a questioning smile at the sound of his name.

'Gen was worried about those beggars in the grey cloaks,' I explained. 'We keep seeing them lurking around, and she's got this weird idea . . .'

Kai's face changed as abruptly as if I'd flicked a switch. Suddenly, he didn't look relaxed and friendly – he looked wary, narrow-eyed . . . afraid. Without a word, he pulled us all back into the doorway of the nearest building.

'How many times have you seen them since you entered the city?' he hissed urgently.

Gen's eyes were like saucers in her white face. 'I don't know . . . maybe . . . a dozen or so?' she quavered.

'*A dozen?* You came through the main gate? The

eastern gate?' I nodded. 'The guards – they flung a coin as you passed?' I nodded again, blankly. 'Then they are watching you. The grey-cloaked ones are not beggars. They are the Followers – the Faceless. And – oh, Zephyr! – they will have seen it all.' He was talking almost to himself now, in a low mutter, his eyes raking the empty street. 'The force-back – that, and a visit to Hob: innocent enough . . . and they have not been near enough to overhear us. They cannot know of the parchment. I pray they do not. Aye, they may know nothing as yet . . . but who can tell when they will close in? And if they find it . . .'

My blood had turned to ice. 'Can't we just go back to the gate, and out into the forest again?' Kenta whispered, her face stricken.

'Nay – they will never let you leave. Even now, their numbers will be gathering and the net closing in. Hush – let me think!'

It was only a moment before he spoke again, low and urgently. 'Follow me. They may not realise you have seen them, or that you know . . . what they are. Walk slowly, and talk comfortably among your-selves. Be calm, for they will smell your fear. And above all, be ready – when I run, follow me closely, for your souls depend upon it.'

With elaborate casualness, we left the shelter of the doorway. Kai led us to the right, in the opposite direction from Hob's shop, and away from the gate. I was sure we weren't fooling anyone – even I could see our little group was huddled unnaturally close together. And try as I might, I couldn't think of a single word to say to any of the others. In tense silence we walked on, as slowly as we could bring ourselves to. My back prickled and it took a huge effort of will not to scan every alley we passed for signs of the Faceless.

At last we turned down a narrow lane, unpaved and in deep shadow. It ran between the sides of two buildings, which almost met overhead. It was dark and dank, and smelled of pee. '*Now – run!*'

Instantly we were off, hurtling towards the distant corner, Kai in the lead, me taking up the rear. Jamie was just in front of me – I was almost treading on his heels. Every nerve in my body screamed at me to overtake him, but his fat legs were pumping like pistons – he was doing the best he could, and there was no way I was leaving him.

As we reached the bend, I risked a quick glance behind – and my heart lurched in my throat. Two – no, three – grey shapes were pursuing us down the alleyway in utter silence, and with terrifying speed. Without thinking, I grabbed Jamie's hand – there was barely room for us to run abreast – and shoved ahead, dragging him behind.

'Oh, Mum, oh, Dad, please help me, please don't let this be real, please don't let this be happening . . .'

'*Shut up, Jamie! Use your breath to run!*'

The others were a couple of metres ahead now . . . and then I saw to my horror we were running full tilt towards a dead end. It couldn't be! But no – the wall didn't reach right to the roof: there was a narrow gap just below the tiles. Kai reached the wall and with a kick and a scrabble he was up, stretching down to grasp Gen's hands. A heave and a shove from Rich, and she was over. I skidded to a halt at the foot of the wall, grabbed Rich round the middle and heaved. He weighed a ton. Kai had hold of his wrists now, and was pulling with all his might. 'Jump, Rich – *help us!*' He jumped, and with a final shove, he was over and gone.

I turned on Jamie. His face was bright red and slick with sweat and snot and tears, his breath rasping in his throat like a hacksaw. 'I can't! I can't!' he wailed.

'You have to,' I snarled through clenched teeth. '*Try!*'

His lip quivered but he reached two plump, trembling arms up to Kai. I spread both hands on his ample bum, and gave him a boost that would've done credit to a space shuttle. He shot over the wall like a cork from a bottle. Without even asking, I grabbed Kenta round the waist and tossed her after him – she was as light as thistledown.

Without looking back, I jumped, and felt my hands grip the top of the stone wall. Kai swung down onto the other side. I gave a heave and a wriggle, and was astride the wall in a second. One quick look back down the alley – and my blood froze. They were so close I could hear their snuffling breath. I swung my leg over, ready to drop to the other side . . . my breeches caught on a nail, and I felt them rip as I fell to the ground.

We were in a small courtyard full of old timber and

broken tiles – and I could see daylight through a gap up ahead. *'Come on – let's go!'*

But Kai stood as if he'd turned to stone, gaping at me with his mouth open. Gaping down at my thigh and the rip in my breeches. 'Come *on* – don't stand there! *They're right behind us!'*

But instinctively I glanced down . . . and through the jagged hole I could clearly see my boxers – my shiny, wine-red satin boxers.

My stomach turned over. But there was no time for that now – no time for anything. I gave Kai a rough shove. *'Go*, Kai – *run!'*

He spun, and raced after the others towards the gap. I risked one final glance up at the wall. A hooded head stared back at me. It was so close that for a second I thought I glimpsed what lay in the deep shadow of the hood – a misshapen lump swathed in strips of stained cloth: damp-looking, seeping, pinkish-grey. The creature hissed as my eye fell on it – I had a sudden, vivid flash of long ago in the bush above Highgate, when I'd come across a dead sheep, crawling with maggots. The stench was the same. Gagging, I wheeled and stumbled away, one hand clamped over the tear in my pants . . . and as I fled, I heard a single rattling gargle of rage.

We pelted through the narrow gap into a deserted street, past a row of derelict houses and down another alley, which led out into a marketplace. Stalls and open carts and wagons lined the street. Wares were laid out on the ground and on trestle tables, and there were people everywhere. Kai skidded to a halt, with a quick glance behind to check that we were following, then wove through the crowds as quickly as he could without drawing attention to himself. We straggled after him, chests heaving and hearts hammering, ducking between the people and praying we wouldn't be noticed.

Kai cut abruptly down a paved sidestreet, with another quick glance over his shoulder. We were close to the city wall now and he broke into a trot. Jamie groaned, clutching his side, and stumbled into a limping jog. Another twist, and Kai ducked through an arched entranceway into a cobbled courtyard strewn with wisps of hay and spattered with dried dung. It was deserted. With the five of us panting behind him, Kai made for the tall wooden doors at the far end, and disappeared inside.

I hesitated, hoping he knew what he was doing. If we'd been followed we'd be trapped. His sweaty face peered impatiently round the door. 'Come *on* – what be you waiting for?'

I caught Rich's eye; he shrugged and nodded. Gen's – she nodded once, decisively. Kenta – yup. As for Jamie, he was operating on autopilot – he plodded blindly after Kai, and disappeared through the doorway. The rest of us followed, me taking up the rear, adrenaline still zinging through my veins like sherbet fizz.

A solid wall of stink hit me in the face like a fist, making me reel and choke. All round me, I could hear the others coughing and gasping. The acrid reek of ammonia, so strong it frizzled my nostrils, and a sulphuric stench of rotten eggs that made me want to puke. With my hand over my nose and mouth, holding my breath, I stumbled after Kai into the gloom.

The dark shapes of the others had gathered at the far wall, sheltered from the entrance by a ramshackle haystack higher than my head. 'Where are we?' I hissed at the shape I thought was Kai.

There was a rueful flash of white – only Kai could grin in a place like this. 'In the glonk stable at Pa's inn,' he whispered back hoarsely. 'The glonk-widdle and rear-enders will cover your scent. Even the Faceless will not sniff you out.'

My eyes were adjusting to the darkness, and I could see that his face had become serious. 'You must leave the city, Adam. Once the gates close at dusk, the Followers will all be free to search – and even here, they will find you. And that be another reason I brought you here. My friends, what I show you now is a secret I have shared only with Hob. Follow me.'

He turned his back, knelt on the filthy floor, and burrowed like a rabbit straight into the heart of the haystack. 'But –' protested Gen faintly.

'But nothing. Think of the Faceless. Do it – and do it quick.'

One by one they disappeared into the hay. Gen, Kenta and Jamie, giving Rich and me one last anguished glance before thudding to his knees and lumbering forward, moaning softly. Rich followed him.

I took a deep, foul-smelling breath, and burrowed into the hay. It was dark as pitch. I squeezed my eyes shut to stop straws poking into them, and groped my way forward with my hands. The tunnel was as narrow as my body, sloping gradually downwards, the earthen floor smooth with use. My lungs were burning. My breath huffed out, and I took another reluctant breath. This time, it tasted of damp earth . . . and fresh air.

My eyes popped open. I could see faint light up ahead, partly blocked by Rich's solid figure in front of me. The tunnel was sloping up again, and there was hard earth on either side instead of straw. Suddenly, with a slither and a grunt, Rich disappeared. I crawled out after him into a copse of thorn bushes and bright sunlight.

We were on the other side of the city wall.

'Heads down, and stay in the bushes until we are certain the way be clear,' breathed Kai. 'Then run for the trees – there is no gate on the northern wall, and few folk come here. It will mean a night in the forest, but you be seasoned travellers – light a fire, and keep careful watch.'

'Do we really have to spend another night in the forest?' whimpered Jamie, almost in tears. 'It's only just turned twelve o'clock – if we set off now, we'd be home . . .' he glanced at Kai, remembering our cover story just in time, 'we'd be . . . uh . . . well on our way back to Winterton by this evening.'

We goggled at him.

'Back to Winterton?' repeated Kai. 'Surely you cannot mean that you would abandon your quest, Pinky?' Jamie scowled, flushing a deeper pink than ever. 'What of your sick friend? What of the adventure that lies ahead? Nay, you must dig deep for the warrior spirit that lies within us all – even you, my friend.

'By morning, your trail will have cooled. I know the byways of Arakesh as well as the Faceless, if not better. I will meet you here at daybreak, and we will see what answers the temple holds, if that is where you choose to begin your quest.'

We spent the afternoon in the woods to the north of the city, eating some much-needed lunch, choosing a campsite to spend the night, and building a bivouac to provide some shelter from wind or rain.

And, in Tiger Lily's case, having a thorough and very pointed cleaning session, to wash away the indignity of being jolted around in my backpack.

Gen cobbled together the tear in my breeches with the sewing kit Nanny had insisted we bring. We played a half-hearted game of tag and hide-and-seek . . . until Jamie wondered aloud what we'd do if we couldn't find someone.

None of us said anything about the Faceless. After all, unless we were prepared to give up, what was there to say? And though Jamie was more subdued than usual during the afternoon, even he didn't mention going home again.

Most of all, we studied the parchment. Over and over again we came back to it, singly and in groups, reading and rereading it, and puzzling over what it could possibly mean.

The Balm of Healing rests beneath the towering trees of stone
Guardian of Inner Voices has whispering leaves as home;
Power rings the walls of iron with silk
And Sightless lies in blindness, pale as milk.
Bright Beauty burns with fire eternal as a gem:
An emerald vision age will never end.

For those who dare defile the steps of five
Lies no escape – they shall not leave alive
Unless bright Serpent Sun to Zenith climb
And fang of light doth pierce the phial of time.

'Each of the five potions is mentioned in turn,' said Kenta hesitantly. 'The *Balm of Healing* is the Healing Potion, of course, and *Inner Voices* could be the Potion of Insight, I suppose.'

'Yeah, and *Power* must mean the Potion of Power, just like it says,' chipped in Richard, cottoning on.

'Which means that *Sightless* means the Potion of Invisibility,' said Gen thoughtfully. '*Sightless*, like unable to *be* seen, maybe.'

'And that means the next two lines must refer to the Potion of Beauty and . . . what was it?' asked Kenta.

'Eternal Youth,' Gen supplied.

'But the rest makes no sense at all,' said Rich.

'Yeah – beyond the obvious, that is,' agreed Jamie darkly.

'I reckon we've got it a hundred percent right so far,' I said. 'But we need to take it a step further. It seems to me each potion is linked to the place where it comes from. Like, the Healing Potion among trees, for example . . .'

'Yeah – right here in the forest, maybe!' chips in Richard, staring round wildly as if a phial of the potion might be lying in full view by the campfire.

'It says *trees of stone*,' Gen pointed out. 'What on earth are trees of stone?'

'*Whispering leaves* sounds like a forest, also,' said Kenta. 'But if that *is* what it means, where on earth would we start looking?'

We gazed around us, at the trees stretching away into the distance, as far as the eye could see. Where indeed?

'I think we stick to our original plan,' I said, in a voice I hoped was as cheerful as Kai's. 'Meet Kai at the tunnel entrance at sunrise, go to the temple, and see if we can't "borrow" a bottle. Who knows? We may be wasting our time trying to figure out the poem – it may all turn out far simpler than it seems.'

But even though I'd made up my mind not to waste any more energy thinking about the poem, by the time we settled down in our sleeping bags for the night I realised I knew the whole thing by heart. Round and round in my head it went, as I lay gazing up at the stars . . . round and round in my dreams, as I tossed and turned on my bed of rustling leaves.

TREES OF STONE

We woke, stiff and cold, in the grey pre-dawn. Breakfast was muesli bars and fruit juice. A fine, misty rain had fallen in the night – not enough to soak us, but enough to put out the fire and rule out any hopes of a hot drink. Jamie, who'd been on last watch, had fallen asleep beside the ashes, a chocolate wrapper peeping from his fist.

It was a bedraggled, disgruntled group that set off in the direction of the northern wall and Kai's secret tunnel. Except for me.

The perfume of damp earth and springtime was all around us; every scent, every sound seemed magnified and unbearably beautiful. Tramping silently over the soft ground, I had a feeling of joy so intense it was almost painful.

Tiger Lily had been missing since we woke, but soon after we set off I noticed her bounding through the trees alongside us, a tiny grey feather caught in her whiskers. She gave me a sidelong look, as if to say that she understood exactly how I felt.

We'd taken note of the location of Kai's tunnel – the wall at that point was fringed by an untidy straggle of thorn bushes hiding the entrance. We smelt Kai before we saw him – a mouthwatering aroma of fresh bread that would have given his presence away at once if anyone had been passing. One by one, we burrowed under the bushes, and he met us with a broad grin and crusty rolls, still warm from the oven.

'*Friends forever*,' he said with a wink, taking the last one himself. 'We have been fortunate. The rain will have erased what remained of your trail. But they will still be searching – especially for you, Adam.' He nodded in the direction of the none-too-tidy darn. 'The customs in Winterton must be different indeed. Here, the wearing of scarlet, like the naming letter "Z", is only for those of royal blood.'

I grinned and tugged down my breeches a centimetre or two to reveal a flash of bare bum – no boxers were better than ones that might get us all strung up on the city walls, I reckoned.

'They searched the northern sector of the city overnight, as I guessed they would,' Kai told us, once we'd emerged into the stable, dusted ourselves off, and slipped out into the empty lane. 'If we keep to the old part of the city, there is a good chance we will go unnoticed. We must be cautious, though.'

'What about you, Kai?' asked Kenta hesitantly. 'Surely they would have seen you with us? I've been worrying all night that you'll get into terrible trouble for helping us escape.'

Kai shot her a smile. 'It ain't the first time a lass has lost sleep over me,' he teased, and Kenta flushed. 'Nay,' he said, more seriously, 'it is said the Faceless track their prey by smell – I know not what lies in the shadows of those dark hoods, but if they have eyes, they do not use them for that purpose. My scent be the scent of Arakesh, and it is strangers they seek. For the time being at least, I am in no danger.'

The streets were deserted, and in the misty light of early morning I began to feel more confident that perhaps we might be able to reach the temple without being seen. The part of the city we were walking through had an air of dilapidated splendour. The streets were wide but empty, and though the houses were large and imposing, many of them seemed derelict. 'I'll bet someone important lives here,' remarked Jamie, gesturing to a tall wall on our left, which stretched ahead as far as I could see.

'Aye . . . and nay. This be the old Summer Palace, beloved of King Zane and Queen Zaronel, but fallen into ruin. They say the gardens were carpeted with emerald, and crystal fountains sang day and night with music sweeter than the birds. Within, the walls were hung with tapestries so finely woven they almost seemed alive; the chambers rang with laughter and echoed to the tales of bards from distant lands.' Kai lowered his voice to a husky whisper. 'But it was also here that King Zane lay upon his deathbed. When his spirit flew free at last, Queen Zaronel's heart tore asunder. And within these walls was born a legend that lives on in tales told by firelight, when voices are low and doors are barred, and dreams stir again in men's hearts.'

A metal gate was set into the wall just ahead, and

we peered curiously between its bars. There was certainly no evidence of any of the wonders Kai described. The gate gave onto a bleak courtyard of dry, cracked earth and the only fountain we could see was a bare, dusty bowl with a broken statue, covered in cobwebs. It might have been beautiful once. Now it seemed a barren place, a residue of sorrow drifting like dust over the splintered flagstones.

'They say Prince Karazeel was crazed with grief when he learned of his brother's death, and in his anguish caused all to be destroyed, overturning every vessel and paving stone, and tearing every precious drapery asunder. And now . . . now Karazeel himself is king. Times change.' Kai's face was grim. I opened my mouth to ask him more but Gen caught my eye and gave her head a tiny shake, as if she thought he had already said too much. I shrugged and followed him away from the gate. Whatever secrets were hidden in the mists of Karazan's past were no concern of ours.

We walked on in silence, the ground rising gradually as we wound deeper into the heart of the city. When at length we reached the open piazza in its centre, the whole of Arakesh fell away on every side. The piazza was like an enormous town square, paved with huge stone flags of a pinkish sandstone similar to the city walls. The Sacred Temple of Arakesh reared up from the centre like an enormous, round, six-tiered wedding cake. The entire second level seemed to consist of vast pillars rather than walls, with creepers and other greenery cascading down. I found my gaze drawn to the top, half expecting to see an ornamental bride and groom perched there. Instead, I saw a shining dome of golden metal.

'They say the dome is a magical timekeeper that counts the hours, and the noonday bell rings of its own accord,' Kai told us. Something in his voice made me glance at his face, where disapproval fought with reluctant pride. 'The temple is one of the wonders of Karazan,' he continued, 'but Pa says it be just a ridiculous waste of gelden.' He shot me a sidelong smile. 'I'll wager you ain't seen nothing like it in Winterton, Adam!'

'We sure haven't,' I admitted. 'Are we allowed inside?'

'Aye, anyone may enter the public hearing room, once the dawn gong has sounded. Let us be bold – those who search will seek you in hidden places, not marching through the portals of the temple. Follow me.'

We straggled across the flagstones to the broad stone steps leading to the main entrance. I felt a chill as we passed through the tall arch into the cavernous hall, and was glad of the reassuring warmth of Tiger Lily, asleep in my backpack.

The entrance led directly into what I supposed must be the public hearing room – and, in fact, appeared to be the entire ground floor of the temple. A pink and white checkerboard of flagstones stretched before us. Tall, arched windows punctuated the circular walls at regular intervals, making the vast chamber light and airy. Huge columns thicker than a man's body reared up everywhere, helping to support the massive weight of the floors above. Only one area was clear of pillars, a wide central aisle leading to the far end of the hall.

'Imagine a game of tag in here,' whispered Jamie. 'These pillars would be even better than trees to hide behind!'

And in fact, instinctively, we'd all moved away from the open aisle, into the shelter of the columns. Using them as cover, we drifted gradually closer to the dais at the far end of the hall. Somewhere, I could hear the sound of water.

On the dais were five ornate chairs, almost like thrones, ranged in a wide arc. Before each of them was a low table bearing a giant set of scales and an array of brass weights. The smallest was tinier than a thimble, and the largest the size of a skittle.

On each throne was seated a man in long robes, holding in his hand a strange staff, tall and slim, with a V-shaped fork at one end. 'The Curators,' breathed Kai. Each man's robes were a different colour: steely grey; an intricately patterned brown; jet black; snow white; and a radiant, shimmering green. 'I bet they have heaps of applications for the green guy's job,' muttered Richard. 'It's the first bit of colour I've seen anyone wearing since we got here.'

'The Curators are among the most privileged in the land, second only to the king and his most trusted advisers. But hush! Here comes an applicant.'

An old man was struggling down the central aisle, wheeling a rickety barrow. Whatever was inside it was swathed in rough brown cloth. The barrow was cumbersome and badly balanced, tilting heavily to one side. The five Curators watched expressionlessly as the man approached and set the barrow down. An usher came forward, and there was a whispered consultation. The man hefted his barrow again, and wheeled it across to the table in front of the Curator in the grey robes.

'The Curator of Healing,' Kai hissed.

The man knelt, bowed his head, and waited.

With a slightly patronising air, the Curator rose and walked up to the barrow. He lifted the cloth with the point of his staff, as if it might be contaminated, and glanced underneath. I could see now that it was a threadbare blanket, and could just make out the huddled form of a child beneath. The Curator raised one dark eyebrow, and let the blanket fall. He poked the kneeling man in the shoulder with his staff and said in a cold, hard voice, 'Come forward and be heard.'

The man shuffled forward, still on his knees. The usher spoke sharply to him, and he turned back to his barrow and fumbled for a moment, then withdrew two heavy leather pouches and laid them on the table. His hands were shaking slightly as he loosened the drawstring of one and extracted ten gold coins, counting them carefully. Kai drew in his breath sharply. 'The price of a hearing,' he whispered. 'Ten gelden – as much as a man might make in a span. *Just to be heard . . .*'

'Listen!' breathed Kenta. The man had started to speak, but his voice was hardly above a whisper, and trembling so much it was hard to make out the words. 'My lord: wise, compassionate and just,' he began unsteadily, 'I approach you in the name of King Karazeel, he of ultimate power and infinite mercy.' Kai snorted. I gave him a dig in the ribs to shut him up. 'You see before you Danon of Drakendale, a humble carpenter. I work at my trade from dawn till dusk, earning but twelve gelden in a span. I am proud to halve six of those gelden to King Karazeel, as the records will show.'

The Curator gave an almost imperceptible nod, and placed the second-smallest weight onto the flat platform at the raised end of the scale. The weight was about the size of a matchbox.

'My lord, I have journeyed three long days with a sick child to attend this audience,' the man continued, his eyes fixed on the array of weights. The Curator inclined his head, impassive. 'My daughter . . .' The man's voice broke, and he put his hands up to his face for a moment before he continued. 'My daughter is our only child, my lord. Until a moon ago she was like a little sunbeam, the light of our days and the hope of our future –'

'Proceed.' The Curator's cold voice cut through the man's words like a steel blade. 'This will not assist your cause.'

'Our daughter fell ill,' the man continued. 'A pain like an axe splitting her skull and her neck so stiff she could not bend it. We were certain she would die.' He sighed. 'But . . . she did not. And yet, neither did she recover. Now she lies like a wraith in a twilight land, neither of the living, nor the dead.' He bowed his head. 'We have begged gelden from kin both far and near, and sold all we have save the roof over our heads, to raise the price for the potion that will heal her,' he said softly. 'I rest the matter in your merciful hands.'

The Curator's pale hand hovered for a moment above the array of weights, finally selecting one about the size of a salt cellar, and placing it beside the other on the raised end of the scale. He motioned to the usher, who brought the first of the bags of gold and placed it on the platform beside the two weights. The scale didn't budge.

The usher hefted the other bag. Even I could see how heavy it was. We watched, scarcely breathing, as he lowered it slowly onto the scale. For a moment, I was sure the balance would tip. The platform dipped a fraction as it took the weight of the bag, and the opposite end lifted for a tantalising second before settling back into its original position.

There was a long, awful silence. Then the man started gabbling desperately, his words falling over each other. 'Please, please, my lord, have mercy,' he begged. 'This is all we have – we can raise no more! Can we not include the ten gelden hearing fee? It would tip the balance! This is our last chance, our only hope! She is our baby, my lord, our only child!' He was weeping now. I couldn't watch; I felt sick. 'I appeal to you as a father! If you have children, my lord, you will know –'

'Enough!' The Curator's voice was like ice.

'Remove this man. I exact a five gelden penalty for wasting my time and attempting to sway the scale by sentiment. Be thankful it is not more. Be gone.'

None of us said anything for a long while. My nostrils were full of the sour, metallic smell of corruption. There were tears on my face, and a hard, hot anger in my heart.

A tall, broad-shouldered warrior in silver armour stepped boldly before the Curators. His page trailed behind him, lugging a sack. When the usher approached, the man shoved him aside. He strode over to the Curator of Healing, threw down a handful of gold and held out one massive arm. His page unbuckled the plate of armour covering the shoulder, revealing a stained and bloody bandage.

'A wound to my sword arm, sustained in combat in the noble name of King Karazeel!' The man's voice rang out among the pillars like a trumpet. The Curator placed a weight the size of a jam jar on the scale, followed immediately by another as the warrior continued, 'Two score gelden have I won in battle this past moon, and halved to the king. I trace my lineage to High King Zilion by direct descent, as my wearing of the crimson sash affirms.' The page removed his breastplate, and we caught a flash of scarlet that flared like a flame in the watery light of the chamber. Another weight joined the two on the scale.

The page produced a bag from his sack, and handed it to the usher. He placed it on the platform of the scale, and the balance trembled. The warrior nodded to his page, and another, smaller bag joined the first.

The balance tipped and the platform fell.

One of the arms of the Curator's chair was fashioned into a kind of rack, for all the world like the test tube rack in science class at school. The Curator selected a slim phial from the rack, rose to his feet, and presented it to the warrior, who took it, and bowed. Then, with a brief word to the usher, he moved across to the table in front of the black-garbed Curator.

'I cannot bring myself to watch this any longer,' Kenta whispered. 'It is so unfair, so cruel . . . that poor, poor man –' her voice caught. She closed her eyes, and a tear squeezed out from between her dark eyelashes. I felt for her hand, and gave it a gentle squeeze. I touched the others lightly on the shoulder, and gestured to them. Without another word, we crept back among the pillars.

Any faint hope that we could somehow talk the Curator into parting with a phial of Healing Potion for Hannah had vanished as if it had never existed. That was the bad news. But the good news was that along with that had gone any scruples I'd once had about stealing the potion.

I leaned back against one of the pillars, closed my eyes, and thought. I thought about whether there might be stocks of the potions somewhere, and if so, where that could be. I thought about the poem, and what meaning it might have in the light of what we'd seen. I tried to think clearly, imagining I was back in the forest, leaning against a tree trunk, with the song of the birds in my ears and hope in my heart.

And suddenly Jamie's words echoed in my mind: '*Imagine a game of tag in here! These pillars would be even better than trees to hide behind!*'

My eyes snapped open. The pillars stretched away into the distance, as far as the eye could see. Just like . . .

'Kenta! Give me the poem a minute!' My hand was shaking with excitement as I reached out and started to unroll it. 'I've just thought – *the towering trees of stone*. Do you think the pillars . . .'

Kenta's face broke into a huge beam. At last the map was open, and I glanced down to confirm the line made sense. The way I thought it did; the way it *had* to do.

In the blank space above the poem was something that hadn't been there before. Something written in the same thick, dark lettering. Something that had appeared out of nowhere, as if by magic. Something that made absolutely no sense at all.

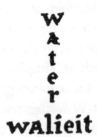

The Hidden Chamber

Kai peered over my shoulder, and nodded sagely. 'Aye, Hob said it be magical,' he said with satisfaction. 'He do have a heavy head, to be sure.'

'That's all very well, but no sooner do we solve one puzzle than another pops up,' complained Richard. 'If this parchment is supposed to help us, then why doesn't it tell us what to do and where to look?'

'Well, Rich, you ain't used to magic, that be clear to see,' remarked Kai. 'Magic be logic, but it be logic hidden from plain sight – round a corner, so to say. These be the corners, your task be to find the way around them.'

'It sounds simple when you put it like that,' said Gen wistfully. 'I only wish it was.'

'If Kai's right, and it is simple logic, then maybe we should approach it simply,' I suggested. 'Let's ignore the new bit for a moment and go back to the beginning. *The balm of healing rests beneath the towering trees of stone.* Who thinks the trees *could* be these pillars? Who thinks the Healing Potion is somewhere in this hall – not just the few phials the Curator has with him, but the main supply? In a cupboard, or under a trapdoor, or even hidden in a hollow pillar – but somewhere nearby?'

Everyone was looking at me, surprised. Then Kai said smugly, 'There you be: logic, plain and simple. Follow your nose and you can only walk forwards. And now, my friends, I must bid you farewell, for now at least.'

'Oh, Kai, no!' protested Kenta. 'How will we manage without you?'

Kai looked ruefully at our horror-struck faces. 'Pa has word of a large party from Shakesh before noon. I must be there to help.

'But be of good cheer.' His dimple reappeared. 'You have your feet firmly on the trail. I am certain Adam be right, and the answer rests between these walls. Aye, I would give my sword arm to help you . . . but magic be logic, and logic be pattern and symmetry. Read your parchment again, and the patterns will emerge. Some may appear from nowhere, as this one has; some be there already, waiting to be seen.

'And one pattern at least I observe: the number five. *Five* potions, *five* steps, *five* of you.' He looked round at us in silence, meeting our eyes one by one. 'So you see, I may be best back at the inn,' he finished softly.

'I hadn't noticed,' Jamie admitted. 'I guess if you really think so . . . you're more used to magic and stuff than we are, after all.' Well, that was putting it mildly. 'I don't suppose there's anything else you've seen that we might have overlooked? Something glaringly obvious, that you can help us with before you go?'

Kai hesitated. I could tell there was something on his mind, that for some reason he didn't want to say.

'Anything at all, Kai,' I prompted. 'No matter how weird it is – we're pretty desperate.'

'There is one thing,' Kai said reluctantly. 'It may be nothing, but there again . . . It be a tale of the cradle Karazan children take in with their mothers' milk, but it may be unknown to travellers from Winterton. It be a women's tale, a legend. But . . . they say there be Guardians of the Potions.'

He lowered his voice to a whisper, and at his next words the hairs on my arms rose and the back of my neck prickled. 'They say the Guardians be serpents, and the serpents reside in the temple.

'That be the name that is whispered among the townsfolk: not the Sacred Temple of Arakesh, but the Temple of Serpents – the Serpents of Arakesh.'

We watched Kai disappear among the pillars with hearts every bit as heavy as Hob's head. Without him it seemed colder, quieter and somehow less hopeful. His words had left a shadow on all our hearts.

We had agreed to find our way back to the Brewer's Butt as soon as possible, 'with your packs laden with potion and your heads full of many a strange tale, I'll wager,' Kai had prophesied cheerfully as he bade us farewell. But for now, it felt lonely to be just five again.

'Let's have another look at the parchment,' Gen suggested. 'Maybe the new message appeared because the magic sensed we were on the right track, telling us we're getting warm and giving a hint about what we should do next.'

We huddled round the parchment again. The message hadn't changed. We stared at it in gloomy silence.

'Well, let's start with the obvious,' I said, hoping I wasn't about to make a complete fool of myself. 'I can see the word *water*.'

'Yeah, but why is it written downwards?' demanded Rich.

'Isn't that what Kai was trying to tell us?' asked Kenta slowly. 'That if something is a certain way, there's bound to be a reason.'

'I thought I heard water before,' I said suddenly. 'Up near the Curators, at the end of the hall.'

Richard got to his feet. 'Let's look for it,' he said. 'That would be better than just sitting around mooning over a mouldy old parchment.'

It didn't take us long to find the water. The curved section of wall behind the Curators wasn't the external wall of the temple, as I'd assumed. It was an arc running parallel to the outside wall, but set in from it by a good couple of metres, which explained why there were no windows in that part of the hall. At the left end of the arc a wall ran at right angles, joining the inner arc to the outside wall. And cascading down the left-hand side of this short wall was a wide, unbroken curtain of water falling into a shallow, rectangular pool. I could vaguely make out the connecting wall behind. On the right-hand side, the wall extended beyond the edge of the waterfall to meet the inner arc, leaving an expanse of bare stone about the width of a door.

'I bet there's a room or something in that space behind the Curators,' Jamie muttered, knocking on the stone with his knuckles.

'This must be the water it mentions,' said Kenta. 'Unless there's another waterfall at the other end of the arc – like a mirror image.'

'A waterfall,' mused Gen dreamily. 'A water . . . fall.' Suddenly her face lit up, and she hopped up and down with excitement. 'That's it! That's why it's written like that! The word *water*, *fall*ing down. *Waterfall!*' She laughed, hugging herself with delight. Her eyes glowed.

'Huh?' said Rich.

'Yeah!' crowed Jamie. '*Waterfall!* Way to go, Gen!'

'So we know we're in the right place,' I said. 'Great job, Gen. It does make sense, once you think of it. And I bet the rest makes sense, too.'

'Walieit,' said Rich experimentally. 'Wa-lie-it? Wally-it? Wally it! Maybe that's it?' he said hopefully. 'Maybe we're supposed to wally the waterfall.'

'Good try, Rich,' said Jamie kindly. 'But how the heck *do* you wally a waterfall?'

'Tie-i-law,' murmured Gen, frowning.

'Maybe it's an anagram!' suggested Kenta.

'What's an anagram?' asked Richard.

'It's when you rearrange the letters to make a new word,' explained Jamie. 'Like in scrabble, or cross-word puzzles.'

'Yeah, right,' said Rich, looking blank.

'Maybe it has something to do with wall! A hollow wall?' hazarded Kenta.

'Or lie? There's the word "lie" in there, in the middle, see? Maybe it's telling us we have to somehow *lie* our way in . . .' said Jamie dubiously.

'Wait!' yelped Gen.

We waited, afraid even to breathe, eyes locked on her flushed, excited face.

'Well, we're waiting!' said Rich impatiently, after a moment or two. 'What are we waiting *for*?'

'No, don't you all see?' said Gen, laughing with exasperation. '*Lie in wait!* The word *lie, in*side the word *wait*! That's what the clue is telling us to do: to lie in wait!'

'Oh, yeah, right,' goes Rich, with heavy irony. 'To *lie* in *wait, under* the *waterfall*, I suppose.'

There was a stunned silence. Then Gen flew at him and gave him a kiss I'll bet you could have heard even in distant Winterton.

'I only hope we don't have to lie in wait too long,' grumbled Jamie. 'I could do with some morning tea.'

We were standing in the narrow space behind the waterfall, with our backs to the cold stone wall. We'd hardly got wet at all going under – the sheet of water was as thin as a pane of glass. Looking through the falling water at the hall was like looking through a pane of obscure glass, like a bathroom window. Everything was blurred and indistinct, and I hoped that was how we'd look to anyone approaching from the other side.

And as it was, less than ten minutes passed before a watery grey shape appeared. We could hear nothing over the rushing of the water, and could probably have spoken in normal voices without being heard. But all the same, Kenta whispered, her breath soft on my cheek: '*The Curator of Healing.*'

We stood like statues while the Curator fumbled in his robes, withdrawing something on the end of a long cord. A moment later the wall behind us moved, sliding noiselessly upwards into the ceiling. With the wall gone, we found ourselves standing between two curtains of water. Through one curtain was the hall of pillars . . . and through the other, the secret room behind the Curators.

Instinctively, we all turned to face the hidden chamber. I stepped forward so that when the wall descended again – as I felt certain it would – we would be on the other side, hidden by the inner curtain of water. The others stepped with me. I could feel my heart thumping in my chest. Behind us, as noiselessly as it had risen, the wall fell.

The Curator moved to the far side of the room. His back was half turned to us, so it was hard to see what he was doing. There seemed to be some kind of cabinet fixed to the wall. He lifted the heavy-looking lid – a wooden rim inset with what looked like a large pane of glass – and rested it carefully against the wall. Stepping back, he wielded his staff over the open casket – uttering some kind of spell or incantation, perhaps? The staff dipped like a wand into the casket. Was he conjuring something? I wished I could see more clearly.

With a sudden flourish he withdrew something

from the cabinet, turning his back on us as he reached for a glass beaker on the shelf above. He stood motionless, head bowed. There was something almost ritualistic about his movements as he dipped his hand once more into the casket, lowered the lid, measured and poured, measured and poured.

At last, he turned to face the waterfall again. Now we could clearly see the rack of phials in his hand – ten or twelve of them, ranged in a neat row. More – presumably empty – rested on the shelf above, alongside the beaker.

I felt a surge of triumph. The stocks of potion must be in the cabinet! And he hadn't needed to unlock it. The potion was ours for the taking once he'd gone back to the audience chamber.

He passed so close to us I could see the cold gleam of his eyes under the hooded lids. As he touched his pass to the door, he muttered something and the wall lifted. He glided through and it fell again, without a sound.

We stood on the inside of the chamber, the water casting rippled reflections on our faces, staring at one another with disbelieving grins of sheer delight.

We'd done it! We were through!

THE BALM OF HEALING

G en was first to move. She skipped through the veil of water and darted across the narrow room to the cabinet, her face alight with anticipation. I felt a sudden, urgent qualm of foreboding and opened my mouth to tell her not to touch it until we were all there together.

She popped up onto her toes and peeped over the edge. Instantly, she let out a shriek – a shrill cry of such horror we all recoiled, and I felt the blood drain from my face. She sprang back and stood pressed against the opposite wall, as if she were trying to burrow backwards through it. Her face was ashen, her eyes staring fixedly at the casket.

We all gawked at her, almost as horror-struck as she was. What had she seen in the casket? My mind raced with possibilities: some kind of monster? Human remains? A curse? A message of doom?

Richard was grinning, somewhat sheepishly. 'Hey, Gen, keep it down, will ya?' he grumbled, in a voice that sounded reassuringly normal. 'Do you want that grey guy coming back to see what all the racket's about? What's the matter? What's in the box?'

Gen opened and shut her mouth like a fish, making little pushing motions with her hands. She didn't take her eyes off the casket. Kenta moved over and put her arm very gently round her, murmuring something in her ear. Jamie edged closer to the smooth stone doorway. I looked at Rich, and Rich looked at me. Together we stepped up to the cabinet, and looked inside.

We saw a sloping lid over a deep, sturdy wooden box. The lid was made of smooth, clear glass, with a wooden rim about the width of my hand. Under the glass was what looked like a miniature desert landscape: a bed of fine, greyish sand; a couple of pieces of dry driftwood; some grey rocks about the size of my fist, arranged in a kind of pyramid. A little pool of water over in one corner. And a tiny mouse, crouched over by the rocks, keeping as still as a stone, as if it was playing a very serious game of hide-and-seek. I felt myself start to grin. Surely it hadn't been the mouse? Typical girl . . .

And then I saw them.

They were so well camouflaged they were almost invisible. One was stretched in front of the driftwood at the front of the cabinet. And I could see only the head of the other one, just visible on the far side of the rocks.

Serpents.

My heart gave a great, painful lurch in my chest, as if it had stopped beating and then kick-started itself again. I swallowed, and took a deep breath. I glanced over at Rich. He licked his lips, and gave me a pale, unconvincing grin.

Over by the entrance, Jamie quavered, 'What *is* it?'

Richard and I both jumped. 'Snakes,' I said, but my voice came out in a funny kind of croak. I cleared my throat and tried again. 'Serpents. Two of them. The Guardians of the Potion, I guess.'

We all stood round the casket, peering in. Well, not all of us. Gen was still huddled against the wall, and didn't look like coming any closer.

'Leave her be,' Kenta whispered. 'Remember what she said at the very beginning, about worms? Well, this is a thousand times worse. For her, this is unspeakable.'

Jamie and Kenta were up on their toes, their breath making misty crescents on the glass. The snakes – going by the one we could see clearly – were about the length of a ruler, and thicker than my finger. Their skins were a uniform silvery-grey, with a shovel-shaped head at one end and a thin, pointed tail at the other. Both were utterly motionless, watching us intently with their unblinking black eyes.

I'd never seen a snake in real life. I wondered if they were poisonous. Not much point in being Guardians of the Potion if they weren't, I guessed.

Then Jamie spoke up. 'Where's the potion they're guarding? All I can see in here is that little pool, and I have a feeling that's just their drinking water.'

It was true. There was nothing in the cabinet except for the serpents, the mouse, the rocks, the driftwood, the sand and the pool of what I had to agree was almost certainly water. So where was the potion?

On the shelf above the cabinet? All I could see were three wooden racks of phials, ten in each, each phial the size of my little finger, with a cork stopper in the top. All empty. And the glass beaker. It had a transparent membrane, like plastic, stretched tightly over the top, tied on with silver thread. I could see a pouring lip through the cover. But it was empty.

Then I noticed one of the forked staffs leaning up against the wall, and for a moment my heart leapt. But what good was a magical staff if we didn't know how to use it?

Desperately, I scanned the room. A narrow staircase led upwards over in the far corner, but the Curator hadn't been anywhere near it. He had stood here, right where we were standing. He had opened the casket, brandished the staff, measured and poured, measured and poured. And he had taken something out of the casket. But what? And where was it now?

'Maybe he took all the potion,' said Richard bleakly. 'Maybe it *was* in here, the serpents were guarding it and now there's none left. Or maybe there's more up those stairs.'

Suddenly I felt a hand on my arm, cold as ice. It was Gen, her hair wild, her eyes red from crying and her skin as pale as snow.

'You're all so *dumb*! The serpents aren't *guarding* the potion.' She slid a glance at the cabinet, flinched, and looked away. 'The serpents *are* the potion.'

We stared at her blankly.

'That's what he was doing,' she said tonelessly. 'The

Curator. He was milking the serpents. The venom of the serpents – that's the Potion of Healing. And that's what we're going to have to do, too, if we want to save Hannah.'

It all fell into place: the beaker; the membrane tightly stretched over the top; the forked staffs. Even the measured gestures of the Curator suddenly made sense. He had simply been moving with extreme caution.

'I've seen people milking snakes on TV,' Jamie was saying. 'There's nothing to it, really. The big thing is to grab the snake right behind the head, so it can't twist round and bite you. The forked stick's for pinning its head to the ground.'

He sounded perky and full of confidence, but I noticed he'd moved a pace back from the cabinet. Kenta and Gen were holding hands. Rich was standing, arms folded, looking dubious.

I looked down at the serpents again. They were the only things in the room that didn't seem to have a problem meeting my eyes. I sighed, and picked up the staff.

'Open the lid for me, Rich,' I said. 'Let's do it.'

With the lid open, I moved round to the side of the cabinet, planning my strategy. One of the serpents had just been milked, and would be dry. Jamie wasn't the only one who watched nature programmes. But which one? What would I do if I was a snake and I'd just been manhandled? I'd go off and hide behind a rock. So my money was on the serpent stretched out by the driftwood.

Snakes are just reptiles, after all, I told myself. *And these are Serpents of Healing – the good guys. Give me the choice between meeting one of these or one of the Faceless on a dark night, and I know which I'd go for.*

I felt my thoughts reaching out to the serpent, soothing him, calming him with my mind, the way I always talked to animals in my head. *Hey there, guy. Let's make this easy on both of us, huh?*

Very slowly and carefully, the way the Curator had done, I raised the stick above the open cabinet, positioning the forked end above the snake. His tongue flickered. I took a deep, slow breath. As quickly and gently as I could, I plunged the end of the staff into the sand, pinning his head in the fork.

Instantly his body writhed, and his tail lashed. Instinctively, I reached down with my other hand and grabbed his body in my fist, just above the tail.

'Rich,' I breathed, 'hold the stick for me – I need another hand.'

I felt Rich's hand above mine on the staff, steady as a rock. I let go, and reached my free hand into the casket. I slid my curled index finger under the snake's neck, just below his head, and put my thumb firmly on top. I nodded to Richard, and slowly, carefully, he moved the stick away.

I lifted the serpent out of the casket, strung like muscular rope between my hands. I could feel him flexing, testing my grip. But I had him. He felt cool and dry and I thought I could feel his pulse beating against my finger. Rich had the beaker ready and held it out, resting it against the edge of the cabinet.

I held the snake's head just above the thin membrane. This was it. I loosened my grip fractionally, and instantly, like lightning, the snake struck. His mouth made a solid *thunk* as his blunt snout hit the tight drum of skin, and there was a thin, squirting sound of liquid hitting glass under pressure. He was clamped onto the top of the beaker; I could see his fangs, curved and deadly, through the glass. And out of them, like liquid squirting from a syringe, spurted twin needles of milky venom.

I held him there until he was spent. Then, as gently as I could, I prised his mouth free and lowered him carefully into the casket, where he slithered away behind the rock.

Richard closed the lid and held up the beaker. The venom lay in a shallow pool at the bottom, gleaming with a silvery phosphorescence, like mother-of-pearl. It was infinitely wonderful.

'Are you OK, Adam?' Kenta's voice sounded dim and far away.

My hands, so steady moments before, were shaking uncontrollably. There was a strange lump in my throat. I nodded, and tried to smile at her. I wasn't seeing Kenta, though . . . I wasn't even seeing the potion. All I could see, as clearly as if she was standing in front of me, was Hannah, in her fairy headgear, smiling at me with sparkling eyes.

★

Kenta poured every drop of the potion into one of the delicate crystal phials. It only just fitted. Without thinking, I pulled my shawl out of my pack and handed it to her. 'I reckon we should wrap it – to protect it. So it doesn't get broken.'

Jamie's eyes darted from me to the shawl, and back again. Slowly, he started to smile. 'What's that, Adam? Funny thing for a guy to have in his backpack . . .'

I felt my face flame. 'It's nothing . . . it's something . . . I just . . .'

'Drop it, Jamie,' said Rich flatly. 'That's cool, Adam – let's wrap it. Good thinking.'

Kenta flashed me a smile. 'Thanks.'

She stashed the precious phial safely away in her backpack, with my shawl wrapped snugly round it for protection.

Richard rubbed his hands together, with a broad smile. 'Now what?' he asked cheerfully. 'Home?'

'Well, yes,' said Kenta hesitantly. 'Except . . . how are we planning to get back through that wall?'

WHISPERING LEAVES

We prodded and poked and tapped and pressed and heaved and shoved, but it was no use. The stone wall was immovable, and deep down I knew the only thing with any hope of opening it was the Curator's magic pass. And he'd taken that with him.

'How about we hide under the waterfall again, and wait till he comes back?' Jamie suggested. 'Then we can sneak out the same way we came in.'

'I dunno,' said Rich dubiously. 'He had ten phials of potion with him, and at the rate he was handing them out, that could last the rest of the morning, easy. And we know the temple closes at noon. I don't fancy being locked in all night.'

There was a gloomy silence, before Gen finally spoke up. 'There's light coming down that staircase. I don't suppose that could be a way out?'

'It can't do any harm to look,' said Rich. 'If it turns out to be a dead end, we can always come back.'

Gen led the way up the stairway, with Jamie close behind. The stairs rose steeply upwards to a small landing, then doubled back on themselves in another short flight. Once we were past the landing we could see a bright rectangle of what looked like daylight at the top of the stairwell. Gen ran the last few steps, and gave a cry of delight. 'Come on up, everyone! It's the gardens – the second storey of the temple!'

The whole second floor of the temple was a lush, tropical jungle. A rambling pathway of pink and white paving stones wound its way through the luxuriant planting, with small fountains here and there, and an ornamental stream, which I suspected ran down through the floor to form the waterfall below.

A wall just over waist high ran right round the perimeter, with creepers and ivy cascading over it. Pillars rose at regular intervals from the balustrade to support the solid weight of the rest of the building, looming overhead. One thick pillar, far more sub-tantial than all the rest, rose up in the very centre. I remembered noticing a similar one on the floor below. I reckoned it must have some kind of structural, load-bearing purpose, probably running right through the centre of the entire building like a spindle, top to bottom.

Nets as fine as gossamer were strung from the ceiling, and birds of every imaginable size, colour and shape flitted, fluttered, perched and swooped. 'It's like being inside a gigantic aviary!' breathed Kenta.

It felt so good to be out of that claustrophobic room with the serpents that we almost forgot why we were there. The girls scampered round, exclaiming over the different birds, and admiring the flowers. Jamie flopped down on a bench and opened a packet of peanuts. Richard wandered off along the path with the studious air of a visitor to a horticultural centre, but his gaze strayed to the perimeter wall more often than it did to the birds. I suspected that, like mine, his thoughts were still bent on finding a way down. As for me, I made my way quietly back to the stairway. I thought I'd noticed a small antechamber at the top, and wanted to check it out.

There was a small, open cubicle at the top of the stairs, with a shelf identical to the one in the room below, even down to the staff leaning against it. In addition to the racks of phials and the beaker, it had a couple of woven igloo-shaped baskets stacked at one end, and a coil of twine.

As I'd suspected, another staircase led upwards, identical to the one on the floor below. But where the entrance to the downward stairway had been only minutes before, there was now a solid wall.

'At least we don't have too many decisions to make,' said Richard cheerily. At least, I assumed his tone was meant to be cheery: it was pretty hard to tell through a large mouthful of potato crisps. 'The only way out seems to be up.'

'I have a feeling we've been set on a track, like an electric train,' said Jamie. 'We have to follow a predestined course or something. I have this feeling of . . . inevitability.' He was lying on his back with his arm over his eyes, so it was difficult to see his expression. His words were brave, though, and I could tell he was doing his best to disguise the slight tremor in his voice.

'Let's have a look at the parchment again, Kenta,'
I suggested.

Kenta hauled it out and unrolled it. Instantly, she
gave a little squeak. 'The magic – it's happened again!
The first clue has disappeared, and now it says . . .'

Looking over her shoulder, I could understand why
she'd been hesitant about reading out what it said.
Frowning, I stumbled through it in my mind:

trbirdap>tr3ee

'Oh, yeah, right: I get it,' said Rich sarcastically.
I glanced over at him. I had a hunch that, like me,
he didn't feel confident with this kind of thing.

Someone – Jamie, I think – heaved a gusty sigh.

But Gen spoke up, sounding excited. 'Hey, guys,
I've had a thought. Forget this *trbirdap* stuff for a sec.
Look at the poem again: the way it's written. Remember what Kai said about things being a certain way for
a reason? Well, see how the poem goes in circles, each
one smaller than the one before? Does it remind you
of anything?'

'A doughnut?' asked Jamie hopefully.

Gen was grinning, like someone with a secret.
'You're on the right track. Go on!'

'A maze?' suggested Kenta.

Gen shook her head.

I put my chin in my hands and stared glumly at the
poem. It reminded *me* of something, all right: every
single lesson we'd ever had at school; every single time
I'd battled to come up with an answer and drawn an

228

utter blank. To me, the lines of the poem didn't even look like words. As far as I was concerned they might as well be stone walls, for all the sense they made . . .

Suddenly I saw what Gen was driving at. I felt my face split into a grin, and she beamed back at me.

'Oh, come on, you two, stop smirking at each other and share the secret,' grumbled Richard.

'The lines of the poem are in circles, like the temple walls,' explained Gen. 'The first line tells about the first floor of the temple, with the pillars like trees of stone, where the Serpents of Healing were. And just like the second floor of the temple is smaller than the first, the second line of the poem is smaller, too. And it says . . .'

'*Guardian of Inner Voices has whispering leaves as home*,' finished Kenta thoughtfully. 'Each line of the poem tells us which potion we should expect to find on each level of the temple. And that means all five potions are right here! We can get all five, and take them back to Q!'

'And I'm prepared to bet a new clue will appear on every level,' I finished up triumphantly, 'telling us what we have to do to get hold of each potion!'

'Yeah,' grumbled Rich, 'and all we've got to do is figure out the clue each time! What could be simpler?'

I gave him a sideways glance. 'Hey, c'mon, we cracked it last time, no problem. Why should the others be any different?'

We crowded round the parchment and gazed at the clue, as if its jumbled letters might suddenly rearrange themselves and reveal their meaning.

'Maybe it works the same way as the last one,' said Gen eventually. 'Maybe this one is: bird *in* trap.'

'And then an arrow,' mused Kenta. 'meaning, *go to* or *head towards*?'

'Hang on a minute: that sign has a mathematical meaning,' said Jamie. 'It means *greater than*. Say you had the number five, and then that sign, and then the number three. Five is greater than three.'

'So what have we got so far?' Gen was frowning fiercely. '*Bird in trap is greater than . . .*'

'Three *in* tree,' said Rich unexpectedly, and blushed.

Gen beamed at him. 'Go, Rich! *Bird in trap is greater than three in tree.*'

'That reminds me of something,' said Jamie. He scrunched up his eyes, and we watched him expectantly. At last he opened his eyes again, and shook his head. 'It's a saying – like *on the tip of my tongue*. Only this one's to do with *birds . . .*'

'A bird in the hand . . .' said Kenta slowly.

'Is worth two in the bush!' yelled Jamie triumphantly. 'That's it!'

'But it isn't,' objected Rich. 'The clue doesn't say that.'

'Yeah, but this is Karazan. Think of Kai, and all his weird sayings. I'll bet you my *sword arm* –' Jamie gave Rich a meaning glance – 'that if Kai was here, he'd be going *A bird in the trap is worth three in the tree*, or something like that.'

There was a short silence while Jamie's words sank in.

'I think you've got it, Jamie,' said Gen respectfully.

Jamie looked down modestly, and Gen jumped to her feet. 'Well, what are we waiting for? Let's go trap ourselves a bird!'

Richard remembered seeing some of the igloo-shaped baskets upended in the undergrowth, and he and Gen went off to check them. The rest of us fetched the other baskets from the storeroom. But first, we took our backpacks off and stacked them at the foot of the stairway. Tiger Lily was wriggling and meowing inside mine. 'I reckon she can hear the birds,' I told Kenta with a grin. 'Tough luck, Tiger Lily: we can't have you scaring them all off.'

Catching a bird turned out to be a lot harder than we'd expected. Gen and Rich drew a blank with the baskets in the gardens: though they seemed to have been carefully positioned, they hadn't caught anything.

We had plenty of basket traps but not a clue how to go about using them. Eventually Jamie came up with a plan: a basket, upside-down, with one edge resting on a tall stick. Twine tied to the stick; stale sandwich crumbs scattered temptingly under the basket. And Jamie himself, concealed behind a dense, leafy bush, ready to tweak the twine and snap the trap shut over the unsuspecting bird.

We settled down a little way away to watch. As we waited for a bird to notice the crumbs, Gen whispered to me, 'Adam – do you think this time the potion will be from a bird? Like a feather, or something?'

I didn't. I'd seen the beaker, the forked stick and

the rack of phials. And I had more than a suspicion that catching a bird wasn't going to be the end of the story.

Half an hour later we were hot, sweating and discouraged. Jamie's trap hadn't even looked like working. The birds had been interested in it: they'd perched on branches all around and twittered merrily to one another, but that was all.

So eventually we'd taken a basket each and leapt round the garden trying to catch one with a mixture of speed, stealth and sheer desperation . . . and we hadn't even come close. Jamie was first to give up, red in the face and dripping with sweat. At last even I had to admit we were wasting our time, and slouched off to release Tiger Lily before she ripped my backpack to bits.

It wasn't five minutes later that we heard a frantic alarm call . . . a sudden flurry of birds fluttered skyward like flung confetti . . . and Tiger Lily came stalking towards us, head proudly erect, and a tiny, bright green songbird in her jaws. She crouched a little way away and watched us, slit-eyed with self-satisfaction.

I rose cautiously to my feet and edged closer. Tiger Lily growled deep in her throat, but she didn't move away. The little bird let out one desperate, strangled '*Chip*,' and was silent again.

I bent down, slowly, slowly . . . and made a lightning grab at the scruff of Tiger Lily's neck. The growl increased in volume. Gently, I put one hand under her chin, inserted my fingers into her mouth behind the bird, and gave a gentle squeeze. Her mouth opened like a dream. I took the bird in my hand, gave Tiger Lily an apologetic stroke, and turned back to the others. Tiger Lily glared at me and stalked away in a huff.

The bird was tiny, about the size of a chicken egg. Its plumage was brilliant green and peacock blue, with a scarlet head and an orange beak. The beak was slightly open, almost as if it was panting, and its bright eyes were half-closed in shock. I could feel its heart hammering in the palm of my hand.

And then I heard a rustle – the softest rustle, but one which chilled my blood – in the undergrowth next to the path.

A PADDED CELL

The serpent that slid out of the undergrowth beside the path was very different from the silver-grey Serpents of Healing. It was fatter and its body had an obscene, squashed-looking flatness. Its skin was a patchwork of mustard and sludge and black, in a geometric pattern running down its back to its tail, as if it had been run over by a tractor and the tread marks had been left imprinted on its skin. The silver serpents had been strangely beautiful. This one looked gross – and evil.

It looked up at the bird in my hand. A forked tongue emerged from its slit of a mouth and flickered, tasting the air.

'So that's it,' Kenta murmured beside me. 'The birds are bait for the serpents. They come . . .' she shuddered. 'They come to be fed.'

I sensed a movement out of the corner of my eye. I didn't want to take my eyes off the serpent, though I was wondering how on earth I was going to juggle the forked stick, the beaker and the bird, with only two hands.

It was Jamie. He had the staff in one hand, the

beaker in the other, and a look of grim resolve on his face. When he spoke, it was in a voice slightly higher than usual. 'You did the last one, Adam. It's my turn.'

We watched in silence as Jamie placed the beaker down within easy reach, moved round behind the serpent, and quickly and efficiently pinned its head to the ground. All on his own he lifted its saggy weight in his chubby, trembling hands; all on his own he guided its head to the beaker and milked it dry.

There was a strange new look in his eyes as he placed the serpent gently down among the leaves, straightened up again, and looked over at me. 'I guess we should give it the bird now,' he said matter-of-factly, 'but somehow I'd rather not. Let it go.'

I opened my hand. The tiny bird lay there on its side for a moment, as if it couldn't believe it was free. Then it gave a little flutter, and was gone.

Carefully, we poured the Potion of Inner Voices into a crystal phial, and Jamie tucked it safely into his pocket.

Then we headed up the staircase, with Tiger Lily padding along behind.

This time the stairway was different. There was no suggestion of daylight at the end, as there had been before. And at the halfway landing, there was a choice of two flights, both leading upwards.

One headed back on itself, just as the previous flight had done, but there seemed to be no doorway at the top. 'It looks like there's just another landing, and the stairs go right on up,' said Rich, squinting up into the gloom. 'But why?'

The other flight branched off to the left, heading inward and upwards towards what must be the centre of the room above. This was the flight we took, by silent consent.

As I'd guessed it would, the staircase came out of the floor of the room above, close to the central pillar. This chamber was noticeably smaller than the garden had been. A greyish gleam shone dimly from the ceiling far above, and it was so dark it took a few moments for my eyes to adjust.

When they did, the first thing I saw was Richard's face, looming out of the gloom. It wore a baffled frown. 'Why the entry through the floor? And where's the shelf with the stuff on it?'

'And most of all,' whispered Gen, 'where's the . . . *you know*. It must be here somewhere. I hate not knowing . . . I hate the feeling it might jump out at me, or drop onto me, or crawl up my leg . . .' I could hear she was close to tears. Reaching out, I put my arm round her and pulled her close.

She was right: there was no sign of a serpent anywhere. The floor was smooth, dark and completely bare. The walls, too, were dark. Still with my arm round Gen, I moved over and touched them. They weren't stone; instead, they had a kind of yielding, padded softness, cool and pleasant to the touch. The padding was in concentric rings, narrower near the bottom and almost two metres wide at eye level, stretching up into the darkness as high as I could see.

'*Power rings the walls of iron with silk,*' breathed Kenta. 'And feel how satiny it is! But something about it makes me feel uncomfortable. It's like a padded cell – and you can't help asking yourself, *why?*'

'*I* can't help asking myself, *where?*' said Gen, with a glimmer of reluctant humour. 'And Tiger Lily doesn't like it, either!'

Tiger Lily was standing on the top step, her tail puffed out and her eyes very wide and dark. I held out my hand to her, but she wouldn't come in.

'Come on, guys – you're psyching yourselves out,' said Rich heartily. But his voice, which had echoed so reassuringly in the hollow stairway, sounded small and muffled in the padded room. 'How about we have a look at the parchment, figure out the clue, and head on up.'

Kenta unrolled the parchment, and shone her torch onto it. Silently, we read the words revealed in the narrow beam.

VAST NOTICE
VAST NOTICE

'Well, nothing springs to mind,' Jamie admitted after a moment.

Gen leaned her head back against the wall and shut her eyes, deep in thought. 'Vast notice,' she murmured. 'Vast notice. If there's a vast notice some-where, how come it isn't staring us in the face?'

'And not just one vast notice, but two,' Kenta pointed out. '*Two* vast notices . . . but where?'

Richard had disappeared into the gloom on the other side of the pillar. His voice came faintly back. 'There's something here,' he called. 'It's a drum.'

Hidden from view behind the pillar was a cylindrical drum as high as my waist, with a taut skin stretched across the top. Tucked in behind it was a rack of phials, but there was no beaker. 'Maybe we have to bang the drum or something,' suggested Rich, 'to call the snake.'

'Hmmm,' said Jamie thoughtfully. 'How does that fit in with the clue, though? *Vast notice* – hard to see how that could possibly mean *give the drum a good whack*.'

'What *I* want to know is, why does it say it twice?' persisted Kenta. 'None of the other clues were repeated.'

Richard had taken the torch, and was walking round the walls, shining the light on them. 'We're sure about the meaning of vast, aren't we? It does mean big, not small?'

'Vast notice, vast notice, vast, vast, notice, notice,' Kenta was muttering. 'Come on, Gen, help me think! *Two* vast notices! *Two* vasts, *two* notices!'

Rich was back in the centre of the room, a scowl of frustration on his face. 'Well, I'm going to bang the drum, and see what happens.'

He crouched down and beat an experimental tattoo. It was surprisingly loud, and the sound had a savage quality in the darkness. I realised one of the things worrying me about the room was its peculiar smell – a faintly fetid, musky odour that was making me feel slightly sick. I wondered if that was what was bothering Tiger Lily.

And then everything happened at once.

Kenta yelped, 'Two vast, two notice! Too vast to notice, *too vast to notice!*'

The wall Gen was leaning against shifted and slithered.

A massive head lowered itself out of the darkness and swung above us, eyes burning like coals in the blackness.

And Gen slumped to the floor in a dead faint.

The reason there was no doorway in the wall was suddenly, horrifyingly clear. And the true meaning of the poem was so obvious I couldn't believe we hadn't understood it right away.

All this raced through my mind as I stared up at the giant serpent, the blood hammering in my ears. Before I realised what he was doing Richard had seized the drum and was staggering with it towards the serpent's head.

'Rich – don't!' Jamie yelled.

'Someone has to,' Richard grunted. 'I'm the only one who'll be strong enough to hang onto it when –'

The serpent's head hurtled out of the gloom like a thunderbolt. Its muzzle hit the skin of the drumhead with a crack like a pistol shot. Richard reeled and almost fell, staggering under the colossal weight. The venom squirted into the drum with the sound of ripping silk.

The serpent wrenched its fangs free, throwing Rich

across the room to bounce off the walls padded by the serpent's own coils. Its head swung up and away into the grey light near the ceiling: a nightmare retreating into the dawn. The entire room seemed to slither and shift as the giant settled itself for slumber once again.

It was over.

And Richard, ashen-faced, lowered the drum to the floor with a liquid, lapping sound, as gingerly as if it were made of glass.

THE POTION OF INVISIBILITY

Richard reached for one of the phials but his hand was shaking so much he almost knocked the whole lot onto the floor. It was Kenta who stepped forward and filled a phial from the drum, her fingers swift and steady. She tucked it safely away in the soft folds of my shawl, then looked at us and gestured upwards, an unspoken question in her eyes. As quickly and quietly as we could, and keeping as far away from the walls as possible, we crept back to the stairway and down through the floor. I was carrying Gen, who showed no signs of waking, and I hoped she'd stay unconscious until we were well away from the horror of that dark chamber.

We turned left at the landing, and climbed three flights of stairs to the room above – the fourth level of the temple.

Tiger Lily was waiting for us, sitting in the sun, her tail curled tidily round her paws. I laid Gen gently down beside her with a sigh of relief – those stairs had seemed to go on forever. Tiger Lily gave Gen an enquiring sniff, and then gave her nose an absentminded couple of licks. Gen's eyelids fluttered open. We all watched anxiously. But it was almost as though she had no memory of what had taken place below; she smiled dreamily, as if she was waking from an afternoon nap, and murmured, 'Sunlight! And look – blue sky!'

It was true. Tall, narrow windows opened to spectacular views of the city, stretching below. The small, circular chamber was flooded with sunlight, as bright and airy as the previous one had been dark and stifling. The familiar stone pillar rose up through the centre of the room and the rack of phials and beaker were neatly laid out on a shelf near the stairway.

Best of all, recessed into one of the walls was a rectangular case, rather like an aquarium. But it was filled with air, not water, and the glass reached only about three quarters of the way up, leaving a space easily wide enough for a hand to be inserted. Resting in clear view on the floor of the case was a pure white snake the size of a pencil, apparently fast asleep.

Rich grinned round at us. 'Well, this is the easy one. Bet we won't even need a clue to help us, let alone a forked stick.'

'Just as well,' Jamie pointed out, 'because there isn't one.'

I'd noticed that, too. I'd also noticed that once again the wall had silently closed over the entrance to the room while we'd been looking at the serpent. I doubted any of us would have contemplated venturing down that staircase again, but now we didn't have an option.

I'd noticed something else as well; something I

didn't mention to the others. Where the upward staircase ought to be was a blank, featureless wall. Sunny and pleasant though this chamber was, it was a prison, with no visible way either in or out.

For now, at any rate, we were trapped.

'Well,' said Kenta gallantly, 'the time has come for you boys to stand aside, and allow the girls to play their part.' She reached down into the case and withdrew the serpent, holding it securely behind the head, just as Jamie and I had done.

This time, though, the serpent didn't writhe and twist. It dangled from Kenta's hand as placidly as a toy. And when Kenta held out the beaker for it to strike, it didn't so much as twitch.

'Do you think it's dead?' Jamie whispered hoarsely.

Kenta was looking pensive, stroking the serpent's blunt lip temptingly against the taut membrane of the jar. 'No, I can tell it's not dead. I can feel a pulse beating in its neck,' she said slowly. 'There's something else . . . something not right.'

'What was the line from the poem again?' I frowned. '*And Sightless lies in blindness, pale as milk*. Maybe that's it! Maybe the serpent's blind, so it can't see the beaker.'

Kenta said nothing. The little snake dangled from her hand, limp as a piece of string.

'Heigh ho, here we go,' sighed Jamie, sauntering over to Kenta's backpack. 'Back to the parchment. We should have known it all looked too easy!'

Kenta replaced the snake gently in its case, and joined the rest of us round the parchment.

FEAR
COME

'*Fear*. That would have made more sense with the last one,' Jamie muttered.

'I don't get it,' said Rich. '*Fear come*. Fearsome spelt wrong? But this little snake doesn't look fearsome.'

'This one *must* be an anagram,' said Kenta. 'I wish I had a pen and paper. Are you any good at anagrams, Gen?'

Gen didn't answer. She was staring at the parchment with a distracted look on her face.

'Cream! You can make the word "cream" out of the letters, see?' said Kenta excitedly. 'And it ties in with the line from the poem, too: '*pale as milk*'. Perhaps we are supposed to feed it some milk, or something. Could that be it, do you think?'

'I don't know quite how to tell you this, Kenta,' said Jamie with a grin, 'but we haven't got any.'

Something – a tiny sound – made me glance over at Gen. She'd turned a ghastly greenish colour, as if she was about to pass out again, or throw up. Kenta was beside her in an instant. 'What is it, Gen? What's the matter? Why are you so pale? Do you feel ill?'

Gen shook her head. She said nothing for what seemed like a long time. And when eventually she did speak, it was in a whisper so quiet we could barely hear.

'It's the simplest one yet. The word *fear* over the word *come*. Fear, over come. Fear overcome. It's a message and it's meant for me. I have to overcome my fear.' She raised her anguished face, and looked up at us, her eyes swimming with tears. 'Five, remember? Kai was right – we each have a part to play. I'm the only one this serpent will give up its venom for.'

'Let's think this through for a minute.' Richard sounded reassuringly adult and in control. 'Are we sure that's the correct meaning?'

There was silence. It seemed we were sure.

He sighed. 'Who says we need the potion, anyway? We've been collecting them along the way because . . . well, because it kind of seemed like the logical thing to do. But we don't *need* the Invisibility Potion. The only one we really *need* is the Healing Potion.'

A look of hope crept onto Gen's pale face.

Jamie was grinning. 'Yeah – way to go, Rich. I vote we pack our bags and head on up –' He gestured over to the stairway . . . to where the exit should have been.

There was a long, long silence.

'Well, how do we *know* it means Gen?' Jamie asked at last. 'You aren't the only one who doesn't like snakes. A snake's a snake, even this little dopey one. I'm scared of it too!'

I felt a sudden rush of affection for Jamie, standing there with his arms folded staunchly over his chubby chest.

I clambered to my feet. 'Good point, Jamie. Let's all have a go.'

Gen shook her head wordlessly. She didn't even bother to watch as one by one we filed up to the case,

245

fished out the limp little snake, and held it uselessly up against the beaker. It didn't take long. Rich replaced the snake in its case, and there was an awkward pause. Slowly Gen rose to her feet. 'I'll do it. I don't have a choice.'

She looked very small and fragile as she walked across to the glass case, her face as white as paper. As she reached the case she paused, closed her eyes and swayed slightly.

'It's OK, Gen, it really, really is,' Jamie was gabbling. 'It's a docile little snake, hardly a snake at all, almost more of a worm – oops, sorry, I didn't mean that. But it's quite cute, when you look at it . . .'

'Shush, Jamie.' Gen spoke absently, her entire being focused on the serpent lying motionless in its cage. Slowly, she reached her hand out, ready to slip it through the opening. But then she froze. Tears were pouring down her face. 'I can't,' she whispered. 'I'm sorry, I just can't. And now we'll be trapped here forever. I've failed you all.'

Awkwardly, Jamie trundled up beside her; bashfully, he took hold of her trembling hand. 'I'll help you, Gen,' he offered. 'Maybe if we did it together . . .'

'Can I go and sit down again by the wall?' Gen whispered in a tiny, ashamed voice. Without meeting our eyes, she crossed the room and sank to the ground as far away from the snake as possible, with her knees curled up and her face buried in her arms.

There was an uncomfortable silence.

'So,' said Rich. 'Looks like that's that. But you know what my old grannie says, Gen? *There's no such word as can't.* Maybe if it was just you it might be different. But it's not. It's all of us . . . even the darn cat . . . and Hannah.' He'd started off sounding frustrated, but now he sounded angry, and I knew the anger was hiding something stronger – fear. 'I don't want to be mean, or unsympathetic. But I don't fancy waiting here while you *can't*, and that gong rings, and the temple closes and it gets dark . . . waiting to find out who'll eventually come in, and what'll happen to us when they do. Just because you –' he spat the word out – '*can't.*'

Gen's thin shoulders were shaking. None of us said anything. Then slowly, stiffly, she stumbled to her feet. Her face was blotched and swollen. 'Do you think . . .' she looked at Jamie, her eyes pleading. 'Do you think that it might work . . . if someone else handed it to me? I might be able to hold it for a second.' She took a deep, shuddering breath. 'I'll try.'

We all hustled forward before she changed her mind. Kenta grabbed the beaker while Jamie fished out the snake. I hovered behind Gen in a way I hoped was supportive, ready to catch her if she fainted. Rich stood apart with his hands on his hips, watching.

'Now, Gen,' said Jamie, 'hold out your right hand. Come on. Just take hold of it gently, behind its head – it won't bite, I promise.' Gen's hand reached out till it was almost touching the snake. She whimpered, and pulled back.

Richard snorted.

'Try closing your eyes,' Kenta suggested. Gen

closed her eyes, and swayed slightly. Her eyes opened again. 'I can't. It's worse when I can't see it.'

'Hey,' goes Rich sarcastically. 'Here's an idea. Don't be so pathetic. Just *do it*!'

Gen looked at him. For a second, her eyes flashed fire. Her lips compressed into a thin line. She reached out and snatched the snake from Jamie's hands. Instantly, it sprang to life, writhing in her grasp and hissing. Gen started to scream, in tiny, high-pitched, hysterical gasps. Her eyes were locked on the serpent, and her hands frozen, the snake twisting between them.

Like lightning, Kenta pushed the beaker under the snake's head; like lightning, the snake struck and the venom spurted. As gently as I could, I prised the snake away – Gen's hands were ice cold and stiff as stone – and replaced it in the cage. Gen backed away like someone sleepwalking, her eyes huge and unfocused, the horrible keening sound going on and on.

'Do you think I should give her face a smack – just gently?' asked Rich hopefully.

But I was staring at the wall, where a doorway had silently appeared. Problem was, it wasn't the one that would lead us upwards, to the next level. It was the one leading down – the one we'd come through what seemed like hours before.

And from it came the faint, unmistakable sound of a cough.

BLIND MAN'S BUFF

We froze. Even Gen was instantly silent.

Jamie hissed, 'Quick – hide!'

But there was nowhere to hide. The only possible place was behind the pillar – and there was no way it would conceal us all. The options flashed through my mind in a second, while the soft scrape of footsteps echoed closer up the stairwell.

'The potion,' I breathed. I ripped the cover off the beaker and handed it to Kenta. Without hesitating she put it to her lips and took a tiny sip. Instantly, both she and the beaker vanished. I groped, felt her hand, felt my fingers close round the smooth glass. I had it again; passed it to Jamie. He sipped, and was gone. Rich. Flick – he vanished. Last, Gen. 'Don't think about it – *quick*!' Gone. There was only a drop left. I tilted the beaker and sipped; felt a weird flickering chill. I held out one hand in front of my face. There was nothing there. Softly as a shadow, I crept to the shelf and replaced the beaker.

We'd done it! I scanned the room – and my heart gave a sickening lurch. There sat Tiger Lily in a patch of sun, preening her whiskers. I lunged for her and snatched her up – just as the tall, cloaked form of the white Curator appeared in the doorway.

Tiger Lily didn't seem at all put out to have her beauty routine interrupted. She reached up one velvet paw and gave my face a pat, as if to reassure herself I was really there. Then she gave my chin a couple of licks.

The wall closed again behind the Curator. He glided across to the shelf and took down the beaker. With an exclamation of annoyance, he fumbled in the folds of his gown, and took out a new cover and tie. He stretched it over the top of the beaker with practised hands, and crossed to the glass-fronted recess. Reached in, withdrew the snake, hissing and writhing. He held it up to the beaker and the snake struck.

And of course, not even the tiniest drop of venom spurted out. In any other situation, there'd have been something comical about the way the Curator held the beaker up to the light to double check it was still empty, with a look of utter disbelief.

But there was nothing comical at all about the look that dawned on his face – a look of slow comprehension, then rage, twisting his features into a grotesque mask.

From somewhere beside me, one of the girls let out the tiniest whimper, almost too soft to hear. Almost . . . but not quite.

The Curator smiled. He shuffled slowly towards us, hands outstretched, groping and patting at the air, like a nightmarish game of blind man's buff.

Tiger Lily started to struggle. She wriggled and

squirmed. I hung on desperately, but with a slither and a twist, she slipped out of my arms. I made a frantic grab – but I couldn't see what I was grabbing at, and missed.

I couldn't see what I was grabbing at.

There must have been a tiny smear of potion on my chin – just enough to work on a little cat like Tiger Lily. She was safe!

Pat ... pat-pat ... pat ... The Curator had turned, and was groping his way towards where I stood, his eyes glittering as they probed the emptiness. But from the floor came a hiss – the hiss of an angry, frightened cat.

The Curator stopped, disoriented. *Waaaaaaaooooow. Sssssssss!* I could see Tiger Lily clearly in my mind's eye – low to the ground, ears flattened, tail like a bottlebrush, eyes fixed on the Curator. But of course I couldn't really see her ... and neither could he. For a moment he looked uncertain. *Waaaaooooooooooow!* The eerie, feral cry unwound again, soft at first, then louder, then trailing away to nothing.

The Curator's hooded eyes searched the ground. His thin, grey lips peeled away from his yellowed teeth in an answering snarl, and he hissed back at the invisible presence on the floor.

And then he was staggering backwards, clawing at his chest, batting blindly at his face. Thin, parallel scratches streaked down his cheeks like someone drawing on a magic slate with an invisible pen, beading with blood as I watched. He took two stumbling steps backwards ... lost his balance ... tottered and fell. His head hit the stone floor with a crack like a rifleshot.

There was a long, long silence.

'Do you think he's . . .'

'Dunno. Hope so.'

'He may have cracked his skull. We should help him . . . I suppose.'

'Get real, Kenta. The only thing we need to think about is whether to tie him up, or get out now.'

'I vote we tie him up. I know some real wicked knots, from Scouts.'

Suddenly I realised the voices weren't disembodied any more . . . gradually, faint as ghosts at first, the figures of the others were taking shape around me.

Tiger Lily materialised on the floor beside the prone Curator, cleaning her paws fastidiously.

'That didn't last long, did it?' said Rich. 'I guess because we only had a tiny sip.'

'It lasted long enough.' I was digging in my pack for Q's rope. I tossed it to Jamie. 'Come on then, Jamie – let's see how good those knots are.'

In no time flat, the Curator was trussed up like a chicken.

Jamie stood back, dusting off his hands on the bum of his breeches, looking pleased with himself.

'How about a gag?' suggested Gen, sounding remarkably cheerful.

Suddenly, I felt a laugh bubbling up inside me. 'Aha! Now that you mention it,' I said, reaching deep into my pack again, 'I do believe I've got the very thing!'

An Emerald Vision

We left the Curator snoring on the floor, my bright red boxers adding a festive touch to the scene. Jamie had amazed us all by producing the Curator's magic pass with a smug flourish that for once it was easy to forgive – especially when it worked first time.

'Four down, one to go,' said Rich cheerfully as we trudged up the final flight of stairs. 'And this one doesn't look too bad either – at first sight, at any rate.'

All in all, things hadn't exactly gone according to plan, and I reckon we all shared the same sense of dread at the prospect of what we might find at the top of the staircase. Once again, though, the room was bright and airy. My eyes scanned the walls. Shelf: check. Phials: check. Beaker: check. Staff: check.

But where the snake's case had been in the room below, there was a blank wall. Well, not blank: a wall entirely covered with what looked to me like weird variations of letters of the alphabet. They stretched up from about waist level to as high as I could reach.

'Cool!' Jamie said beside me. 'Runes!'

'Not runes,' Gen contradicted. 'Letters of the

alphabet. Look – there's an *s*, and there's a *q* . . . and there's another *s*, over there.'

'Yeah, but *that* one's not a letter of the alphabet, is it?' Jamie objected.

'I think some of these may be from alphabets of different languages,' Kenta chipped in. 'That sign over there: the circle with the line through it. I think that's Greek.'

'Yeah, you're right, Kenta: and see there? That's pi, the Greek letter pi you use to calculate the area of circles and stuff like that. Maths rules!'

'I see an *e* over there!' said Rich, not to be outdone.

Sure enough, as I stared at the wall it gradually became less of a meaningless jumble. Here and there was a letter I recognised, some repeated more than once, but the vast majority were weird squiggles I'd never seen before.

But no matter how carefully I scanned the wall, I couldn't find the one I was looking for: a squiggle that might give us a clue as to where the snake was hiding. Even though there were enough letters – or runes, or symbols, or whatever – to fill a dictionary, the Serpent of Beauty and Eternal Youth was nowhere to be seen.

I listened to the others exclaiming and arguing with a growing feeling of unease. The triumphant buzz I'd felt at seeing the Curator hit the deck was wearing off, and I was starting to think logically again. And logic told me that some time – sooner rather than later – someone was going to wonder why he was taking so long and come looking. And when they found him, he'd be tied up in enough knots to sink a battleship, with a royal issue pair of satin boxers stuffed in his mouth.

It had seemed like a good idea at the time. But now I desperately wished we'd simply left him lying there, out cold and looking like staying that way. After all, he'd only *heard* Tiger Lily, not seen her . . . and without the rope and boxers, there'd have been no proof the rest of us ever existed. But it was too late for wishing. Way too late.

Now, whoever found him wouldn't have to be a genius to figure out that there was something unusual going on . . . and work out where the culprits must have gone. The Invisibility Potion had saved us last time, but it was finished, right down to the last drop.

Just as before, I was betting the only way out would be up – once we'd cracked the code that revealed the snake and the hidden door to the stairway. And I was uncomfortably aware that we were leaving solid ground further and further below us. For all we knew, we were following each successive clue, and every successive stairway, deeper into a trap – a trap from which, like the poem said, there'd be no escape.

'Guys,' I chipped in, 'this is all real interesting and educational – but I think we need to get started on working out the clue and finding the snake. Because unless he's on an extended morning-tea break, they're going to come looking for that white Curator pretty soon.'

Kenta scurried over to her backpack and produced the parchment without another word. This time, the message was longer.

**I am the beginning of eternity
The end of time and space;
The beginning of every end
And the end of every place.**

'It's a riddle,' said Gen, hot on the trail.

'And it's cryptic,' agreed Kenta.

'What's cryptic?' asked Rich.

'It means the meaning is hidden – not straight-forward,' Jamie explained.

Richard groaned.

'Could it link in some way with the main poem?' Kenta suggested.

'Bright beauty burns with fire eternal as a gem:
An emerald vision age will never end.'

'Eternal . . .' murmured Gen.

'Maybe we need to approach it logically again,' suggested Jamie. 'Ask ourselves what the poem is describing. What *is* the beginning of eternity? Or, what *is* the beginning of every end? It sounds like a contradiction to me.'

'Unless it was a circle,' said Rich slowly. 'Circles don't have beginnings or ends.'

'Good thinking, Rich,' said Jamie. 'Are there any plain circles on the wall?'

But there weren't.

'I've got it!' said Kenta suddenly. 'It mentions beginnings and ends twice. That must mean they have special significance. It must be the beginning and end letters of the alphabet – *a* and *z*!'

But no matter how carefully we looked, we could

see neither the letter *a* nor the letter *z* anywhere.

'I don't suppose it could be those letters in a different alphabet?' Rich said desperately. 'Like, maybe, Russian or something?'

We all stared blankly at the wall. No one needed to point out that the chances of any of us knowing what *a* and *z* were in Russian were non-existent.

'I know the *Greek* for *a*,' said Jamie suddenly. 'It's alpha. It looks a bit like *a*, too. Look – that's it over there!'

'Now we're getting somewhere!' said Gen excitedly. 'Alpha, beta, gamma . . .'

'Delta . . .' supplied Kenta.

There was a pause. Rich and I exchanged a glance. For a moment it had looked pretty promising, but there again, it was a bit much to hope that three kids would know the whole of the Greek alphabet.

'Pi?' offered Jamie hopefully.

Gen's face was screwed up in concentration. 'We haven't got time for this! We have to hurry! Oh, why can't I *think*! I know it – I *know* it! I just can't – alpha and . . . alpha and . . .'

'Omega!' squeaked Kenta triumphantly.

'Yes! Omega! And it's like . . . an upside-down horseshoe, I think. Is there one? Oh, please let there be one!' Gen was hopping up and down, her face glowing.

'I saw something like that a second ago, I'm sure,' said Jamie. 'Yeah, look: over there!'

Rich marched over to the wall. 'What do you reckon? We push them, or what?'

With one finger, he pushed the alpha sign, and then the omega. Nothing happened.

'Maybe you have to press them at the same time,' suggested Gen.

Rich did. Nothing.

'Or cover them up with your hand – kind of . . . warm them up, maybe?' hazarded Jamie.

But that didn't work either.

And then it hit me. 'Jamie – *the pass*!' I couldn't believe we hadn't thought of it before. 'The Curator's magic pass! Let's forget about the clue – who needs the darn potion, anyhow?'

Jamie scurried over to the wall and swept the pass up and down near where we'd come in. Up and down, back and forth. He turned it over and tried again. Nothing. I watched the hope fade from his face; bleakly, he shook his head. 'The other one opened easy, first time. Sorry, guys – it's just not working. Maybe they only have access up to a certain level.'

'So . . . back to the clue,' said Kenta reluctantly. 'The previous ones haven't required any special knowledge – we've been successful using simple common sense. Why should this one be different?'

'Hard to see where the word *simple* comes into it, though,' said Gen wryly. 'The symbols have to be the key, and they're anything but simple. There must be something we're not seeing. Don't some symbols have . . . oh – a philosophical meaning or something, kind of condensed down to one character? Maybe it's one of those.'

'Yeah, right – and we just have to figure out which

one,' muttered Rich, staring gloomily at the wall. 'Easy, huh?'

Gen rolled her eyes in his direction impatiently. 'I bet the answer's staring us in the face. Like, say . . .' she read the poem over again, lips moving as she mouthed the words silently. Then her face lit up. 'Infinity, perhaps?'

'And there's the sign for infinity!' yelped Jamie. 'Over there, see: an eight, lying on its side!'

But the sign for infinity didn't work either.

'You're very quiet, Adam,' said Kenta, looking over at me. 'Have you any thoughts?'

I shrugged awkwardly. 'Nah, not a single one,' I admitted. 'I wish I had. I feel totally useless. This is the kind of thing I'm worst at. Puzzles and riddles and poetry and stuff like that. It'd have to be dead simple for *me* to figure it out. Something real, real basic.' I glanced down at the poem. 'Like, the letter *e*, or something.'

'Well, you contribute in other ways, Adam,' said Kenta, giving me a shy smile and putting a gentle hand on my shoulder.

Gen was staring at me like she'd seen a ghost. 'What did you just say?' she croaked.

'Nothing, forget it.' I shrugged.

'You said: *the letter e*. The answer *is* the letter *e*! It's the first letter of eternity, the last letter of time and space, the first letter of end and the last letter of place!'

'But *which* letter *e*?' said Rich. 'There are two of them.'

'No, there aren't: there are three.'

'No, *four* – look, there's one over on that side.'

But I was betting there'd be five. And sure enough, Kenta spotted a fifth one hiding away up at the top.

Relief flooded through me in a tide so strong my head swam. *Please, please – let it work!* Each of us covered an *e* with the palm of our right hand. And without a sound, two things happened.

The wall covering the exit doorway faded away to nothing . . . and so did the flagstone beside Kenta's left foot. She leapt back with a little shriek of surprise, and moments later we were all leaning over it, even Gen.

There in the cavity left by the flagstone was the most beautiful creature I had ever seen. It was a snake, of course, but as it slid with silken grace round its pit, the sunlight flashed and played on its skin like light on a precious emerald. You longed to touch it. Every couple of circuits it would rear up and spread its hood like a cobra – a hood iridescent with blues and greens and turquoise deep as the sea, like the colours of a peacock's tail.

This time, Kenta insisted it was her turn to milk the serpent of its venom. But Rich and I hovered close. In spite of its beauty, there was something about this serpent that made me feel uneasy. It was a lot bigger than any of the others except the giant black one; there was something in its eyes I didn't like, and I had a sense that it was somehow more aggressive.

But all went smoothly, and soon Kenta had handed me the phial of shimmering emerald potion, and was kneeling to replace the serpent in its pit. As she let go it reared up, spreading its hood and hissing angrily. It wove to and fro, like liquid green fire. Its eyes glittered, and its forked tongue flickered dangerously.

Gen, who'd been sitting near the edge of the pit, scooted backwards hastily. And in that instant, its attention drawn by her sudden movement, the serpent struck. With the speed of light, its head flashed forward and its fangs fastened on Gen's hand, outspread on the floor.

I leapt forward and prised its jaws free and threw it roughly back into the pit, wishing there was a lid to slam over it. Every drop of colour drained from Gen's face, and she swayed, staring at the twin drops of blood beading the back of her hand. Rich goggled, his face a mask of shock. But it was Jamie who grabbed Gen under the arms and tugged her away from the brim of the pit, out of harm's way.

Kenta crouched beside her, peering anxiously into her face. 'Gen – Gen, are you all right? Do you feel short of breath? Do you feel pins and needles in your hand? Heart palpitations? Oh, I wish I knew more about snakebite!'

Amazingly, the calmest of us all seemed to be Gen. She took a deep, shaky breath, and when she answered she sounded reassuringly normal – even impatient. 'Don't panic, Kenta. It hurts, like after an injection. I feel . . . numb.'

'*Numb?*' repeated Kenta, alarm flashing onto her face like a neon light. 'Quick – let me take your pulse!'

'No, not *that* kind of numb – just numb with

horror. I feel like I've been bitten on the hand, and it's sore, and I'm in the middle of the worst day in my whole life . . . and I wish I was home. That's all.'

'Well, when you think about it, maybe there isn't too much to worry about,' chipped in Rich encouragingly. 'Luckily it's just been milked. And let's not forget which serpent it is. Rather than expecting Gen to keel over and die, you'd expect . . . well . . . something . . . *different* to happen.'

There was a pause while we digested his words. We stared at Gen. She flushed – a bright pink tide that started off at the bump at the end of her nose and worked its way outward, till even the tips of her sticky-out ears were glowing like traffic lights. She darted a little, shy, hopeful glance up at us. 'Oh! Am I . . .'

'Nah, not so you'd notice,' admitted Richard. 'But who knows? Maybe it takes time to work. Or maybe you need a lot more than that for it to be effective – especially if there's, like, a fair bit to do.'

There was an awkward silence. Then Jamie jumped to his feet. 'Come on – we don't have time for this! I'm sure Richard's right and the snakebite isn't dangerous. But right now our first priority is to move on – and fast. Here's the potion – tuck it away safely, Gen. I reckon you've earned the honour of carrying this one! Look – the floor's closed over, and the doorway's open. Let's just hope the stairs lead down, and out of here!'

No Escape

From nowhere, an unwelcome thought formed in my mind. It was something a teacher told us a mountaineer said about climbing Mount Everest: 'Never forget that when you reach the summit, you're only halfway.'

I looked at the open doorway, and, like Jamie, I hoped with all my heart the steps would lead downwards, and out of the temple.

But they didn't.

Once again, the stairway led up – up not two flights this time, but four, up into the metal dome at the very top of the temple.

It was a small, windowless chamber. The only light came from a long, thin slit in the roof high above us, almost as if someone had sliced into it with the blade of a knife. It was unbearably hot. Almost at once, I felt beads of sweat pop out on my forehead and upper lip.

'The view from up here would be amazing, if only we could see out,' Kenta whispered. Her voice echoed with a strange, metallic intensity.

'Are we all here?' I asked. 'Rich? Jamie? Gen – are you still OK?' They all answered. 'Can anyone see Tiger Lily?' There was silence.

I had a sudden, vivid memory: Tiger Lily sitting at the edge of the emerald serpent's pit, her golden eyes fastened hypnotically on the snake as it slid in its endless circuit. Tiger Lily crouching in the same spot after the pit had closed over again, staring at the bare floor where the snake had been.

'Shoot,' I muttered, 'I'll bet that darn cat's still down there. Wait for me, guys – I'll be back in a sec.'

But when I turned to head down the stairs again the doorway had vanished, leaving only a bare wall.

It was growing hotter by the minute.

'Get out the parchment, Kenta,' Rich said. 'Maybe it'll show us the way out.'

'Yeah, and do it quick,' gasped Jamie. 'I'm stewing.'

Now that my eyes had adjusted to the gloom, I could see this room was very different from the ones below.

It measured perhaps eight strides from end to end. Again, it was completely circular, but this time there was no central pillar. Instead, in the middle of the room was a pedestal about waist height, with something protruding from the centre.

The dome-shaped metal roof radiated heat in almost tangible waves. The slit of light hurt my eyes when I looked up at it. Suspended in the darkness above us was a gigantic metal disk. Reaching my hand up, I could just reach it. It was cold and inert, and so heavy it didn't budge when I pushed against it.

'Adam, don't,' whispered Gen. She sounded scared. 'What if it falls on us?'

Kenta shone her torch onto the floor. For the most part it was tiled, as it had been on the previous levels. But here, the tiles were inlaid with two huge metal plates, joined by a short strip running through the base of the pedestal.

'The floor is a representation of a set of scales, I think,' Kenta whispered. 'The pedestal is like the centre of a see-saw. Do you think it's symbolic of the scales used in the Chamber of Hearings? See how one of the ends is circular, and the other square?'

'Stop waffling and pass over the parchment before we all fry,' said Richard impatiently.

But when we opened the parchment up and peered at it in the light of the torch, there was no new message. The circular poem was there, and the four lines underneath, but the space above was blank.

'Maybe the information we need is in the last part of the poem, and we don't need an extra clue,' Kenta said.

'Put the parchment on the table,' Jamie suggested. 'Then we can all have a better look.'

We moved up to the pedestal, and Kenta carefully opened out the parchment.

I reached out one finger and touched the strange protrusion sticking up out of the centre. It was made of glass or crystal, like one of the phials we'd collected the potions in, only bigger. I wondered whether it could have some kind of ritual significance. Perhaps the Curators came up here and poured some of the venom into it as a kind of sacrifice, or something. Maybe we were supposed to pour some potion in too, to reveal the doorway leading down and out. If so, I hoped it would be the same one we'd come up. I was desperate to find Tiger Lily again.

A soft gasp from Kenta broke into my thoughts. I looked over her shoulder at the parchment. Where the blank space had been only moments before, a message was appearing: two words, growing gradually darker and more distinct as we watched.

ecApe no

Gen started to cry.

A trickle of sweat ran down my spine like a cold finger.

'Even I can figure this one out,' said Rich. I knew his words were meant to make us smile, but they had a desperate, hollow ring.

'But that's not how you spell *escape*,' said Jamie.

'Maybe not,' said Rich grimly, 'but this isn't a spelling test.'

The heat was like a furnace. My ears were starting to ring, and I felt light-headed. Next to me, Gen slumped to the floor. We needed to think – and fast. But my brain had gone numb. There was no way out I could see. No escape, just like the message said. I knew time must be running out – it could only be a matter of minutes before they came for us.

But we did have one option left. It was a last resort, but it was still an option – the only one I could see. It was our ticket home, and I could feel its reassuring shape against my back, through the fabric of my rucksack.

I tried to remember exactly what Q had said. *When you make your re-entry, do so from the same point you arrived at, as exactly as possible. Logically, the interface between the two worlds will be strongest there.*

It might not work from here. And it would mean leaving Tiger Lily behind.

'Guys,' I said, 'there's one more thing we can try.'

We stood in a huddle behind the pedestal, the parchment stashed in Kenta's backpack. The others were all holding hands. I could feel Rich's, big and damp with sweat, clamped firmly on the back of my neck.

Jamie was muttering the last four lines of the poem over and over, interspersed with the occasional, 'Spelling does *so* matter, Rich.' He sounded close to tears.

On the pedestal in front of me lay the micro-computer. It was switched on, and its screen glowed with a greenish fluorescence in the gloom. It looked weirdly hi-tech on the simple stone table, as out of place as something out of a science-fiction movie. I had a sudden, intense misgiving about what I was about to do.

I would have given everything I had to feel the solid, sleeping weight of the little cat in my backpack.

I squinted at the keyboard, searching for the right keys in the dark. I found them with my fingers and lifted the computer up in front of my nose. Peered at it again to make sure, then closed my eyes, ready to press.

Suddenly Jamie yelled out, '*One pace backwards!* It's not 'no escape'! It's *one pace*, written backwards. Spelling *does* matter, Richard! Quick, everyone, let's try it! Take one pace back, *now!*'

Richard's hand tightened on my neck. Still clutching tightly to one another, the five of us took one long step backwards, into the centre of the metal square on the floor.

As we stood there, a single ray of light as fine as a laser beam shot down from the slit in the roof above us, pierced the darkness, and struck the crystal phial. The crystal shattered the white beam into a multitude of rainbow colours that lit the chamber with a blinding flare of radiance.

Jamie yelled triumphantly:

'*Unless bright Serpent Sun to Zenith climb*
And fang of light doth pierce the phial of time!'

And in the same split second, the floor tilted away beneath us, and we dropped like stones into nothingness. As I fell I saw the other end of the scale swing up to smash against the huge disk suspended above.

A tidal wave of sound boomed after us into the black void as the noon gong sounded over Arakesh. Even falling, spinning through the darkness as I was, I flinched from the barrage of sound.

Instinctively, my hands clutched, clenching into fists . . . and my fingers clamped tight onto the keys of the computer.

THE GREY ANGEL

Sound and light and black shards of darkness battered me from every side. I was falling, falling, weightless as in a dream, with the same sick feeling of having left my heart somewhere above me. I bounced and crashed against invisible walls, my brain rattling in my skull.

The roar of the gong carried me with it like a wall of water, bearing down on me, overtaking me, tumbling me over and over, bruising my body and searing my lungs like fire. Then I was rushing up, up, through deep, dark water, the sound of the gong ringing in my blood, pressure exploding my brain.

I was flung like a rag doll onto the shore of our world at last, bright light cleaving my skull like a sword, retching and spewing, too weak to breathe.

'Adam? Adam – are you OK?' It was Kenta's voice, but it was far away.

My ears felt full of water. My body had turned to lead. I could feel small waves at the water's edge sucking at me, tugging me back to the soft embrace of the ocean. If I could only roll over, I would reach it and it would take me back, floating, weightless, drifting . . .

'Adam!' A hand was shaking me roughly, dragging me back. I moaned, and tried to pull away. '*Adam!* Open your eyes – you're scaring the girls!'

I wrenched my eyes open. My face was wet – from water, or sweat, or tears. I could feel a familiar roughness under my cheek, and something hard hurting my forehead.

I lifted my head. It weighed a ton.

The computer room at Quested Court slowly swam into focus. I was lying sprawled on the carpet under my computer desk with the leg of the desk digging into my forehead. I pushed myself up into a sitting position. I felt sick and heavy, as if gravity had suddenly doubled. Breathing was an effort, as though I was trying to suck treacle into my lungs, instead of air. Everything looked misty and indistinct, as if there was an oily film over my eyes.

The other four were staring down at me with worried faces.

'Are you OK?' quavered Gen.

'Yeah – I guess.' My tongue felt thick and swollen.

'It was easy for me this time,' said Jamie jauntily. 'I got knocked about a bit, though, and I gave my head a bump. But hey – we're back! Doesn't it feel great?'

I stumbled clumsily to my feet.

'Has anyone seen –' I croaked.

Richard shook his head.

That was it, then. Tiger Lily was gone.

Suddenly Jamie clamped his hands onto his breeches, an expression of horror on his face. His face turned bright red and his voice dropped to a whisper. 'I think I've wet myself.'

I looked down at him. There was a dark stain on the seat of his breeches, but . . .

'It's OK, Jamie, I don't think you have,' I said numbly. 'I think it's the potion. The phial must have broken.'

'Which one was it? It wasn't . . .' Gen's voice was the merest whisper.

'It was the one from the garden. The brown serpent. Inner Voices.'

'I've got the beauty one,' said Gen, turning slightly pink and digging in the pocket of her tunic. 'Or rather . . .' She held out her hand for us all to see. Sticking to her fingers like coarse, wet sand were the crushed remains of the phial that had once contained the emerald potion.

'It was the re-entry,' said Jamie. 'Maybe you can't bring things from one world into another – or not such delicate things. Maybe there's some kind of – I dunno – sonic force or something that destroys them.'

We looked at one another, the same thought in all our minds.

White-faced, Kenta slipped the straps of her backpack off her narrow shoulders and set it down on one of the desks. She undid the toggle and drew out the parchment, unrolling it and sliding it carefully from between its protective covers.

It was completely blank.

Reaching into the bag again, Kenta pulled out my

shawl. Her hands trembling slightly, she untucked the ends and opened it out.

There among its soft folds, safe and intact, lay the phials containing the Potion of Power . . . and the Potion of Healing.

Because he had been waiting for me last time, I'd expected Q to be sitting in the computer room, watching the clock for our return. But he wasn't there.

We trailed to the door and out into the corridor. There was no sign of anyone. The passageway was dark and silent, with that echoing emptiness that settles on houses at night when everyone has gone to bed.

The sound of the grandfather clock ticking in the hall was as loud as footsteps in the silence. As we passed, it wheezed, and struck once. Half past ten.

'What should we do?' whispered Jamie. 'It looks like everyone's gone to bed. But it's not *that* late, and . . . I'm *hungry*.'

I had a hollow feeling too, but it was disappointment, not hunger. It was so unlike Q not to be waiting for us. It seemed odd that he would just have gone off to bed, leaving us to blunder back to a dark house and no welcome. The clock ticked on, counting the seconds away.

Suddenly, I knew.

'Quick – he's with Hannah. *We have to be quick!*'

I turned and ran up the stairs, with the others behind me. Left at the top, along the dark passage to Hannah's door. I could hear the blood thumping in my ears. Silently, I eased the door open. Someone groped for my other hand. It was Kenta. She slid something into it – something cold and smooth that tingled.

Across the room Q was hunched over beside the bed. The soft nightlight illuminated his face. He looked like an old, old man. I felt Richard's hand in the small of my back, giving a gentle shove. Hesitantly, I walked forward into the room.

Everything looked the same: the clown picture on the wall, the rocking horse in the corner, the doll's house, the cuddly toys arranged on the armchair in the corner. It was tidier than a little girl's room ought to be.

I walked softly across the carpet to the bed. Q looked up at me like a man in a dream, with no sign of surprise. He gave me a slow smile, the saddest smile I'd ever seen. 'Welcome home, Adam. You're just in time to say goodbye.'

I looked down at the little figure in the bed. The tubes were gone. The battered teddy lay beside her on the pillow. Death hovered in the room like a grey angel.

'Take her hand, Adam.'

I put my big, rough paw round the little hand that lay curled on the sheet. It was very cold. Her eyes fluttered open and rested on me for a moment. I couldn't tell whether she even recognised me. They drifted shut again.

'Q,' I whispered, my voice sounding rough as sandpaper in the stillness, 'we've got it. Look.'

I opened my hand.

'She's still – there's still time, isn't there?' My eyes scanned the bedside table. It was cluttered with bottles and tumblers and containers of pills.

I reached for a plastic medicine measure. I eased the cork out of the neck of the phial, and carefully filled the spoon. There was still half the potion left. I replaced the cork, to keep it safe. I had no idea how much we needed. I had no idea if it would even work.

I felt a sudden pang of unease, and pushed the memory of the silver serpents to the back of my mind. A voice spoke harshly in my mind. *She's dying anyway. This is what it was all for. Do it – now.*

I glanced across at Q, who made a helpless, fluttering motion with his hands.

Gently, as if I was lifting a newborn kitten, I slid my arm round Hannah's shoulders and raised her up. It was like lifting a bundle of dry sticks wrapped in velvet. Her head flopped. I lifted the spoon to her parched, cracked lips.

'Hannah,' I whispered urgently, 'open your mouth. It's medicine. It will make you well again. You have to have it.'

The tiniest frown flickered across her face, and her lips tightened. Hannah had obviously had enough of medicine. But my heart lifted. The spunky Hannah I knew was still in there, faded faint as a shadow.

'You *have* to! Come *on*!'

But her lips stayed stubbornly closed. A wave of panic rose up in my chest like bile. If she refused to take it . . .

'Hannah, *come on*!' Just as I'd done with Tiger Lily and the bird, I cupped my hand under her jaw, felt for the twin ridges of teeth under the fragile skin, and gently squeezed. She gave a little mew, like a kitten, and her mouth opened a tiny crack.

Quickly, I slipped the spoon in and tilted it. And at the same time, I tipped her head back, to stop her spitting it out.

Hannah hiccuped and coughed. She made a rattling, gurgling sound . . . and she stopped breathing. My heart turned to ice. She was choking. I wanted to shake her – to shout at her and shake her and force her to be well. I wanted to fold her in my arms and hold her close, and let my strength soak through into her frail little body. I wanted to turn the clock back and leave her to drift into death peacefully, instead of choking her on snake venom from an alien world.

I lowered her gently back onto the pillow, held her hand and prayed.

She gave another little cough. A tiny translucent bubble popped out onto her lip and sparkled there, as iridescent as mother-of-pearl in the soft light. And as I watched, the dry, cracked lip under the bubble smoothed over. It was a dewdrop on a rose petal.

Hannah's lips parted, and she gave a deep sigh. Her eyes opened.

'Q,' she whispered, 'I'm thirsty. Is there any lime juice?'

She struggled to sit up, but she was so weak she wobbled and fell back on the pillow, like a newborn foal. 'I feel like fish fingers, with lots of tomato sauce. And jelly,' she told us from the pillow, a dreamy look on her face. '*Strawberry* jelly, with hundreds and thousands.'

EPILOGUE

It was after breakfast the next day, and my mind was hazy with the sweetness of waffles and maple syrup, and the warmth of the golden sunlight pouring in through the window.

Sitting at my desk in the computer room, I linked my hands above my head and stretched until my shoulders creaked.

Outside in the garden, I could hear the others calling to each other and laughing, and occasional shrieks from the girls. It reminded me of another time – a time that seemed very long ago. I smiled to myself. Part of me wanted to run out and join them, but I could do that later. Right now, I had something more important to do.

Carefully, I smoothed out the e-mail address Cameron had given me. It was a bit smudged, but I could just about still read it. Double checking every letter, I typed it in. Then, frowning with concentration, I wrote: *Hey ther Camarun. Gess wot? I mayd it!*

For a moment, I could almost see him – the goofy smile, the Coke-bottle glasses. My friend. *One of my friends.*

Searching for the next letter on the keyboard, my eyes were drawn to the three keys.

Alt. Control. Q.

Already it was hard to believe it had really happened. That I could go back again, if I simply reached out and pressed them.

It would be that easy.

They drew my fingers like a magnet.

I took a deep breath, and gave myself a mental shake. The adventure was over. So why did I have such a strange feeling that for me, it was just beginning?

The Karazan Quartet

Dungeons of Darkness

Everyday life hasn't changed much
for Adam Equinox since his adventures
in Karazan. But brimming with new confidence,
he feels ready to tackle anything.

Suddenly Adam is faced with a new
and even tougher quest.
Can he survive the dangers
that lie at the outer limits of Karazan?

Available from 1 October 2005